THE OAR MARKER

THE OAR MARKER

D L Coleman

The Oar Marker
Copyright 2022 by D. L. Coleman

Published in the United States of America by PRIVATE LIBRARY™

ISBN (paperback): 979-8-88831-331-2
ISBN (ebook): 979-8-88831-332-9

Cover Design by the author
Book Design by Maureen Cutajar, www.gopublished.com

Printed in the United States of America
First Edition

Contact publisher at e:pvtlibrary@gmail.com

Or

Private Library
P.O. Box 1346
Buies Creek, North Carolina 27506-9998

10 9 8 7 6 5 4 3 2 1

DEDICATION: This book is dedicated first to those who read it, then to those who suffered the kinds of losses portrayed in this story that were so prevalent in the late 1960s and the era of our nation's involvement in the Vietnam Conflict. That includes members of the military as well as families and friends, many of them who still suffer long after the initial tragedies.

ACKNOWLEDGMENTS: My gratitude to Bob Mears, a fellow Newport News High School alumnus, whose keen eye for detail while reading the manuscript allowed corrections of the many errors I tend to make while typing and just plain missing stuff. And to my daughter, Eugena Coleman, who also helped, especially in the requirements for computer functions, as well as some copy editing, because I am the dumbest guy in the world with computers and forever cyber challenged. Any remaining errors are on me.

1

Life can be awfully tricky when you're not paying attention. Like a freight train is coming and you don't even know you're on the track. Nobody would have seen it coming, not in a million years, how things could turn on a dime and go in a completely different direction, just because you met somebody. I know we never saw it coming, or we did and didn't know what it was. That's the way it was with my buddy Will when he met Mary.

I'm Layton Dockery Cavanaugh, by the way. Doc, I'm called. Will and I were best friends since first grade and were here at school on athletic scholarships. We were just two jocks standing in a registration line, trying to get classes we needed and could pass. Must have happened a million times a year this way at colleges around the world. But this was not colleges around the world. This was Williamsburg, Virginia, U.S.A. It was the 1960s and we didn't have a clue.

It was right before lunch when the whole thing started, just after morning football practice. The heat was in the nineties and the gnats were all over the place, gnawing on the student body, who were on the sidewalks and under the trees in lines queued up outside the gym. Will and I were in lines next to one another, and Mary, the first time either of us laid eyes on her, was about twenty feet ahead with a group of girls we didn't know. It was a harder line, some kind of advanced biochemistry, so I wouldn't have noticed it, anyway, and Will saw her first. Not because of the biochemistry part, but because she was pretty. What else?

"Lots of pedigree. Requires something special, something creative. She'll expect and appreciate it. I'll get the extra effort award."

Then I noticed her. "I better do this, Will. This girl will hurt your feelings. She's too much for you."

"That's what you think."

Will saw Dicky Humphrey a couple lines over. Dicky was a frat brother. Will took Dicky's cane. Dicky was legally blind, by the way, which made you wonder what illegally blind could mean.

"Hey, goofy, give me my stick back. Now, Will. I can't see without it."

"How come you don't wear sunglasses?" Will said. "You're a bad example for blind people."

"I'm a rebel, bird brain. Give it back."

"They see you with no sunglasses and they think they can do the same thing. Next thing you know, we can't tell who's blind and who's not."

"Five minutes, Will. I want it back."

Will kept going. He borrowed sunglasses from another student nearby and gave me a *watch this* look, then walked up beside Mary's line, tapping the stick on the ground, like an expert blind person. He bumped into her.

"Oh, excuse me. I'm so sorry." He grabbed Mary's arm, faking confusion and disorientation.

"Oh, I'm so sorry. Excuse me. You okay?" She helped steady him, and I could tell he liked her hands on him.

"Oh, no, no, my fault. I'm really sorry. You okay? I'm always doing this."

"I'm fine."

They exchanged *I'm fines* and *really sorrys* overkill. And he noticed how her voice was a refined drawl, kind of lilting, like she was already thirty-five.

"This is kind of new to me," Will said. "Do I know you? Your voice isn't familiar."

"No, we've never met."

"We're close to the door, aren't we?"

"Yes." She said it without looking.

"Good. My name's Will." He stuck out his hand.

She looked back at him and shook it. "Pleased to meet you." She turned away again.

"Will Wythe. What's yours?"

"Mary." She said it without looking.

"How far are we from the steps? I don't want to trip." He did the little hand-out-in-front-of-him thing, feeling around. She seemed uninterested, maybe even a little annoyed. High-strung type, I was thinking.

"Just a few feet. Can't miss it."

"Easy for you to say."

She looked like she almost answered but didn't.

"You don't like sightless people, do you?" Will said.

"I beg your pardon." She raised an eyebrow.

"I can tell. That's okay, though, don't blame you. I'm used to it by now. You wouldn't believe I used to be popular."

The other girls were now giving Will a curious look.

"Of course, when you lose your sight, you lose your friends," he said.

She turned back to him. "Look, uh—."

"Will."

"Will. How did you get here?"

"I was dropped off."

"Look, Will, if you want, why don't you stay here, next to me, hold my arm if you like. I'll make sure you get registered safely." She rolled her eyes at the other girls. I now figured her for the kind who rescued lost puppies and hated herself for it.

"Oh, would you? You don't mind?"

"No, of course not. It'll be fine."

"Thank you. I'm sorry to be a bother."

"You're no bother." She took his arm, straining for patience.

"You know, I used to think I could walk around this campus blindfolded."

She gave a phony grin.

The lines were creeping along and Will said little, until they'd climbed the steps to the doorway of the gym. He didn't want to get inside, in close quarters, where somebody would give him away.

"Oh, God, my registration form. I don't have it." He fidgeted like he might find it by patting himself down, even felt the space in front of him again, like the thing was hanging out in mid-air.

Mary rolled her eyes once more.

"It must be back at the dorm." He said it like how could he ever get back there on his own.

Mary gave the girls a look of exasperation. "And where is that? Your dorm? Don't you have friends?"

"I used to. It's just behind the gym here, not far. I think I can make it. I appreciate you helping me. See you. Well, not really *see* you, but you know." He took a couple steps and did the almost-tripping number again and she reached for him.

"Look, maybe I'd better go with you, before you break your neck. How long have you been like this?"

"Since spring break."

"How do you get around?"

"My sister drops me off. She can see."

"I can help you back to your dorm real quick, but I can't wait for you." She asked the girls to hold her place. "Come on. Where is it?"

Will walked closely at her side, getting that occasional reassuring hold on his arm. When they stopped in front of the dorm building, he thanked her.

"Look, I feel like I owe you something for being so nice. SPD's having a party Saturday night a couple blocks from here. Why don't you go with me."

"Sorry, I can't. I'll be busy."

"That's okay, I don't have to go."

"Thought you didn't have any friends."

"It's an open party, everybody's invited. Think they'd actually invite a guy like me to a private party?"

"I can't. Thanks anyway." She turned to leave. "Quit feeling sorry for yourself. It's not healthy."

"So you have a boyfriend."

"Kind of."

"Here?"

"No, home."

"Where's that?"

"Charleston."

"There are at least two Charlestons."

"South Carolina."

"But you didn't say that. You said it like there's only one Charleston in the world."

"So?"

"So that's an insult to the people of West Virginia, at least, for you to just ignore their existence like that. It's not fair to all those ridge runners."

"Then don't tell them I said it. We'll spare their feelings."

Smartass, too, he was thinking.

"Out of sight, out of mind. Your boyfriend, I mean."

"That's for me to say, and I don't think like that. Bye."

He called out to her. "It's the blind thing, isn't it? Sorry to embarrass you."

She stopped and walked back to him. "Look, it's nothing personal, uh—."

"Will."

"Will. I appreciate the offer. Really, I do, but I'm very busy most nights, including weekends, so, generally, I don't date."

"You work or something?"

"Something."

"Why are you so busy? You trying to make Phi Beta Kappa or something?"

"I'll make Phi Beta Kappa anyway."

"Pretty cocky."

"Confident."

"Ever take a break?"

"I volunteer at a hospital in my free time."

"A candy striper?"

"Not exactly."

"A nurse?"

"No, premed major."

"Biochemistry, figures. What do you do at the hospital?"

"Why are you so curious?"

"Don't know, you seem so different from the girls around here."

"How would you know? You don't know me."

"Yes, I do. You're beautiful. I can tell."

"I didn't know it snowed here in August. And you don't know what I look like."

"I'm not talking about physical beauty, although I'm sure you are."

"Maybe it's not just snow. Maybe a sewer line burst. Either way, I need a coat and boots. Have to go. See you. Good luck, Will." She turned and walked away again.

"What's your last name? Sorry I didn't ask."

"Poythress," she said over her shoulder, not looking back.

Will took off the sunglasses and watched her walk away. It was the first time he could ever remember being turned down flat.

2

He was William Longman Wythe. Not Why-the, understand, but Wythe, as in With. I pronounce it only because few not from the area get it right at first. He loved football and would spend his life involved in the game. She was Mary Collette Renee Reedlaw Poythress. Poythress with or without the h, she said, because it was kind of a tongue twister. She would study medicine and cure childhood diseases. They were the best friends I ever had, before or since, including my wife, of course. In fact, my wife in large part because of them.

I'm thinking about all this now, while here on campus at the pond, in the little clearing in the patch of woods across from the football stadium, where I come every year to pay my respects and feel closest to them. I've claimed it as kind of a personal memorial to them, you might say. Others claim it for their own reasons, mostly romantic. I'm standing in the middle of the painted wooden bridge that arches over the pond, a favorite spot for lovers and hopefuls, both students and others, for generations. It's October now, mid-day Saturday. It's sixty degrees, overcast skies, no glare in the eyes. Only a mild breeze, and autumn leaves are falling like crazy. Almost kickoff time and I can hear the crowd getting louder. Playing V.M.I. A perfect day for football in Williamsburg.

I can still spot it sticking out of the ground, over in the brush, though each year it seems to sink deeper, or the ground swells, whichever. Ever so often I pull it up some and pack the dirt around it, to keep it from going under. I'm speaking of the paddle end of the wooden row boat oar Will cut off and carved his and Mary's initials into that day, when he came back to the dorm all excited and exclaiming how Mary would be the girl he would marry and spend the rest of his life with, though she didn't yet know it. No one has removed it. And it's not an authorized marker, but after they left no one we knew at the time dared move it, out of respect for their memory, I suppose.

Doc was a nickname Will hung on me our freshman year, but not from the Dockery. I had started school as a premed student and hit Biology and Chemistry 101 like stone walls. I had planned on being this great surgeon and ladies' man someday, like Richard Chamberlain playing Dr. Kildare on TV. When I realized all the medical schooling in the world wouldn't make me look like that, the profession lost a lot of its appeal and I switched to pre-law. But the name stuck, first as kind of a friendly joke, then like a tattoo or a scar. In fact, the guys made up a little song to razz me about it:

> *Hickery, Dickery Doc*
> *Doc went up the clock*
> *The clock struck One*
> *And Doc was done*
> *'cause he flunked Bio One-O-One*
> *And the frog lived ever after.*

Cute. Real college boy cute.

Frankly, I never got the hang of the microscope and wondered if I might be learning disabled. And I couldn't kill the requisite frog. I couldn't do it in high school, and I couldn't do it here, either. If the world was waiting on me for a medical breakthrough, it would wait until hell froze over, if I had to kill something to find it. I had once planned on sneaking into the lab at night and dropping a goldfish in a tank of sulfuric acid, just to see it disappear, like I was told it would, but I backed out at the last minute, didn't have the stomach for it.

Before "Doc," I'd always been called L.D., in grammar school, high school, everywhere. It was my father's doing. I think he figured since he would always be gone, why get too chummy. You don't miss or feel guilty about an L.D. as much as you might a Layton, which my mother always called me, until a few months before she left to join Dad, both physically and in calling me L.D. I could see it coming, just by the switch. Kids don't miss much.

Will and I grew up just twenty-five miles down the road, at the end of the lower peninsula, overlooking the James River, the Chesapeake Bay and the Atlantic, where we spent so much of our life on the beaches and waterfront, and playing the ever-loving game of football. His academic situation was a lot more serious than my D plus in Biology and C minus in Chemistry, the former I overcame in summer school. We were starting our junior year and he had a flat 2.0 GPA and was borderline academic condition for pulling his second D in English in two years, very much a no-no. A no-no because the Queen's English was both a huge hurdle and a rite of passage here. It was taken very seriously, like a test to get into heaven or something. But flunking was also a hurdle and a common occurrence, as well. Some of the brightest students in the country had always come here, along with the rest of us, but the grading standard was always the toughest, too. An A in the Ivy League, or at Duke, or some other expensive place, might have gotten you a B minus here, if you were lucky, but you wouldn't count on it. Will and I barely met the requirements, though our SATs were promising. Jocks were no exceptions and received no special treatment, so it was a battle. He was the better running back by a thin margin and out-weighed me fifteen pounds. I was the better student by an equal degree and was faster. But neither of us were Phi Beta Kappa or Heisman Trophy material. We did dream of a long shot at the pros, he as a running back and I as a receiver, because of my lighter weight and speed. Don't we all.

This particular semester was crucial for Will, not that I was to-tally immune. At the time, outside our safe little place in the serenity and historic ambiance of Colonial Williamsburg, and liv-ing a carefree life, the whole damn world seemed to be turning upside down, the draft and Viet Nam snatching people all around us like you wouldn't believe. And grades were important.

Which was the furthest thing from Will's mind up on Jockstrap Corner, where about twenty-seven of us were sitting on the brick wall, like a bunch of crows on a fence, having our fraternity meet-ing. The Corner was at the edge of campus where it met with one end Duke of Gloucester Street, the pedestrian main way that went up the center of the colonial and commercial district, with all the shops, exhibits, restaurants, and the stockades, where the tourists stuck their heads and hands in and had their pictures taken, looking goofy. It was kind of a hangout, mostly for guys ogling tourists, and a lot of Monday-morning quarterbacking. We had just the one practice that day, in the morning, because of a scrimmage sched-uled the next day, so we had the afternoon off and held our meeting. We didn't have a frat house, like regular fraternities. In fact, we didn't officially exist, as far as the college was concerned. We didn't take it that seriously, either, all the brothers-for-life crap, and nobody would pay the rent, anyway. Though most of us wore Kennedy haircuts, Will and I shorter versions of it during the foot-ball season, and we were all preppy dressers, except maybe some of the guys from up around New York and northern New Jersey, who did all right until it got to their feet, wearing strange-looking shoes that would frighten small children. We were the SPD, just a loose bunch who met wherever we could and, according to the weather, usually outside and when we had the time.

I had just finished telling my old story about Will, which always drew a big laugh, even from him. The one that happened in U.S. History class our junior year of high school, when the teacher asked Will what was the significance of December 7, 1941, in American history, and he had said, dead serious, before he realized it, "A date that will live in infamy, the day the Japanese attacked Pearl Bailey."

We were falling off the wall, like knocked-over bowling pins, when Kenny Miklos, Will's roommate and the team center, got there and reminded Will he was late for his meeting with the coach.

"What meeting?"

"The note I left on your door this morning when you wouldn't wake up, after I pounded on it for five minutes. That meeting."

Kenny Miklos was one of our offensive captains. It was not just an honorary title. It had real duties with it, including, among others, making sure players knew the plays and showed up at meetings on time, one of his strengths and one of Will's weaknesses, the meeting part. And he took it very seriously, as he tended to take most things in a gruff, straight-forward manner. Kenny didn't have time for slowpokes. He was going to be a great journalist, like his heroes, Murrow, Cronkite, Sevareid, and Ernie Pyle. He was going to be right in the middle of all the great historic events of his lifetime and make sure the rest of us knew the score. That's why he majored in history and wrote for the school paper, and why he prided himself on knowing everything that went on around campus. It was his calling. That and the screaming need to escape his family's little wholesale grocery empire back home in Pennsylvania, if only to prove Greeks could do something besides be in the food business.

"Guess I'd better get over there," Will said.

"Smashing idea. And while you're at it, you might as well forget about Mary Poythress. She has a boyfriend, doesn't date here, especially jocks. She hates jocks, I hear."

"You know her?"

Kenny was in his element now. "Rooms with Shelley Michaels. Got here in June for summer session. Transferred in from Georgia. A blue-blooded Huguenot from Charleston. Lives down there on the battery. Old man's big in real estate, owns half the town. Uncle runs the newspaper."

"Huguenot. Isn't that a religion or something?" Will sometimes played dumber than he was, which he wasn't.

"Can't get one over on you," Kenny said. "Better get over to that meeting, Will. Serious."

Will left and headed for the coach's office under the stadium bleachers.

Dickey Humphrey said he wished he were rooming with Shelley Michaels.

Kenny jumped on that. "You wish you were rooming with anybody. What are you doing, rooming with that runt botany major? Guy wants to live in a flower garden the rest of his life. No shoulders. Coke bottles for glasses. No personality. Give me a break. What's happening to our already low standards here?"

"Guy's old man owns a beer franchise in Richmond. That's only about forty miles up the road, if you check your map."

"Then it's settled, he's in. We can't blackball a guy like that. It wouldn't be right."

"I knew you'd agree."

"I love you, Dickey. You've always been my favorite," Kenny said. He patted him on the head.

Ds carried only one quality point and did not count toward graduation requirements, even if your overall grade point average was above the required 2.0 on the 4.0 scale. So Will was repeating the second semester sophomore English Literature class. Normally, he would have gone to summer school for it, as he had the previous year for another course, and as I had both summers for my own deficiencies. But we both had military commitments, too, his six weeks of Army R.O.T.C. training and mine the equivalent Marine Corps Platoon Leader Class at Quantico. But Will opted out of school this summer, just past, because he wanted some free time, and to make some money working. So here was this English course hanging over his life like a bad dream, and he would have to do it all again and try for a C, sitting in a room and listening to brainy types saying things like, *allegory, iambic pentameter,* and *onomatopoeia*, making him want to run and hide in the woods. Tough stuff for a Phys. Ed. major who just wanted to coach football. This was what the coach wanted to see him about, for sure.

3

Coach O'Neal was in his late forties, average height and about two-thirty, with a slight gut—not too bad for a former guard—and a silver band of hair around an otherwise bald head. His voice was raspy from years of yelling and from sucking on those stubby, stinking cigars of his that made it seem he'd never been properly weaned. But he was a good coach, well-liked and respected. He was also the boss, and Will was late. Coach was leaned back in his squeaky swivel chair, with a foot up on his rickety old desk, and taking a drag off his stogie, when Will walked in.

"Coach?"

"Am I, really?" Coach said. A wry sense of humor, too. Almost forgot to mention that part. "I'm glad you could make it over here at such a late hour. Somebody appoint you coach?"

"Well, I just heard—."

"Because if you want to be the coach and run things, I'll just clean out my desk here and get out of your way."

"No, it's just—."

"Great, then I'll just stay on and continue setting the schedule here, and handle all the other nuisance details that you don't have time to bother with."

"I just got the message from Miklos."

"I see that. I was going to kill myself if I hadn't heard from you. Awfully thoughtful of you to stop by, and I appreciate it. I could be other places, you know, but I've been here, waiting, just to see you."

"What is it, Coach? Something wrong?"

"Couple things. Have a seat."

Will pulled over the hard wooden chair, just as squeaky as everything else in the office, and sat in front of the desk.

"I want you to spend more time with Humphrey this semester," Coach said, meaning Dickey. "Hang around with him a lot in your spare time, learn how to read and write the English language. It's our native tongue, you know.

"I spoke with your professor, Dr. Antise. You drew the toughest of that whole bunch over there this semester, and I'm really sorry about that. I tried to help. But if you don't get a C, you're out, you lose your scholarship, and you'll be out of school, too, because you'll be under a C average. And since the draft board has your number, you know what that'll mean. We've been over all this before."

"Yes, sir. I'll pass it. I promise, Coach. I won't let the team down."

"I certainly hope not. We need you. We need everyone to pull his weight. I can't stand over you guys every minute and make you learn, or unscrew your heads and pour it down your necks. So hang out with Humphrey."

"I will."

"Which brings us to the other thing."

Will just stared. What else could top this?

Coach took his time, seemed to soften a bit, studying Will's face. "I got a call late last night from Tim Davis's father. It was a courtesy call. He thought we'd want to know. The team. Tim died four days ago. In Viet Nam." He let it sink in. "His body will be home today. His funeral is next Wednesday. You can tell Miklos, so he can notify the rest of the team. He doesn't know yet. I told you first because you were Tim's roommate."

Miklos wouldn't like that.

Will felt like his nerves collapsed. He was wobbly is his seat for a moment. His vision narrowed, like he was light-blinded, and the breath went out of him an instant.

Tim Davis had been an All-District defensive back in high school, in Fairfax. He'd come to school here with big hopes. But his grades went down the tubes, and he was out of school by Christmas of his freshman year. He was picked up by the draft and volunteered for Army Special Forces. The last we saw him was the previous spring when he came to watch practice and hang out with us for a couple days, before leaving for the Far East.

"I've got to go to the funeral," Will managed to say.

"That won't be necessary. Coach Tuttle will be going up to represent the team."

Will considered that a moment. "Well, I, uh, think it would be the right thing for me to do, to go, myself. Maybe I could ride with Coach Tuttle."

Coach O'Neal looked at him like Will had missed something. "The whole purpose of Coach Tuttle going is so we don't miss any practice. We've got a game coming up. You might have heard. Furman? They're a college, you know. They'll be here for the opener and we have to be here to meet them. It wouldn't be fair if we didn't. Means we have to be prepared, too. We've done this a number of times before, practice. Surely, you remember."

"Well, it's just that Tim and I were good friends when he was here, Coach. I know his family pretty well, met them a couple times. I think they'd expect to see me there."

"With all due respect to Tim's family, and your friendship with him, I think they'll have enough on their minds, without being on the lookout for you. But it's a nice thought and that's why Coach Tuttle is going. There'll be a big spray of flowers and a signed card from the team. You can sign your name real big, if you'd like, like John Hancock, to ensure you won't be missed."

"I can make up the practice."

"Sure, we'll have the whole team fall out an extra day, just to accommodate your schedule, Will. Sunday would be okay. Screw studying or resting, or church. Maybe we'll bring out a buffet lunch, make it a picnic. Heck, maybe we'll invite the Furman guys up. No use them being better prepared than us. We'll bring them up here, stuff their bellies at the picnic, then knock their pork butts all over the field. Might even be national champions, working the picnic strategy."

Will started to give a little grin, to show his appreciation for Coach's strange sense of humor, but changed his mind halfway in.

Coach and Will stared at one another, cautiously, like they were playing chess with their eyes, then Will nodded no. He knew he was laying it all on the line, his starting position, maybe even his scholarship, by contradicting the coach's wishes. Serious business.

"Sorry, sir, but I've got to go. It's just something I've got to do. I'll make it up any way I can. No use for the team to suffer on account of me."

Coach O'Neal turned a little red as he studied Will. "What is this, Will? You knew Davis only a semester."

"Well, we weren't close, not like family. But I've never had a friend who died before, especially in a war. I'd hate for his family to know I didn't go."

The red went out of Coach's face. He tapped his fingers lightly on his desktop. "You know, I thought a lot of him, too. I'm the one who recruited him, after all. Decent young man, lot of talent. Nice family, like yours. And I'm sorry for his death. Really, I am. But the world doesn't stop every time someone dies, as tragic as it is."

"But I'm stopping for this funeral because he was a friend of mine, and I owe it to his family. I'd do the same thing for you, Coach."

"Don't go killing me just to prove it." More finger tapping. "And I suppose if you're going, Cavanaugh will want to go, too, because you two are joined at the neck like some carnival exhibit."

"Yes, sir, he'll want to go. Yeah."

"Yeah, bullshit." Coach rubbed the back of his neck and leaned forward. "How many will want to go?"

"Probably all of us who knew him."

"And a couple more who didn't, just for the ride, I guess, and for the refreshments. There won't likely be a buffet at the funeral, you know. You can tell those knuckleheads who're going up for the snacks, they can forget it."

"I know."

"Okay. At least you'll be thinking as a group. We'll take a couple vans, go up as a team. See the co-captains at the meeting today, give me a head count. But we're practicing when we get back, seven-thirty until we get it right."

"Thanks, Coach." Will started for the door, then stopped. "Did Mr. Davis say exactly how he was killed, Coach?"

"No, he didn't say how he was killed. And it's not important. But I know exactly why he was killed, and that's damned important."

Will stepped closer, like he missed something else. "Why?"

"We'll go over that before we leave."

Riddles, Will thought. Always riddles with this man. At least he got by it. Thinking about Tim Davis being dead and Mary Poythress being alive was all he needed now, on top of a C in English Literature from the toughest professor on campus, No Peace Antise.

4

We had a good scrimmage with the Apprentice School Saturday morning, a good practice for both teams. It was hotter than hell and we played on their field downtown, in Newport News, at the shipyard stadium. I scored two touchdowns to Will's one, one a thirty-six-yard run, the other a nineteen-yard pass play. Will ran a twelve-yarder, but he piled up more yardage than anyone on either side. Things were looking good for our season opener with Furman, and nobody was injured; couldn't get better.

That night, we had an ambush party at Rick Bowman's. He lived only a couple blocks away in a big colonial house—what else in Williamsburg?—with a large, lit-up backyard with trickling water stuff and plants and statuary and topiary that would never be the same again. His parents were in Florida and said he could have a few close friends over for a quiet evening if he wanted to. He wanted to and there were about two hundred people going in and out of there, with all the fallout you might imagine. It was fairly civil by college standards, but two hundred people couldn't be quiet and orderly if they were all dead and in a graveyard. In fact, when Rick's parents got back a week later and talked to the neighbors and saw what happened, his old man just about beat the living hell out of him.

I got to the party before Will. I took Pam with me, though she could've gone with anybody she wanted. Seemed I was always taking Pam somewhere, but she was hard to shake sometimes.

Pamela Flanagan and I went together off and on since high school. We knew one another from the eighth grade and screwed one another's brains out since the tenth. She was very serious about the relationship and never dated anyone else, even though I strongly encouraged it. I dated everybody I could because I was kind of like a whore, anyway, as long as the girl was clean cut and nice looking. Pam was a decent, very attractive blue-eyed platinum blond, a drop-dead knockout in a bathing suit, too, and tanned like a beach goddess. And smart, could've had anybody. But she had a profound fondness for me, or weakness, whatever you call it, that I never really understood nor appreciated. I honest-to-God believed that if I'd asked her to she'd have jumped on a gurney and let the Red Cross suck every drop of blood from her fabulous body, just so I'd have some on hand for emergencies. It was frightening. The only reason she went to school here was because I did. When she thought I might be going to V.M.I. or Virginia Tech, which I seriously considered once, she applied to every school in the western half of the state, just so she could be close by. She really did adore me and I didn't know how to handle it. And I didn't know if I wanted to.

We got to the party at Bowman's just after dark. The beer and wine were running like a sieve already, thanks in large part to Dicky Humphrey and his wonderful new Botany major roommate-pledge discovery, whose old man owned the beer franchise. There was no room to move inside, so Pam and I grabbed a beer and went to the backyard. Will came in a few minutes later, without a date, figuring to pick somebody up, and a few of us stood around talking about the scrimmage earlier and the Furman game the next week. And, of course, the bad luck about Tim Davis didn't go unnoticed.

Just then, I spotted Mary Poythress and her roommate, Shelley Michaels, coming through the back door into the yard with wine coolers. Shelley was cute, a petite girl with big, brown eyes and short, dark hair. She was on track for Phi Beta Kappa and everyone knew it. I never could figure why these tiny girls were always so smart. I whispered to Dicky and nudged Pam and Kenny.

"That's her?" Pam said of Mary. "Lord, she is beautiful."

"What's so funny? Who?" Then Will noticed her. "Oh."

"Yeah, 'Oh,'" I said. "That's one girl you won't be picking up tonight, Will."

"She's probably queer, anyway," he said. "Won't go out with a blind person, but lies about it and comes to the party because she thinks I won't be able to see her, even if I'm here."

Pam said, "Just because she wouldn't go out with you, Will?"

"She could've been more honest about it."

"Yeah, like you're really blind and honest."

Will reached for Dicky's cane.

"No, hell, no," Dicky said, snatching it back.

"You ought to quit carrying that thing," Will told Dicky. "You're going to blind somebody with it."

"Here." Dicky handed it over. "But bring it right back, after she turns you down again." Dicky wasn't going anywhere. He was with Carol Foley, his steady, who was inside fetching another beer. Foley could drink like a hog fish and was always leaving Dicky standing around.

Will said, "Watch this," and started toward Mary, doing the stick-tapping number again.

Shelley had turned her back a moment to speak with someone nearby, leaving Mary looking around.

Will tapped his way over, bumping into Mary from behind.

"Oh, excuse me." Will stared out the way blind people do because there is nothing to look at.

Mary barely noticed, and Will went to squinching his eyes and sniffing the air. "Mary? Is that you? Mary Poythress?"

It took her a second to recognize him without the sunglasses. "Oh. Yes, uh—."

"Will. How soon we forget."

"Right. Will. Sorry I forgot."

"It's okay. I don't blame you for not coming with me. I mean, what would it look like, you here with a blind person? People would talk and think there was something wrong with you, too." He did the little sarcastic lip-curl grin. "Besides, you might end up pitying me, and where would that lead?"

"Oh, please. Would you?"

"It would've been nice if you'd been honest about it. Blind people understand, too, you know. And we have feelings. Lucky my sister was coming this way, so she could drop me off. Another exciting night in the life of the sightless. Now, if I could just find somebody to talk to or be kind enough to fetch me a beer."

Mary's jaw was moving around now. And it looked like she might unload, but Shelley turned back in time.

"I see you two have met," Shelley said.

Mary was relieved. "Yes, this is the guy I was telling you about, the guy in the registration line. Will."

"Not this Will," Shelley said. "This Will is not blind. This is Will Wythe." She gave him a friendly punch in the gut. "Don't pay him any mind."

Just then, Will quit staring out and looked directly into Mary's very surprised eyes and gave her a big smile, like he'd just pulled off the biggest caper of the century.

Mary didn't seem to think it was funny. She looked disappointed, if not a bit hurt. "Oh. I see that now. How gullible and foolish of me to think I might have been helping someone who deserved it."

Shelley said, "Will's on the football team with Rick Bowman. They're both Phi Deltas."

"Is that so?" she said, glaring at him.

"He's a halfback," Shelley said. "Backfield people tend to be goofy like that, not very stable. But he's nice, we'll keep him."

"Oh, really? Must be terrible," Mary said, still glaring.

"What's terrible?" Will said.

"I mean, being a halfback, all those vertebrae missing. Weak back."

"Cute."

"How long before you make fullback?" she said.

"Oh, I see, a smartass."

"No, what you see is the smart. The ass part you'll never see."

"Who says I want to? You take yourself pretty seriously, don't you? Why don't you lighten up. I'm just trying to be nice."

"Bullshit. Why don't you go back to quarterback and start all over, Will. Come back when you have a full backbone, instead of preying on the handicapped to meet people because you're too insecure to be honest."

Shelley's jaw was dropping. "God, what's happening here? Did I miss something?"

"No, I think you've seen it all with this character," Mary said.

Will threw up his hands. "Oh, I'm a character now."

"No, you're a jerk."

"Why don't you kill me then, get all worked up about it. Can't take a joke. Jeeze." He looked at Shelley. "You actually room with this girl?"

"How did you know that?" Mary said. "You spying on me, too?"

"You know," Will said, "I used to date a girl like you—."

"No, you didn't. A girl like me wouldn't date a jerk like you."

"She was a Huguenot. Strange people, those Huguenots. Very peculiar people. You wouldn't happen to be one of them, would you? A Huguenot?"

"And you ridicule a person's religion, too. What a prince."

"This is escalating," Shelley said. "He's just kidding, Mary."

"No, he's just a kid, himself, and I don't have time for it. Shouldn't have come. Think I'll just leave." She gave Shelley her glass and turned toward the gate.

"Wait, I'll go with you," Shelley said.

"No, you stay. I'll be fine."

"Just like a Huguenot to walk away," Will said after her. "Don't leave on account of me, Hugo. I'll leave and you can stay." He looked over at us. "Damn Huguenots, always walking off on you."

"Drop dead," Mary said back over her shoulder.

"Whatever you say, Hugo." Suddenly, Will dropped dead-like to the ground, like he'd been killed instantly, which drew a big laugh from everybody close by.

"What's this all about?" Shelley said.

"Why don't you ask her." He got up and brushed himself off.

"You two meet in a former life or something?"

"No big deal. She's a stuck-up snob, is all."

"I can see her point, Will. What'd you do to her?"

"Nothing. I swear." He told her his side of their meeting the other day. "Just a little joke, you know, having some fun in the registration line. What else are registration lines good for? She gets all worked up about it. She's got a superior attitude."

"No, she's just very serious-minded. She's also very nice when you get to know her."

"How would she ever meet anybody? She hates people."

"No, just you. I'll talk to her."

"Forget it. It's not important. Sorry if I upset you."

"No, it's fine. She probably shouldn't have come. It's my fault, I insisted. Thought it would do her some good to get out."

"So what is she, a shut-in? A mental case of some kind?"

"No, Will, quit. She walked you back to the dorm, didn't she? How can you say that?"

"She was just being a do-gooder. She did it for herself."

"She's very upset today, is all. Something happened last night that affected her."

"She get a smudge on her white tennis outfit over at the Huguenot country club?"

"You've got to stop with the Huguenot business."

"Jeeze, Shelley, don't tell me you're a Huguenot."

"No, I'm Presbyterian, but that's not my point."

"I know, I know. I'm sorry. You know how I am. I'm just goofing around. Tell her I said I'm sorry, if it'll make her feel better. Then tell her to drop dead for me."

"I will not."

"Well, she told me to drop dead and I did it. What if it'd been Dicky who'd asked her out? A real blind person? How would he have felt?"

"She doesn't date. She told you that and it's true. We've been rooming together the whole summer and she's never been out. No lie."

"That's her problem."

"No, it's her choice." Shelley looked at the two glasses of wine she held. "Let's drop it. I've got work to do here. Want one?" She held it out.

"No, I'll get a beer in a minute. You want to hang out with me tonight? We can take a ride, and get something to eat later, you and me and Doc and Pam."

"I don't know. I better get back with Mary."

"You her mother or her roommate? She'll be fine, like she said."

She thought about it. "Well, okay. But we'll stop by on our way out, let her know where I'll be."

5

We got a buzz on from the beer and wine, not that we drank that much. We were dedicated athletes, Will and I, and went kind of light on it, and it didn't take much. While the party was still going strong, the four of us, Will, Shelley, Pam and I, left and went to the delicatessen that was wedged in the corner of the block across from the football stadium. We took Will's car, a '60 Chevy coup, because mine was a sports car and seated only two. We stopped by to see if Mary was home, which made Will a little nervous. She'd left Shelley a note saying she went for a walk and would be back shortly. The deli was only a block away. Luckily, there was room. No football game yet, so no crowd, and a lot of parties were going on around town. Mostly, it was an older group in the deli, graduate students and locals, more leaving than staying, and the music wasn't too loud. I hated loud music.

Soon as we walked in, who did we see but Mary Poythress. She was sitting alone at a booth, near the front, looking out a side window at who knew what, because there was nothing to see but the streetlight. There was a mostly uneaten sandwich on a plate in front of her. She didn't see us at first, or if she did, she didn't let on. As we passed to take the booth behind her, Shelley and Pam stopped to talk with her, invite her to join us. Shelley introduced Pam. Will and I felt the awkwardness, especially Will, who was wrestling with the need to say something. Mary was conscious not to look our way.

"I'm afraid I wouldn't be very good company," Mary told them. "I was just leaving, anyway. I'm tired." She assured Shelley everything was fine and was glad to meet Pam. She just needed to get back and rest, had to be at the hospital in the morning. She wrapped her sandwich in a napkin and got up.

Will and I let Shelley and Pam in next to us.

Will was facing the door, watching Mary as she stopped at the counter to pay her bill and get a takeout bag.

"Penny for your thoughts," Pam said to Will.

"You're over-paying him," I told her. "Let's order."

Shelley giggled at that. "You his financial advisor, Doc?"

"Just these big accounts," I said.

The waitress set down the pitcher of beer and glasses. We ordered and she left.

"Bunch of wisenheimers," Will said.

"Can't blame you for looking," I told Will. I winked at the girls. "You look like you've never seen a Huguenot before, Will. Beautiful, aren't they?"

Shelley was trying to restrain a laugh.

Will was almost laughing, too, and said to Shelley, "Didn't you realize what you were getting into when you started rooming with this Huguenot? Did you know her background? What am I suppose to tell the F.B.I., when they come around asking questions?"

We all thought that was funny as hell.

"Tell'em to bite one," I said.

"You all are terrible," Shelley said.

"I'm sure she's a very wonderful person," Will said. "Not really making fun of her, you know."

"Well, you've been fired from the Welcome Wagon," Pam said.

I went silent for a moment, while looking at the cute waitress attending another booth. She noticed and gave me a nice, long look of approval. I'd seen her a couple times recently. I filed it away.

Pam noticed both of us. She gave me an elbow shot to the ribs, and looked hurt but used to it, as usual. The look she gave the waitress was something else. "Damn nerve," she said.

I muttered something like, "Sorry." It was lame.

Will asked Shelley, "So what was the big deal horrible thing that happened to your roommate, Hugo, last night, you were telling me about?"

"Someone close to her died."

"Oh." Which was also lame.

"A little girl at the hospital," Shelley said. "Mary went into work last night and the girl had died. She works with seriously and terminally ill children. That's why she wants to go to med school, to study childhood diseases, do research and all. Her younger brother died six years ago when he was eight."

"Of what?" Pam said.

"Brain tumor."

"Grief," Pam said. "Poor girl."

"You mean poor brother," I said. "He's the one who died."

Will said, "Did anybody bring a rock? I need to crawl under something."

"You didn't know," Shelley said.

When the waitress brought the sandwiches, Will lifted the corner of his. "I think I can get under here."

"Always the diplomatic one," I said. "And I'll eat the sandwich so you have no place to hide."

"Mind crawling under a strawberry shortcake, while you're at it?" Pam said. "And another pitcher of beer?"

"You know," I said to Pam, "you sure are getting to where you're saying a lot of funnies, hanging around with me."

"Clown college."

"Is there no end?"

"You didn't do anything terrible, Will," Shelley said, "besides being yourself." She gave a cute grin.

"I don't mind being a pain in the ass," Will said, "but not at somebody's disadvantage, especially a girl's. I'll apologize to her."

"You're an officer and a cattleman," I said.

We dug into the food, talking less and enjoying the music from the jukebox. Pam grew extra quiet. I looked at her for a reason and could see her eyes glistening.

Will kept looking at the door.

The only one who seemed to have nothing particular on her mind was Shelley, the brightest mind at the table.

6

We split up after leaving the deli. Will and Shelley decided to go back to the party at Bowman's, since he wasn't going home to Newport News and she wasn't sleepy. They dropped Pam and me off at my car, where I left it parked on the street, next to the dorm. It was a year-old Austin Healey ragtop, dark British racing green. We'd earlier thrown our laundry, including Will's, into the trunk, our main reason for going home. That and for me to make church in the morning so I could stand around out front and talk sports with the guys. The price for doing it was attending Sunday school, at least, if not the sermon, depending on who was there.

It was one a.m. when we parked at my father's cabin cruiser at the boat basin. The basin opened up through a narrow inlet from the James River cut under the two-lane Sixteenth Street bridge connecting our neighborhoods. A boardwalk rimmed the basin. Pam and I lived only a few blocks apart, she on one side of the bridge, and I on the other, on Chesapeake Boulevard, overlooking the river, itself. The view from the riverside was great. You could see the Navy base in Norfolk, four miles across, and the dozens of military and merchant vessels at dock and in the channel lit up like a city. The field next to the basin was a favorite parking place for kids, as well as for local cops on duty, to sneak up on cars and see naked girls, and couples fornicating, among other things, before finally running them off, of course.

A nice breeze was blowing in off the river, which eliminated the mosquito problem for a while and cut down on the incessant heat. The water only faintly lapped at the boat. We boarded and opened the windows in the cabin. The boat was outfitted as much for comfort as fishing, because my father liked to party as much as throw a line in the water. That made two of us. But because he was never home, the boat was idle, except when I used it. Will and I used it for double-dating, and sometimes for parties on the river and out in the Chesapeake.

Pam and I locked ourselves in the cabin and had sex, as usual. More honestly, I think I was the one having sex, while she was actually making love to me. She was very passionate and always cried when doing it, like it was some kind of religious or other deeply spiritual experience, which was great because it made it so much better. So much so that at times I felt guilty for not reciprocating in a like manner. But there was always a thin line of fear I found impossible to cross. I truly did not want to lie to her. I admit I was rakish, and I never denied it. I simply could not commit. I liked to think I was too young for it. Being twenty was my excuse. But she always said to me when we finished, "I love you so much, L.D." It was like a soft ringing in my ear, a reassuring hand on my shoulder.

It was getting too hot in the cabin, so we went to the stern and stretched out together on the chaise, after I rolled out the canopy overhead to keep off the dew. Pam lay between my legs and rested her head on my chest. I loved the smell of her hair like this. And the residual female scent of sex was intoxicating. Sometimes I found myself holding on too tightly.

"L.D., I wish you wouldn't flirt with other girls when you're with me," she said. "It's humiliating and disrespectful. And it hurts."

"I don't mean for it to be. You know that."

"But you still do it, knowing how I feel about it."

"I promise, I'll try not to do it again."

"If I see that bitch again, I'll scratch her eyes out."

"Just one eye. Leave the other so she can study."

"Piss on her. She can get Dicky to teach her how to be blind."

"Dicky's all booked up."

"Do you get the feeling Will is stumped by Mary Poythress?"

"Yeah."

"She seems really nice. Shelley says she'll graduate early with a double major and make Phi Beta Kappa in grad school."

"That's two of them in the same house. The place will explode from hyper-intensive brain waves."

"Are you trying to sound intelligent?"

"Gee, you think I could?"

"Nah, forget it." She gave me a gentle punch in the gut. "Let's don't go home just now. Let's stay here awhile."

"You win."

"I mean, he actually dropped to the ground and got his clothes dirty. That's a first. There's something going on there."

"Say goodnight, Gracie."

7

The chilly air woke us in one another's arms at five-thirty, just before sunrise, and we left the boat. I dropped Pam off at her house, then went home and went to bed.

Aunt Evie came into my room to wake me about eight. She drew the curtains.

"You're going to church, aren't you?" she said.

I yawned and stretched. "Yeah."

"I'm fixing breakfast." She stopped at the doorway, hesitant to tell me. "Your mother called yesterday, honey. She tried to reach you at school." She hesitated further. "They won't be able to make it to Homecoming in October. She'll try to make it Thanksgiving. Christmas, for sure. She sent some money for you. I'm sorry, L.D." She went back downstairs.

Sunlight sprayed the room. I sat on the edge of the bed a moment, looking out the windows, across the boulevard at the river and my early morning thoughts, which weren't much. No great surprise. So what else was new? They were hardly ever around anyway. It's pathetic when you have to look forward to bumping into your parents at a college homecoming, in order to see them. But I guessed there had to be enough in it for them to make them want to come home.

My father was an engineer who traveled the world building dams, tunnels, bridges and roads for his employer, a giant engineering and construction company. My mother stayed home for years, then dumped me into military school in eighth grade and took off after him, staying in luxury hotels, apartments and villas in exotic places like Singapore, Brazil, South Africa, Europe, and shopping his money away almost as fast as he could make it. Of course, they agreed early on this was no life for a child, so they sent money home and I stayed away at school and with my Aunt Evie, my father's older sister, in our big house, where I avoided the solitude—hell, the loneliness—by staying with my friends as much as possible, as often at Will's house as my own. It was amazing how you could be in a house in the middle of summer, temperature in the nineties and, literally, shake like a leaf from the cold, which actually happened when I was younger.

Not that my Aunt Evie wasn't okay. She was great, the closest thing I really ever had for years to a regular blood mother, but it wasn't the same. She had her own baggage to deal with. Her husband, a fighter pilot during the war, disappeared in the Pacific. She heard rumors of his being captured, tortured and beheaded, and she never got over it, never took up with another man, either. What she did was drink. She was an attractive woman—still kept the men at bay—was immaculate in her dress and housekeeping, cooked well and was sociable. A lot of people liked her. She was nice to my friends and was always available for me, as long as she could stay awake. But she smelled of booze—her friend, she called it—slurred her words, and her eyes always looked like they were glazed over with Karo syrup. Not the person you would want representing you at the P.T.A. meeting. In fact, when I left military school and enrolled back home in ninth grade at Newport News High, she went with me to sign the papers as my guardian. She was dressed to kill and, at ten a.m., already had a couple belts in her, and went down the halls tipping to one side, then another, like she was doing some funny Latin dance step. Fortunately, it was during classes and none of the students saw her. Mostly, I took her for granted for the good she offered, and avoided her when possible, for the rest. Probably said more about me than her.

The church was just around the corner, on Blair and Maple, a short block off the riverfront, so Aunt Evie and I walked together. I stayed for Sunday school, then went home. She stayed for the sermon and chatted and gossiped with the other women. She didn't drink on Sunday mornings, but after church, if there were no non-drinking company, her calendar was wide open the rest of the week. She'd be sitting up front, enjoying the choir and not hearing the minister, but her mouth would be moving all kinds of ways, and her mind would be on that gin and whatever waiting for her back at the house. I changed my clothes and read the newspaper, until she got home and set the table. It was the only time at home I did not mind, the spring and summer, when the dining room was warmed by the air coming through the windows, and the smell of food, which made it tolerable, and all the boats and ships in the water.

Sometimes Aunt Evie would bring home a guest or two for Sunday dinner, usually older folks, mostly blue-hairs, occasionally the minister and his family, but this Sunday she didn't. We sat alone at opposite ends of the dining table, which seated eight, ten with a leaf.

"What time you going back?"

"Five or six," I said.

"Your laundry will be ready by four, I suppose."

"Thanks."

"All this good food. You should've brought Pam over."

"She had to go over to her grandparents. Her family actually likes to see her."

"What about William?" She always called him William.

"He stayed at school."

"I'll package up some of this to take back with you."

"We don't take bag lunches to college, Aunt Evie." I said it nicely. "Don't bother with it."

"Shame to waste it. I thought sure you'd bring somebody with you."

"Call the Starvation Army."

"I saw Martha Lynn at the grocery store yesterday." She was speaking of Will's mother. "She's worried about William's grades, and all."

"He knows the score."

"God-awful mess we've gotten ourselves into over there, all I can say." She was referring to Viet Nam, of course.

"Long as it's over there and doesn't affect the football schedule."

She looked like she had been hurt. I thought of her and her dead husband, and Tim Davis, and felt kind of cheap. "Just kidding," I said.

"And you watch your grades, too, and work hard, honey. Try to make the dean's list." She reflected on that. "Now wouldn't your momma and daddy be proud of that."

"They'd be on the first flight."

"Well, they would be proud. I know they would. I know it's hard for you to see sometimes."

"It's hard for me to see all the time."

"You've got to give them credit, L.D. They love you very much and you know it."

"Really? She could come home, she doesn't work."

"It's more complicated than that."

"Not for me, I took math."

"I wish you wouldn't be like that, honey, a snappy answer for everything."

"And I wish I didn't feel like it. I wish they wouldn't try and make me feel like a charity case, a darn orphan or something. I feel like I'm going to get a bill for all this."

She seemed hurt again, not angry, but I wasn't in a mood for apologies.

"I wouldn't exactly say that," she said.

"She won't be home for Thanksgiving. You can count on it. Christmas, either, neither one of them. Not that I give a crap."

"Yes, you do. And I know they'll be home for Christmas, both of them."

"I'll make it a point not to be here."

"You're a lot luckier in some ways than a lot of people your age, L.D."

My look told her she had over-spoken, and her look withdrew the comment.

"Sometimes," I said, "I think I'd like to save up all the money they send home and put in the car and run the damn car off the seawall," which was across the street.

"Then you're going to look awfully funny pushing that little two-wheel scooter up and down the street all the way to Williamsburg and back on the weekends." She grinned and looked into her spiked ice tea glass.

It was a funny thought. "I didn't say I'd do it right now. I have to save up a carload of money first."

8

That same Sunday morning, Will got up in the dorm at nine, unable to stop thinking of Mary Poythress. A few hours sleep did not do him much good. He was still tired and feeling like an idiot. Maybe if he played the noble role, maybe that would do it, get the date with her. That would put things back the way the universe was suppose to operate. Wasn't that really what it was all about? Guys went to school to prepare for a career and screw as many girls as possible. Girls went to find husbands who would be good breadwinners and easy to live with. Sure, the girl majored in something as a cover. She was going to do medical research, or go to New York and be a famous fashion designer, or actress or artist, or teach school, or be a pillar of the community, raising funds for the less fortunate, and all that other lofty crap. But let a guy throw a ring on her finger, then stand back and watch. She'd drop out of school before her next class and go to work somewhere as a clerk for a chance to live in the guy's nest. All a lot of bullshit, far as Will was concerned. But she, this Mary girl, deserved the apology, and he would give it to her, and the sooner the better. Use that to make his next move.

Will learned from Shelley Michaels that Mary volunteered on the fourth floor at the hospital in Newport News, in the children's ward. He could have gone home that night and been closer when he got up, but he and Shelley didn't leave the party at Bowman's until three a.m. His mother would throw a fit because he did not go home, but sent his dirty clothes in his place as a token of his love, which, I supposed, made me the unofficial Ambassador of Laundry who would take the heat for it.

Will wanted to look like he belonged there, so he wore a coat and tie to the hospital. It was Sunday morning and he would blend right in with the doctors making morning rounds. It helped that he looked a couple years older than his age. Hopefully, security guards would not be a problem. But we were both experts at getting into hospitals when we weren't suppose to be there. When you have a hospital in your own neighborhood, while growing up, you acquire those skills.

Will walked through the double doors from the emergency area, making it look like he was working there, and into the lobby where the elevators were located. He was wearing a stethoscope around his neck. The guard nodded and pushed the button for him, and Will spotted the nurses' station just to the right when he stepped off the elevator.

The nurse on duty did a double take, probably because she had never seen him before. Probably thought he was good-looking, too. Whammo combination, doctors and good looks, very rare.

Will gave the nurse his best smile. "Where can I find Miss Poythress?" The smile really said, *Where can I find you?*

The nurse gave it back. "I'll call her up for you." Probably thinking, *So I can keep looking at you.*

"No, no, don't disturb her. I just want to talk with her in private a second."

"Last room on the left." She pointed.

"Thank you."

"Any time." She watched him walk away, tilting her head one way, then another, to visualize the different angles.

Will looked into the room.

Mary was sitting in a chair at the bedside of a skinny little boy of eleven or twelve who was strapped with tubes, I.V.s, and all kinds of gadgets Will couldn't tell from beans. She was dressed in a nice skirt, a frilly blouse and dress shoes, like she might be going to church or somewhere after finishing up here, or maybe already had been to wherever it is Huguenots go on Sunday mornings. She was reading a story, or the Bible or something, oblivious to Will.

Will leaned on the doorjamb and watched. She looked good sitting there with her back to him, legs crossed, figure a thin hour glass; small waist, rear end a perfect heart shape.

Be my valentine.

In a few seconds, the boy noticed Will, which made Mary stop reading and look back. She was momentarily speechless, and not happy.

Will gave a little wave with a *me again* half-smile.

Mary tried to sound formal, like he was a total stranger. "Can I help you?" she said.

"Aren't you going to introduce me?"

"I'd have to know you to do that." She looked at the boy to see that he didn't know Will. "Maybe the nurse can help you." She pointed the way.

Will walked past her and to the opposite side of the bed.

"You're not supposed to be in here," Mary said.

"What do you know about where I'm suppose to be? I'm Will," he then said to the boy, sticking out his hand.

The boy shook it weakly. "I'm Steven. Are you her boyfriend?"

"No," Mary said quickly.

"No, I think that would be you," Will said.

The boy grinned. "Okay with me."

Mary was seething at the way this was going. "You're not authorized. The nurse will call the security guard."

"Are you a doctor?" Steven said.

"No. How'd you like a football? A real one, a college football? I'll bring you one."

"Yeah, I guess. That'd be great."

"If you don't mind, we're busy here," Mary said.

"Steven," Will said, "you think it'd be okay if I speak with Miss Poythress a second, out in the hall?"

"That won't be necessary," Mary said.

"Yeah, I guess," Steven said.

"Please. It won't take but a second. It's important."

"Okay, if you promise to leave and not come back," she said.

"Only to bring the football to Steven."

"When are you going to bring it?" Steven said.

"Next couple of days or so, maybe sooner. Don't tell the nurses, they won't let me come up."

"Your presence is corrupting," Mary said.

Steven seemed puzzled. "If you're not a doctor and you're not her boyfriend, then what are you?"

"He's the football man," Mary said. "He visits hospitals and drops off footballs. Before that, he was blind, then he switched to medicine. Hold my place, I'll be right back." She handed Steven the book.

"What is it?" Mary said when they were in the hallway by the door. "What is it you could possibly want?"

"Just to apologize. For the way I acted."

"You make it a bigger deal than it is."

"I try."

"Great. Apology accepted. Now leave. You're not suppose to be up here, and I've got things to do."

"I'm going, don't worry. You don't have to be so hostile about it. I got out of bed early and put on a tie and everything, to come all the way down here and do this."

"So what do you want, a Nobel Prize for Apologies? I'll nominate you. Now get lost." She turned away.

"Must be awfully painful," Will said.

She stopped. "I beg your pardon."

"To lose so much. Be sour all the time. Never laugh at anything. Staying busy. Work, work, work."

"What are you talking about?" He did not answer. "You're immature."

"But I'm amusing and lovable."

"In your own mind."

"That mean you don't love me any more?" He could see the answer to that in those gorgeous but pissed-off eyes of hers.

"It's okay, I won't bother you any more," Will said. "I'm sorry for upsetting you. But the apology stands, even though it's obvious you can't accept apologies gracefully."

He stepped past her and back into the room and told Steven, "I'll bring the football by. I promise, buddyro. See you later."

Will left Mary standing in the doorway, watching him leave.

Well, it was done, but she sure didn't buckle at the knees, like he was hoping she would. Where did he ever get a dumb-ass idea like that?

9

Will told me later about the grand apology that didn't work out.

"But I've still got to take that football to that little boy because I promised. You'll have to go as my junior intern."

"Always glad to lend my medical expertise," I said. "Better do it now, though. You won't have time this week. We'll have to break curfew, too."

"We'll take your car, look like rich young doctors when we pull up next to the emergency room."

"Mary Poythress isn't going to be there. Is she? I don't want her to see me with you. She'll never go out with me."

"Not so fast, you rat fink. It ain't over for me yet. Besides, she won't be there, if she was there this morning. Volunteers don't work those kind of hours. Fact, I think Miklos was right, that's girl's not going out with anybody."

"Then why do you keep trying?"

"Good question."

"Let's take him a real jersey, too," I said. "Your ball, my jersey."

"No, I want the kid to have my number so he can talk me up. She'll come in next time and say, 'Oh, Steven, where'd you get that beautiful Number Twenty-one jersey, and that wonderful football?' Of course, she'll already know. And he'll say, 'Oh, that big, handsome, super jock hero you were so nasty to the other morning brought it to me out of the kindness of his big heart, because he's honest and dependable and noble. Aren't you sorry you blew it with him?' And she'll be sorry as hell and call me and beg me to go out with her so she can screw my brains right to the ground."

"Yeah, it seems to be working, so far."

We skipped curfew and borrowed lab coats from guys we knew who were science majors and actually passed labs, to go with the stethoscopes we already had. Those and a line of bullshit about a mile long would get us anywhere in the hospital we wanted to go. I carried the football and jersey in a gym bag.

It was nine p.m., visiting hours were over, and people were pouring out of the place. We kept a sharp lookout for anyone we might know, since this was our hometown. We acted very casual and took our time working our way through the E.R. and into the lobby to the elevator, stopping briefly a couple times to talk shop around the guard. He was an older guy. Hopefully, he wouldn't know anything about medicine.

"So what was your diagnosis?" Will said, so the guard could hear, while we waited at the elevator.

"Plyethoric nyarhemia," I said.

"Treatment?"

"I decided on a left ventrical quadrastat of the tibula figueroa."

"That's good. Did Dr. Willets concur? Great. I want you to see Dr. Lacy in the morning. I'll call him and tell him you're coming by. He's doing a parallel procedure Tuesday morning. You can assist. You'll learn a lot from him, he's done a hundred of them."

"Good," I said. "I was hoping to get a chance to see one up close."

The guard was thoroughly in outer space when the elevator finally arrived and emptied. That or he just didn't care. We liked to think it was our talent. On the elevator, we laughed like two morons trapped in a toy store.

"Great," Will said. "Now if you ever learn to use a microscope, you'll make a brilliant lab student."

The floor was cleared of visitors. Will and I acted real doctorly. We told the nurses we were dropping something off to Steven as a favor.

The kid was hooked up the way he was earlier that morning when Will was there. He couldn't have gotten off the bed if he'd wanted to. He lay gazing out the window at the darkness. Made you wonder if he was waiting for something magical to appear, like an angel, or a miracle, or Tinker Bell, that would get him the hell out of the place.

Will led the way into the room. "Hey, Steven, you awake?"

"Yeah. Hey, you came back." His voice was weak.

"I told you I would, didn't I? This is my buddy, Doc."

"Hey, partner." I shook his hand.

"Hey, you a doctor?"

"No, just a nickname. It's Will's fault."

"Show him the stuff," Will said.

"Yeah, we brought you this ball. And this jersey to wear." I took it out and handed it to him. The jersey would fit like a nightgown if he ever wore it, since it was made for shoulder pads. He seemed too tired or weak to do much except clutch the ball loosely. But his eyes were excited about the whole thing, even though he seemed a little proud or embarrassed maybe, being treated like a kid.

"This a college football?" Steven said.

"Genuine college pigskin."

"Made from the finest college pigs," I said. "You play football?"

"Yeah, but I got sick. Not a real team or anything. I like baseball most."

"What position you play in football?" Will said.

"Quarterback and tackle."

"Deadly combo," I said. Stick to baseball, I thought.

Will and I saw the humor in the unlikely picture of one guy playing both those positions in the real world.

"Had any visitors today?" Will said.

"My mom and sister and brother. They just left."

"What about your dad?"

"He's overseas, in the army. He'll be home Christmas."

"I know the feeling," I said. Only Steven's dad probably would come home.

"Good," Will said.

"You Mary's boyfriend?" Steven asked me.

"Not yet, but it looks like I might be soon."

"That's what you think," Will said. Then to Steven, "This guy's got the prettiest girl in the world and he's not satisfied. Watch your girlfriend around him, Steven. He'll try to steal her away. This guy collects girlfriends."

"That's a lie, Steven. I never bother another guy's girl."

"I don't have a girlfriend yet. But both of y'all like Mary. Don't you?" He looked like he might be worried about it.

"She say anything after I left this morning?" Will said.

"Nuh-uh."

"Seem mad or happy or anything?"

"No."

"There you go," I said to Will. "It's that stunning effect you have on women, leaves them speechless." I signaled him to drop the Mary thing. Steven seemed a little jealous.

Will picked up on it. "Ah, it's not important. I think she likes you anyway."

Will got a bright idea. "Hey, what if we get you some tickets to a home game? You and your mother, and brother and sister, can go sometime. Of course, Mary would have to go, too, to help out and all."

Steven struggled to lean up on his elbows. "That would be al-right, if I could go. I'd have to ask my mom and the doctor." There was a glimmer of hope there.

"When do you go home?" Will said.

"I don't know. They haven't said yet."

"How long you been here?"

"Five months, this time."

"This time? How often you come here?"

"Been coming for treatments since last year."

Will and I exchanged glances.

"Well," I said, "we didn't bring all this stuff for nothing. You'll have to go to a home game, and bring the football and wear the jersey. You can even meet with the team and coaches, and cheerleaders."

"Okay, I'll try." He flopped back down like he already knew he wasn't going anywhere.

"Is it okay to prop you up?" Will cranked up the bed.

We didn't know it at the time, but Mary Poythress was by the door, listening. Christ, she must have lived there.

"We keeping you awake?" I asked Steven.

"Naw."

Will took the ball from him and spun and flipped it in his hands. "Know the best way to hold the ball when you throw a pass, Steven?"

"I think so."

"Well, I'm going to show you the college way. That way, when you get well, you'll be way ahead of everybody, playing on a different level. Maybe even play for me someday."

"You can play quarterback on offense," I said, "then switch to tackle on defense, a double threat."

Will and I giggled. A little joke at the kid's expense.

Will demonstrated placing the fingers on the threads of the ball. "This is the way I did it last year in the big U.VA. game, when I faked the pass that saved the day." He did a little drop-back movement. "The crowd was on its feet, the noise was deafening." He cupped his hands to his mouth and blew a crowd sound. "It was now or never, showdown time. Turnbull—he's our quarterback—took the snap and pitched left to me. I faked one of my usual deadly runs to draw in the defense—they were keying on me anyway—

then went to throw down the sideline, on the run, to Doc here, who was wide open and was supposed to catch the ball, but, unfortunately, had stopped to chat with the cheerleaders. See, I told you about him and the girls. So I immediately reversed fields and out-ran everybody to the far corner to score by using my blinding speed, breaking tackles all the way. So hard to get good help these days, you know."

I told Will, "Give him the ball back. See, Steven, he's a ball hog."

"You guys are crazy. But y'all won, huh?"

"Uh, well, not exactly," Will said. "They cheated. See, we were about to win and one of their guys snuck behind the clock and moved the hands, so time ran out. U.VA. guys are like that."

"Which made us lose by the skin of our teeth, by only twelve points," I said. "Another couple hours and they'd have fallen asleep on the bus and we'd have clobbered them."

Steven laughed, seemed to enjoy that.

Then Mary walked in, pretending our presence was a surprise. She was still dressed the way she was earlier that morning. "Oh, excuse me."

Damn, she was good-looking. I exchanged nods with her.

Will almost died.

She hesitated an instant, then went to the bedside. "I'm leaving now, Steven. Anything I can do before I go?"

"I don't think so. Thanks, Mary. When you coming back?"

"In a couple days, Wednesday night for sure, to help you with the new homework assignments your mother left. Okay? I'll be in the lab Tuesday night, try to get up to see you, but no promises."

"Yeah, that'll be good."

I extended my hand to Mary. "I'm Doc Cavanaugh. L.D."

"Pleased to meet you." Polite but insincere.

"I believe you've already met Will." Trying to start something.

"Seems I can't stop meeting him."

Having recovered quickly, Will said to Steven, "I'm going to use my influence with Mary here to get the nurses to let you wear your jersey, Steven."

"Make sure you check with me about that," she said.

"Better than these goofy hospital clothes," Will said. "Ain't that right, Steven?"

"I guess."

If Mary's looks could have killed. "The nurse will be here in a minute. You'd better go now. You might be late for surgery."

"Cute," Will said.

"I'm talking about your own, of course, the frontal lobotomy."

Will said to me, "Hey, Doc, I think I'm getting a human reaction here." Then to Mary, "You're not going to fink on us, are you?"

Mary didn't answer.

"You mean you've been here all day?" Will said to her.

Her quick look said it was none of his business, but it didn't have that edge to it.

Will told Steven, "I'll get with Mary about the tickets. Maybe she can help."

"Help what?" Mary said.

"I'll tell you about it later."

"We don't have a later."

"Champ here is going to a game, if his doctor and mother can swing it."

She looked at them both. "That so?" Then to Will, "Can I talk with you on the way out?"

"Thought I'd never hear you say those words."

"Don't get any ideas."

"I want to pack in as many ideas as I can before the lobotomy."

"Tell you what," I said, picking up on it, "you two talk while I go look up lobotomy. I'll meet you at the car, Will. Nice meeting you, Mary."

After I was gone, Mary left the room just ahead of Will and waited for him down the hall.

"So what is it?" Will said when he got to her.

"As if you have no idea. First, you're not suppose to be up here. Second, you have no business promising things you can't deliver."

"Like what? I brought the football, didn't I?"

"You don't even know this boy. He's not going anywhere. You should check with his doctor before you say things you don't mean. And can't do."

"Who says I can't do it?"

"He's terminal. Don't you understand? He's not going to any football games. He's not even going home. He's not going any- where. According to his doctors, he'll be lucky to live until Thanksgiving. It's offensive and cruel for you to come in here and create disappointment and upset things."

Will absorbed that for a second. "Then why are you teaching him his school work?"

Mary seemed tripped by the question, took a second of her own to answer. "Because it's what his mother wants, and I volunteered to help."

"Yeah, well, I'm volunteering, too."

"No, what you're doing is chasing skirts, namely mine at the moment, no telling how many others on the way out the door. And I told you, I'm not interested." She started to walk off, but managed to turn only her shoulders before Will's response stopped her.

"Would you like to have lunch one day this week?"

She couldn't believe it. "You know, you're probably the most obstinate person I've ever met in my life. *No.*"

"At least that makes me number one somewhere with you. Doesn't it? That's an improvement. I'll pay for the lunch, of course."

"Save your money, Will. It's likely you've got a long, hard life in front of you, and you're going to need every dime you can get." She walked away.

"Whatever you say, Hugo. Good to see you show an interest in my future." He watched her. He sure did like the way she said his name, like she had known him forever.

She almost paused, just a brief hesitation, but kept going.

"What kind of crap have I got us into, Doc?" Will said, when he got to the car and we drove off.

"Us? What's this *us* business?"

"We volunteered to take that kid to a game."

"We didn't volunteer anything," I said. "And you just volunteered first to get some tickets. I just said he could meet the team."

"The kid's dying."

"I kind of figured that. But what can we do? His mother can take him."

"Well, we can at least get him to a game, I guess. Can't back down on a promise."

"I can't believe this crap, Will. We went through all this just for you. And you went in the hospital to sneak up on a date with Mary Poythress and came out with a date with the kid."

"Kind of got it bass awkward. Didn't I? But I believe she's softening up a bit. Did you notice?"

It was a wonder we didn't have an accident and kill ourselves laughing all the way back to Williamsburg.

10

The next morning, just before leaving home for class, Shelley Michaels could hardly believe it when Mary told her about Sunday.

"Twice he went down there? My *gawd*, he must really have the hots for you."

"He looked pathetic, like a little boy, when he apologized."

"We were out until around three in the morning and he never mentioned you after we left the party. You ought to take him up on it."

"I thought you liked him," Mary said.

"I do, as a friend. There's nothing serious between Will and me. We've dated a few times, made out a little bit, but that's all. Some of us at Hampton used to hang out at the beach with the Newport News crowd. That's how I know him. He's a great guy, but we've never had sex, if that's what you mean. Besides, I want to be a serious scholar and travel the world, and Will wants to be a football."

"I wouldn't ask. It's none of my business."

"Well, we haven't anyway, just so you know the history, in case you're ever interested."

"His friend is really cute," Mary said.

"Doc? L.D. Yeah, Doc's cute, but Doc's also dangerous, if you care anything about your feelings. Love'em and leave'em Doc. A string of broken hearts from here to Nags Head. Don't get me wrong, he's a nice guy and a lot of fun, but he's not serious material."

"That so?"

"Doc's a beach bum at heart. If we had surf on the east coast, that's what he'd be doing. You met his girlfriend the other night. Pam?"

"They go together?"

"She goes together. He goes wherever he wants."

"She's so beautiful, though. Must be the sex."

"And she's just as nice and sweet. But Doc doesn't get it. He's not into long-term commitments, or any commitment that I know of. My advice, unless you're actually looking for a little quick fun—and I don't think that's you—is stay away from him."

"What about Will?"

"So you care."

"No, I was just thinking, just curious. He just keeps coming back."

"Don't tell him that, it'll go to his head."

"I don't have time for dating now."

"Will has never gone steady with anybody, either. He's always dated a lot of different girls. He's like Doc that way, but at least he doesn't string anybody along. With Will, I think he'd be a great catch if he ever fell for somebody. But you can't be too sure, you know, since there's no record to go on."

"Great catch if you're fishing. But who's fishing?"

"And by the way," Shelley said, "don't ever call him William. He doesn't like it. Something about being named after an uncle he hates, who used to give him the Dutch rub when he was younger.

"But I'll tell you something, if he drove down to Newport News twice in one day to see you at the hospital, well, he's never done that before that I know of. Good sign. Usually, the girl goes after him."

"Last thing in my life I need is a good sign. Too much complication."

"Don't take this the wrong way, Mary, but your mother must really be a bitch to live with."

"She can be. She's also very wonderful. And complicated. It's just not easy, with all that's happened, my brother and all."

"I understand, but you need to get out more, no matter what she thinks. So you think maybe you'd like to go out with Will?"

Mary was standing at the bathroom mirror, doing makeup. "Maybe sometime. But don't tell him that."

"Make him crawl."

"He's got to be strong."

They thought that was very funny.

"Isn't it great to be a woman and still have options?" Shelley said.

I had to admit, sometime later when I heard about it, that I was a little hurt by Shelley's evaluation of me as a rake, like there was something terribly wrong with being twenty and single and wanting to stay that way awhile. It gave me that cold feeling I sometimes got at home, like I was somehow different, not really one of the rest of humanity, missing something. Girls were always thinking ahead, about life pictures and how a guy might fit in. Just what the hell was that all about? Of course, the remark about my being cute, and about "a little quick fun," helped me get over it, so I guessed I had some redeeming value on this earth, even though the implication was that I was limited and vacuous because I didn't fit into someone's idea of a life picture guy.

Except for Pam. Pam loved me and saw me in her life for the long run, even if I didn't see her and admitted it. Well, that was one.

But it still gave me that lonely feeling, like it would all end after college because, well, the party would be over and everybody would go their separate ways, then meet somewhere else and not tell me. And what use would I be then? What in hell would I do?

11

Will wanted to be slick. He learned Mary's schedule, so he thought, and wanted to go through the building and come down the corridor to the front and just happen to meet Mary as she was coming through the door of her class, some high baloney science course. But it didn't happen that way. Mary had changed her schedule around, and Will waited and waited, easing his way toward the front, looking like a pervert hanging around a hallway, until class started without her. He thought she might be late, or maybe even skipping, since she was so bright and probably could get away with it. Which made him late for his own class, like a dummy.

And who did he see when he got to his own class and tried to sneak into the lecture hall unnoticed? Mary. Right there, up front. What in hell was she doing in this flaky art history course? How, as a double major in the hard sciences, could she stoop that low, without a bag over her head, to what must have been for her a crib course, but to Will an easy elective, if you could call a course easy here? Where did this girl get time for all this crap she did?

Will found a seat a row behind her, a couple spots over, and couldn't stop looking at her. Mary didn't know he was there, not until Dr. Sandridge reached over and passed up to Will a copy of the syllabus and she happened to glance around, see him, and roll her eyes. Will tried to pretend he didn't notice her. Sure.

Dr. Sandridge stepped back behind the lectern. He was an older guy, tall and lean, who always wore a suit with pastel shirt and bow tie, and carried his books and papers up high in his armpit, kind of brainy-fied.

"Now," Dr. Sandridge said, "if you're ready, Mr. Wythe, we'll get started. I'm glad we could all make it on time this morning so we could be here to welcome you when you finally arrived."

That got a mild laugh from everybody but Mary, who didn't want to encourage Will, probably. Dr. Sandridge enjoyed the stage, and he was a big football fan, so he knew Will. Art guy gets one over on jock, I guess.

A student in back asked if class would be dismissed early, since it was the first day. Of course, everybody liked hearing that, but most knew better.

"You must be new here," Dr. Sandridge said.

"Yes, sir."

"Still looking for your homeroom, I see. What correspondence school have you been attending, young man? You're trying to leave before you get here. Trying to defy some natural law of physics? Go back to your correspondence school and you'll never have to get up in the morning."

More laughter, better than getting out early. Even Mary was enjoying the humor. And Will enjoyed watching her. What do you know, she could smile.

"But to answer your question, Mr.—?" Dr. Sandridge said.

"Meyer."

"Mr. Meyer. To answer your question, sir, yes, you can leave early, assuming this is an elective for you. And I suspect it is.

"The only people we hold against their will, under penalty of death, are Art majors. The rest of you don't have to be here, and we don't have to have you here. But I suggest, before you make your hasty retreat, you look over the handout you just received, as it explains quite clearly the course content, as well as the rules of engagement. Either that or you go to Add-Drop. For you freshmen, like Mr. Meyer here, that is a place where you can go to seek refuge from a course or professor you thought you might like but now frightens you. Attendance will be recorded at the end of class and seats reserved for those of you who are still here.

"Does that answer your question sufficiently, Mr. Meyer?"

"Yes, sir."

"Thank you. Inane question time is now over. Are there any questions on matters reasonably important, before we proceed? Good. Today's subject is You." He accented the You.

Dr. Sandridge cut the lights and walked to the rear of the classroom to his projector, where he began flashing slides on the screen up front of paintings by well-known and dead European artists.

"You have forty seconds, each slide, to make a rough drawing, while I give you the names of the artists, the paintings, and a brief history of each. They will be on your mid-term and finals."

The scrambling for paper and pencils created a brief explosion, after he mentioned the exam part.

The paintings were all depressing—death, sadness, gloom, misery. Will wondered how this could be called art. Art was suppose to be wonderful, beautiful, colorful, uplifting, even if in a faggoty kind of way. But, then again, Will's idea of art to this point was executing the perfect play on the football field or pounding out an ashtray with a ball-peen hammer in high school metal shop.

Then the slides of the street urchins popped up.

"They were the throwaways of society," Dr. Sandridge was saying. "They were abandoned or sold for today's equivalent of fifty-to-two hundred dollars by parents and others who couldn't, or wouldn't, provide for them, didn't want a child who was sick, or deformed, crippled, retarded, or otherwise handicapped. They were newborn to five or six years old, and lived no longer than that, usually. Eight was old age for them. Their procurers—pimps—put them on the streets daily for whatever demand there was—sexual, usually—anything that was perverse, or too dirty or dangerous for anyone else..."

Will was stunned by what he was seeing and hearing, paintings of children, filthy, crawling the streets, with emaciated bodies, nubby limbs, begging for food and money, hungry for attention, or for the right to live another day maybe, or for whatever. He stopped drawing and stared at the image on the screen. He felt nauseous now, breathed faster, sweated, shifted in his seat and rubbed his hand over his mouth. He stopped looking at the slide. He cleared his throat as quietly as he could, looking around the classroom, self-conscious. He missed the next slide, similar in subject. What in hell was Dr. Sandridge trying to do, kill somebody? He closed his notebook and eased out of his seat as quietly as possible and left the room, unnoticed.

Fat chance.

In the hallway, by the door, Will sat on the bench, his face in his hands, dealing with this thing that just slapped his emotions silly. He was doing this when Mary came out.

"You alright?" she said.

"I'm fine."

"No, you're ill."

"Just tired. Not much sleep, riding the roads all last night apologizing to ungrateful people." Couldn't resist the jab.

"Sure, the world owes you a big truckload of gratitude."

"No, just you."

"Liar. The paintings got to you. Now you know what Dr. Sandridge meant when he said the class was about *you*."

"Bull."

"Embarrasses you. Doesn't it? Something touches your humanity and you're ashamed of it, ashamed to admit it."

"You must have the wrong person."

"You're William, aren't you?" She accented the William.

Will's jaw moved on its hinge.

"Guy who'd carry a dumb ball down a field and score a field goal, or whatever you call it—."

"A touchdown."

"A dumb touchdown then, and rant and rave and scream like an idiot, so proud about it in front of thousands of like-minded cretins—."

"They're called fans."

"Cretin fans. But let him witness the suffering of others and he wants to run and hide. Wonder what your cretin fans would think if they could see you like this."

Will looked her over. "You've got it all wrong."

"Then go back and finish the class. Why run from it?"

"Actually, I'm planning on it, for your information. What's it to you? I just needed some fresh air, all that freshmen breath in there."

"Sure."

"You some self-appointed grand counselor or something?"

"No. I wouldn't have expected to see someone with your limitations in this class anyway. But since I have, there's something we need to talk about, and I didn't want you to get away."

"That's a switch. So talk."

"Not now. After class."

"Must not be that important."

"I'm sure it's not to you," Mary said, "but it is to me. What are you doing after skipping this class because you have no guts?"

Will looked up again. His eyebrow lifted this time. "I'm not skipping this class, and I'm free until eleven."

"I'll meet you here after we're out. You can walk with me to the commons, while I tell you what you have to do."

"You can't walk by yourself?"

"I'm blind, I can't see."

"Want to lead me with a ring in my nose? You've got a heck of a nerve, you know it?"

"Yes, but apparently you don't, not when it comes to something that really counts."

Will was pissed, but Mary went back into class before he could formulate a decent comeback. All he could muster was a mumbled, "Sure thing, Hugo." He waited a long minute, not wanting to appear he was doing it because of her, which he was, of course. But he was not looking at any more of those dumb-ass slides, either. He could get the drawings from someone else. He did not know art was dangerous. Put warning signs up, or a lifeguard or something around the place, for Christ's sake.

But Will did not wait for Mary after class, either. Not exactly. He was losing credibility, if he ever had any, and figured he'd better get out with as much dignity as possible. So he went out the side door after class and got to the commons ahead of her. He sat alone at a table near the doorway, so she couldn't miss him, and pretended to study.

I say pretended to study because Will couldn't actually study during the day. It was mentally impossible. It had to be at night, dark, with the whole day behind him, and nothing in front but sleep. It was that little slot of time in between the two when he had to study, if at all. It was the only time his brain could accept knowledge, school stuff anyway.

Now it was Mary's turn to be pissed. She stopped in front of his table and dropped her books down a little hard.

"So what are you, some kind of jerk, trying to be cute? I waited for you."

"My, my," Will said, "is that a violent streak I detect?" He was sipping a bottle of Coke and enjoying the moment. "I don't take orders well."

"I guess that makes you a real rebel, a regular James Dean. How dramatic."

"I didn't think we had anything to talk about. And I'm not your pet donkey. You can walk yourself. Besides, I'm no longer interested in going out with you. So what's the point?"

"Oh. Well, that's a relief to hear. That mean you won't be showing up everywhere I go? Could you drop the art class, too? It's bad for your health, you know."

"I just think we should see other people."

"Funny. I got a call from Steven's mother last night, after we left the hospital. Steven called her, all excited about the great football game he was going to with you and your friend, Doc, to meet the team, the cheerleaders, coaches, the whole thing. She called his doctor and he said okay, under certain conditions. So now she's as excited as he is. So the sooner the better."

"Oh, so the doctor agrees with me then. Did you tell him you didn't think it was a good idea? That kids with terminal diseases shouldn't have fun, shouldn't laugh or be happy? Better call him before he does something stupid."

Mary looked like she wanted to reach over the table and smack his stupid head off and watch it roll across the floor. Instead, she handed him a slip of paper with the address and phone number of Steven's mother.

"I told her you'd call her and work out the details."

"Hey, I can't do this myself. What about you?"

She picked up her books to leave. "Well, I'm sure where there's a *Will*iam, there's a way. She accented the William again.

"I need help with this."

"You need help with a lot more than this."

"Wait. Look, I want to do my part. Really, I do, but I don't have time for all this."

She stopped. "Then why did you start it?"

"I don't know, I kind of felt sorry for the kid. I wanted to make him feel good. That make me Hitler?"

"He doesn't need your sorrow. He needs you to make sure he gets to that game."

"I have to play in that game. I have to be there early. I practice every day. I'll get the tickets, and I'll even take him back to the hospital. But I can't take him to the game. It won't work, there's not enough time."

"You'd better make some, or it'll break his heart if it doesn't work."

"Why don't you bring him up here and sit with him during the game. I'll take over afterward."

"Can't, I'm committed. Besides, I didn't make the promise, you did."

"I didn't really specify which game, you know."

"I know, I did that." She gave Will a big smile and left.

"Way to go, Hugo."

12

Wednesday morning, we met in front of the stadium, where the vans were parked for the trip to Tim Davis's funeral, in Fairfax. Our fraternity wore the green blazers with embroidered shields, gray slacks and school lapel pins, since Tim had been an S.P.D. brother, and we still considered him one. We had a meeting of the Stonewall Jackson Club the night before and collected the hairs to go into the coffin, assuming it was okay with the family. If not, we would do it anyway, but those hairs were going into that coffin, one way or another. It was the least we could do for Tim. We knew he would appreciate us doing something goofy, since he had been kind of a practical joker, himself.

Maybe I'd better explain the hairs. The Stonewall Jackson Club was something Will and I started in tenth grade and carried with us to college. What happened was, every February, when the track team went up to the state indoor championships at V.M.I.—Virginia Military Institute, in the mountains at Lexington—we visited the campus museum that honors the revered Confederate general, Thomas Jonathan "Stonewall" Jackson, who had taught there before the Civil War, and we would hang around, looking at all the stuff. The museum was an old brick building on the main street that ran parallel to the parade field, where all the marching was done, and which, if you followed it off campus, led directly onto the campus of Washington & Lee University, then into the town of Lexington, where you could buy pizza, and three-point-two beer if you looked eighteen.

What caught our eye right away, the first time we went in, was the big glass case on the left as you walked in the door, which covered Little Sorrel, Stonewall's horse. The horse had been skinned and remounted after death and put there to be with the general's other memorabilia. The glass case was to the wall, against a chair rail, which allowed us enough space to get our arms behind it and into the opening, about five inches, so we could actually touch the horse, a no-no. But we did it anyway.

The lady in charge of the museum was about thirty-five and kind of nice looking. She had blondish hair and wore glasses, and dressed well. Will and I were considering the risk of flirting with her, but were distracted by the horse. Each of us reached in and snatched a single long hair from the horse's tail, like it was a great coup or something. We carried the hairs in our wallets, in the picture folders, the whole next year, until we went back up again. Then we put the hairs back and snatched different ones. No particular reason, I guess, except the challenge of getting past that very nice lady, and to have something no one else had that we could brag about. And since we still had dual meets and football games with V.M.I. every year in college, it gave us an excuse to keep doing it. We took in a few members along the way, but not more than eight or nine active members at any given time. If we grew too big, the horse wouldn't have a tail. Tim had been an honorary inductee, you might say, because he had dropped out of school before getting his first hair. So we wanted to make sure he got it, and then some, as a way of honoring him and making him a full-fledged member.

Of course, we did not want to approach Tim's family with something this stupid at a time like this. We also did not want to get caught acting suspicious around the coffin. So what we did was, we decided Dicky Humphrey would do the honors. Nobody would likely turn down a blind guy. He would approach the family spokesman and ask permission to place the small tin box of unidentified, but very wonderful mementos into the coffin and that would take care of it.

"What if we get there and he's being cremated?" Dicky said.

"Leave it to you to think of these questions," Will said.

"We can't burn those hairs," Kenny Miklos said. "They have historical importance. They're really a long-term loan, not a gift."

Sounded just like museum talk. "He's not being cremated," I said. "I checked."

Coach O'Neal, and Coach Tuttle, a tall, lanky man and former offensive end, were coming toward us from the office under the bleachers.

"Alright, gather around and listen up," Coach O'Neal said. "I want to have a word with you before we leave."

Will and I looked at one another. Philosophy time.

When everybody was bunched up between the vans, and still, Coach said, "I don't know how many of you have been to a funeral for someone killed in war. I don't suppose it matters at this stage." He looked around to see if anyone had. He was fiddling with a football in his hands. "But they're different from other funerals. There is something about the pain and the sense of loss that's a little different, a little bit more than the rest.

"I've seen war, fellas, and I've seen people killed. I'm sure some of your fathers have, too. And I've seen them buried, been to my share of funerals for them. Today, we're going to the funeral of a young man we all knew and liked, but didn't know long enough or well enough to be greatly pained by his death. Let's don't kid ourselves, we'd forgotten him, until someone told us he was gone. He'll be a distant memory almost before we get back here tonight. That's why I didn't think much of us all going up, like it was a hayride, like ghoulish hypocrites crowding around a graveside ogling the dead, like maybe some social obligation to show up, just because he was a brief acquaintance. Neither of us will shed a tear today. Sure, we're sorry he's gone. He was a decent, likeable young man. He was our pal and teammate and all this other business for a few months, then he was out of our life.

Poof. Gone. But we didn't cry when he left. Did we? Didn't chase after him. Did we? Or insist he stay? No, we let him go. And now we all want to go out of our way to help bury him.

"The other people there won't be like us. They'll be different. They'll be family and life-long friends, people who really loved him, people who will really cry, who will suffer real pain. Particularly his mother. I especially want you to look at his mother when we're there. I ask you to watch her the whole time, not take your eyes of her, and imagine she's your mother. You'll see her pain and you won't understand it, but you'll know it's there.

"Nobody suffers like a mother, gentlemen. Sure, the father, the brothers and sisters and others will hurt. And they'll carry the pain and loss. But they'll adjust and move on. Tim's mother will move on, too, but she'll never adjust to the pain and the loss. Every day for the next thirty or forty years of her life, she'll wake up every morning thinking about her son. And every night, when she goes to bed, she'll still be thinking about him. Because nobody suffers like a mother. And mothers don't forget.

"Tim won't be bothered by any of this, of course. It's over and done for him, it's painless. He'll never know we were there, either, never appreciate our coming. And his family will hardly notice, if at all. Maybe a nice card later, and that'll be it.

"So what I'm trying to say is, if it makes any sense at all, is I guess we're really doing this for ourselves. Tim did what he wanted to do for himself, and we're doing this for ourselves, and everyone else involved are doing the suffering. It's just a field trip for us.

"And don't get me wrong. When your country calls, you've got to go. I did, and I'd do it again. And I know you fellas would, too. But Tim didn't have to go, not now he didn't.

He quit too soon, he threw in the towel. He came here eager to set the world on fire with his talent, a good student, a better athlete. And when it didn't happen fast enough, he grew impatient and quit. And the war gods were waiting. He was just a soul lost in time and space. And that's why we're taking this ride today.

"These are getting to be treacherous times, fellas. Your decisions in times like these can kill you, like it's done Tim. And you have a responsibility to your mothers, your families, before anyone or anything else. Sacrifice is the grim reaper, with its own time and place. It'll seek you out when it wants you. When it knocks on your door, you'll have to answer it, one way or another, but you don't have to go looking for it, you don't have to invite it in.

"You're probably wondering why I'm preaching like this. Probably because I'm stupid or hard-headed in thinking that, maybe if I do, somehow something of what I say might find its way through the cavernous recesses of at least one of your young and impetuous minds, and maybe cause you to go right, instead of left, at some juncture so the rest of us don't have to go to another one of these funerals and pretend we're deeply moved by the whole thing. I might be wrong, but I said it anyway."

Coach O'Neal handed the football to Turnbull, our quarterback. "Here, everybody sign it, then load up. I'll give it to Tim's family, for what it's worth."

We signed the football and quietly got into the vans. One of the guys helped Dicky put the three green and white S.P.D. wreaths in the back. Nobody said a whole lot on the way up, but I believe we were all thinking the same thing, feeling kind of awkward, more like guilty, for even considering going to the funeral. Coach had a way of putting things in perspective, I'll say that much for him. Now we had to go watch all these real people cry and hurt, and feel like morons about it. I almost felt guilty for not dying so they could bury me, too.

Will said, "Maybe we should wait until we get there, right in the middle of the service, then drop dead on the floor. Old Tim would get a kick out of that."

"We can't die," I said. "We've got a game Saturday. It would be irresponsible. And our mothers would suffer for the rest of their lives. Yours anyway. Good luck locating mine with the bad news. She'd be holed up with my dad in Bumfuck, Egypt, somewhere."

13

Tim Davis's church was more than twice the size of mine, a huge white stone building colonnaded across the front, with wide steps. It sat atop terraced grounds with sculpted hedges all over the place and a manicured lawn that cascaded down to the sidewalk and street. Very stately, more like the capitol house in Richmond, or maybe the train station there on Broad Street, but real churchy. Inside, colored light sprayed all the Jesus and shepherd stuff over everything through the stained glass windows. It was filling up fast with the well-heeled, both the genuinely and dutifully sad, and the usual sniffles and tears, and whispers, and their perfumes and colognes. The place smelled like a department store.

The baritone pipe organ music didn't help much on my end. Must have been written to drive you to the depths of depression, something someone with a better vocabulary at the time might have called draconian. Sounded to me like background music for the Russian Revolution. I always got funerals confused with weddings, anyway. Not sure why, maybe because both represented something terminal and had pipe organ music, in my experience, and that always scared the hell out of me when I was a child, so they seemed the same.

The S.P.D. floral wreaths had been set in place among the

others, and Dicky had successfully negotiated placement of the metal box with the hairs in the coffin, in full view.

We joined the line to view the body.

Tim didn't look dead and there were no visible wounds. How could somebody look so alive and dapper, yet be so totally and forever gone? He looked like he was faking, maybe taking a nap, like if I nudged him he'd startle and ask me what the heck I was doing. You want to reach out and touch the dead, you know. I'm not sure why, maybe to make sure they're actually dead. Try one last time to revive them, perhaps something innate that drives one to fight for life, even someone else's.

Hell, I'm sounding like Coach O'Neil.

We were crowded around the coffin, where no one could hear, when Will said, "Hey, Tim, wake up. We've got a game coming up and we need your sorry ass. None of this quitting bullshit. And bring the hairs with you. They're loaners."

We giggled, but it really wasn't funny. Don't know about the others, but Will and I had never seen a young person who was dead, and didn't know how to feel about it, I guess. We used to sneak into the neighborhood funeral home when we were younger, just to look at the dead folks laid out in the coffins. But they were always old and were supposed to be dead, anyway, far as we were concerned, so it was no big deal, not like this here.

"We can't do it," Kenny Miklos said.

"Can't do what?" Dicky said.

"We can't leave these hairs in this coffin. It's not right. They belong to the state, to V.M.I. It's government property, a part of history. Stonewall's estate."

"Since when did you get so sensitive? Besides, I thought about that, left just one of them in there. The rest are right here." Dicky patted his left breast coat pocket.

"You're a man of strong moral conscience," I said.

"That's still too many," Kenny said. "It's still not right."

"Look," Will said, "there're still plenty left. We're the only people in the world who're taking those hairs. If other people were doing it, the horse's ass would be bald."

"You damn Greek Yankee carpetbagger," Dicky said. "Always something."

We all snickered at that, including Kenny.

The coaches gave us the look of death.

"Move the line," Coach O'Neil said.

We took our seats closer to the back.

The front two rows on each side of the aisle were reserved and now filling with the immediate family and closest relatives.

Tim's mother was young looking, and pretty, as mothers go, but this day she looked seventy-five over forty, a complete wreck, held up by Tim's father and sister Kelly as they walked her down the aisle to the front pew. When they were seated, Kelly kept looking back over her shoulder to where we were. Looking for Will, I figured, maybe some sympathy attention. She was thirteen now and had a crush on Will, met him a couple times when her family visited Tim on campus. Kid sister falls for brother's roommate. Her tears were thick as syrup and only the surface tension kept them from bursting like a dam down her face.

It was hard listening to the eulogies because every time someone said something good and sweet and memorable about Tim, which was all of them—I mean, who's going to say something bad?—some others, mostly up front, exploded with grief. It was like all there were aware that from this point on they were seeing him in the flesh for the last time, and would never know him again, except as a memory. It reminded me of the old war films where the sailor was buried at sea, his coffin slipping overboard into the water, a place of darkness, fear, and loneliness, where no one wanted to follow.

But that was nothing compared to what happened when the church part of the service was over and people started filing out to their cars for the procession to the cemetery, a mile away.

We moved slowly through the vestibule, then lingered out front, following everyone else's lead about where to go. That's when Kelly, bawling her eyes out, confronted Will, right there in front of everybody.

"Why didn't you stop him, Will?" Kelly said. "Why didn't you do something? Why didn't you help him? You were his roommate, his fraternity brother. You could've helped. Now he's gone. He'd still be here. Friends are supposed to look out for one another. Why? I'll never understand."

"I—I'm sorry, Kelly. I don't know what you mean."

Tim's father came over. "Please, Kelly, honey." He put his arm around her. "I'm sorry, Will. Please forgive her," he said.

"Yes, sir. I'm sorry—."

"No apologies necessary, Will."

"It's not fair," Kelly said. "You didn't help him. None of you did. Now he's gone and you're all here. I hate you. I hate all of you. Why don't you just go back where you came from." She buried her face in her father's chest.

Mr. Davis nodded to a lady nearby who came over and led Kelly away.

"I'm sorry, fellas," Mr. Davis said. "She doesn't mean that."

We all said it was okay, we understood.

"Please," he said, "I hope you're staying for the graveside service. Thank you so much for coming. My family and I appreciate it. Tim would be happy to see you all here. His time at school, I think, and playing ball with all of you, was the happiest time of his life." He shook hands with us and rejoined his family.

"Jesus H. Christ," Kenny said. "What the hell was that?"

"He'd still be here if it weren't for me?" Will said. "Did you hear that?"

There were people looking as they passed us, maybe wondering if there might be some truth to Kelly's accusation.

"What the hell did she mean?" Will said. "Like it's my fault Tim died?"

"Who knows?" I said. "Don't worry about it. She's just a kid. Come on, let's go."

We went to the vans and got in. But something clicked in Will at that moment. The whole way to the cemetery he didn't speak, just sat silently staring out the window, his eyes squinting, trying to understand his world, like a patient being transported from one funny farm to another.

"Snap out of it, Will. Your eyes are growing together," I said when we were parked at the cemetery.

"I'm not going," Will said. "I'm not getting out of this damn van."

"So you just came up for the ride or something?" I said.

"You heard what she said to me. The way those people looked at me."

"They looked at all of us because we're ugly as hell. She said it about all of us. Doesn't mean crap. She's a kid, she's upset her brother was killed. She's just pissed off at the world. Come on."

Coach O'Neil overheard us from a few feet away and stepped over. "Two things," he said. "This isn't about any of us, and it was your idea to come up here, so let's go, quit licking your wounds."

That night, after football practice, before hitting the books, I stopped by Will's room. He was alone and lying on his cot, staring at the ceiling.

"Where's Dicky?" I said. "I thought y'all were suppose to be studying."

He was slow responding. "In the morning, after class," he said.

"This is serious stuff. You know what Coach said."

"Screw Coach."

"What's your problem?" I sat down on the cot across from him, which would be vacant until next semester, since Will's roommate had been injured in practice and was still in the hospital.

"I keep thinking about today. I've never been humiliated like that in my life."

"It was a new experience for you."

"I keep thinking about what Kelly said. I'm just wondering what her point was. I mean, what the hell did I do?"

"Well, you aren't going to find it on the ceiling."

He sat up. "You think there's anything we could've done about Tim, I mean? I've been racking my brain."

"I don't see what it could be."

He was silent a little longer, then said, "There's one damn thing for sure. I've got to get that little Steven boy to the game Saturday. God help me if I don't and something happens to him in the hospital. They'll blame me for it. Never hear the end of it from Mary Poythress, either, be run off campus."

"Yeah, the world just unloads on you," I said. "I think all this Viet Nam crap is all your fault, too. Wait'll they catch up with you for that."

"I'm serious. I'm taking him to the game, and you're helping me."

"How are we suppose to do that? We already talked about it."

"We'll just have to get up early, drive down to the hospital, pick him up and bring him back."

"And leave him where, while we're suiting up and playing?"

"The team can adopt him for a day, take turns looking after him. Coach okayed his coming. We'll bring him in the locker room, he can sit on the sidelines."

"Yeah, and he has all this medical equipment strapped to him and there's a big pile up, with him under it. Then you will get blamed for it."

"You're a fatalist."

"No, I'm a realist."

Will thought a moment. "Sure is easier to say stuff than it is to do it. You know it?"

"The world is revealing itself to you."

"I don't think we're ready for the big decisions, Doc."

"Speak for yourself, you goofball."

14

W ill skipped his next Art History class, trying to be the mystery man, make Mary Poythress wonder what happened to him, like she didn't have anything else to think about. All this against my better advice of showing up and just ignoring her. But he wasn't good at ignoring her, so maybe he was right.

On Saturday morning we got up a couple hours early and drove down to Newport News in Will's car, to the hospital. Steven's mother, Linda Harnley she introduced herself as, was with him in the room. She had a worried look, like she might be having second thoughts. She looked in her thirties, was kind of petite, attractive, and wore glasses that gave her a kind of librarian-like sexiness. But she had that haggard look a lot of service wives have when they're left alone with a house full of kids and everything to do by themselves, while their husbands are gone forever. Saw a lot of that with all the military bases around here. She was sizing us up, trying to spot the thing about us that would give her the confidence to let her son go with us. It was the same look I got numerous times when I was a scrawny kid with a push mower and a neighbor would look at me and wonder, *Should I let this kid get near my grass?*

The nurse came in. She looked like a prison guard and a judo expert. I was thinking maybe we could use her in the Furman game.

"Oh, I think these two strapping young men can handle Steven for a few hours," she said. The way she looked at us made me feel like a pork chop.

The nurse gave us instructions about the oxygen tank and mask. Not necessary to have it on the whole time, just if he gasps or seemed too tired. Shouldn't be a problem, just make sure someone is with him at all times, use the umbrella. Not too much direct sunlight—Jeeze, the game was outside. He could have pizza or whatever to eat, in small bites, but has to eat everything slowly, not stuff, he chokes easily. And we'd better bring him back safely.

"Had breakfast yet?" Will said.

"Yeah, Mary brought it to me this morning," Steven said. He was very excited, and clutched his football. The kid was ready.

"There you go," I said to Will, "Superwoman strikes again."

"She still here?" he asked Steven.

"She's in the lab."

"That girl's always in some lab."

"He'll be okay," I said to Mrs. Harnley. "The whole team will be looking out for him."

"But how can they do that and play ball, too?" she said. Her voice was the same size she was, had a nice quality to it, but you had to listen closely.

"We don't all play at once. We take turns."

"Believe me," Will said, "they'll be fighting over Steven. He'll be the safest guy there."

That made her smile.

The nurse helped us downstairs to the emergency room door, where we were parked just to the side. Linda Harnley's eyes welled up, and she hugged and kissed Steven like he was going off to war. I think she was just happy to see him doing something.

I drove while Will sat in the back with Steven and kept an eye on the oxygen tank. That tank scared the hell out of us. What if we had to use it? What would that mean? Jeeze. But with the windows down and the warm air blowing in and all over him, Steven held his football and took it all in, like he was seeing the world for the first time. It looked like a pretty good day was coming up.

15

It was a good game and we barely won. Will's parents couldn't come, as they usually did, because his uncle Lewis, the Dutch rub guy, was in the hospital out of town and they had to visit him. Mary showed up and helped, of course, and stood over Steven with an umbrella the whole time near the end of the bench, where the cheerleaders made a fuss over him and a lot of the equipment and water were located. Obviously, she didn't know anything about football. Every time a play came to our side of the field anywhere near her, she was like a deer in the headlights. The only time she seemed relaxed was halftime, when no one seemed to be killing anyone else. Once, in the third quarter, when we were on defense, and Will and I were standing on the sidelines waiting to go back in, our guys tackled a Furman halfback and the whole pile rolled right up to Steven's feet, almost hitting him. Mary jerked his wheel-chair back and liked to went nuts, dropping the umbrella and turning one way, then another. Steven's eyes were as big as the numbers on his jersey, but the smile on his face said it all.

We wheeled Steven into the locker room with us after the game, while Mary waited outside, kind of like a stage door Johnny.

"Well, you ready to take on the town?" Will said to Steven when we met Mary and Pam outside. "You think you can keep up with this wild bunch?" he said to Mary.

"I'll rally all my strength and probably get by," she said, giving it back to him. "What do you have in mind?"

Pam stepped next to me and locked her arm in mine. "Great game, L.D. You were great."

"First we eat," Will said. "Head for the corner," meaning Jock-strap Corner, "eat some pizza. I'm starving." He nodded to Steven. "And we champs get hungry after a big game."

Generally, our energy level was subdued after a game, what with being so tired and the soreness creeping over us from all the hits taken. But Will seemed to find a reserve, probably the show-off factor. We walked the couple blocks up Richmond Road to the cor-ner, and Will and I and Mary took turns pushing the wheelchair.

Will then jumped out front of us fast, up the sidewalk, pushing the wheel chair and making cuts left and right, like a running back in a game, spooking more than one pedestrian for about thirty yards, before tiring and slowing down. Steven's eyes were big as saucers. He gripped the sides of the wheelchair, holding on for dear life.

Mary gasped and threw up her hands. "Stop. God, you'll kill somebody. What do you think you're doing?"

He stopped and waited for us. "Just tourist bowling," he said. Then to Steven, "Good run, champ. Think it was a touchdown. You've got a great future as a running back."

"I'll take him home later," Mary said, waving him off. "You don't have to bother."

"I think I'll be alright with it, Hugo. I said I would, and I will. And you keep saying everything is a bother, and it's not."

"Don't be ridiculous."

Will thought about that. "Okay, I'll carry him back, you carry the wheelchair in your car."

"No, I'll use my car. It'll fit just fine."

"*We'll* use your car. I'll pay for the gas."

It was crowded and noisy inside with chatter and music from the jukebox. Red and white checkered tablecloths, high ceiling with paddle fans and the smell of beer and pizza and toasted ham and cheese. We finally got a table, thanks to several good folks and their sympathy for Steven's wheelchair predicament, with Mary pushing and Pam trailing, while Will and I nodded our thanks and slid in behind them like we were bodyguards or physical therapists or something.

We parked Steven at the end of the table and slid into the booth and ordered right away, but no beer, out of respect for his presence. We could do that later, since there would be numerous parties around campus. People we knew, or knew us, stopped by the table to congratulate us for the win. Other team members and families were there, and the din of talking was comfortable if not a little loud, though the background music wasn't. Nothing like Williamsburg after a game. The merchants would make a killing.

"That was dangerous," Mary said of Will's little run down the street with Steven. "Anything could have happened."

"But it didn't." Will said.

I interrupted. "We're not driving, so it's okay if Pam and I have a beer, I guess." I looked for the waitress.

Pam said, "No, I don't think we need any now." She glanced at Steven, in case I missed the point.

"That's okay," Steven said. "My dad drinks beer when he's home. And my mom, too, sometimes, when she watches T.V. at night. I wouldn't mind one myself." He was hopeful. He'd come this far, he must have figured.

"Future football greats don't drink," Will said. "You'll be going into training, soon as you're out of the hospital."

"Besides," I said, "we don't want to get arrested. You get drunk, you might tear this town up. Then they'll come for us."

Steven snickered. One of the guys.

Mary was silent a moment, like she was wondering about her comfort level in our little group.

"You thought I was going to do something stupid and dangerous, didn't you?" Will said to Mary.

"You did do something stupid and dangerous."

"You have little faith in your fellow man." He let hang for a second. "You know," he then said, "my grandfather is the smartest man I know. He used to tell me, growing up, still does sometimes, that, no matter who you are, where you come from, or what you do in this life, the only thing that really matters at the end of the day is having a roof over your head in a safe place and falling asleep under it with people who care about you. You know how he knew that?"

"I haven't the slightest idea," she said, "but I'm sure you'll tell me. I'd just like to know how you know it."

"My grandmother told him, then he told me." He grinned. "And if she said it, he believed it."

"Your point being?"

"He trusted her. Still does. Sometimes you have to trust somebody. Like Steven, here. He trusted me and he's still alive and well, and getting ready for the next big home game."

Her eyelids went up, recoiling.

"Another home game?" Steven said, sitting up higher, hopeful.

Will said it a little too quick. "Well, yeah. You can't quit on us now, champ. We have nine more games on the schedule, four of them at home."

"Then the Rose Bowl," I said. "Probably play Notre Dame or Southern Cal. You'll have to ride in the Rose Parade, on a float."

"When is the next home game?" Steven said.

"Week after next," Will said. "And we need your support. Playing V.M.I."

Mary gave Will a look of no confidence. Something else for her to deal with from this reckless jock.

Will said, "And Mary will have to come, too, because she's the only one of us who knows how to work this oxygen gizmo." He looked at her and smiled. Gotcha.

She was tongue-in-cheek, patted Steven on the shoulder. "Steven knows he can always count on me when it really matters." Then to Will, "And you have a very hard head."

"Thank you."

"He could play without a helmet," Pam said, giggling.

"There's a thought," Mary said.

"Again," I said to Pam, "your recently- acquired humor is infectious."

The pizza came and we dug in. Will and I ate like apes. Pam was civilized. Mary ate like she was being watched and judged by eating critics. Her breeding, no doubt. That or she wasn't hungry. She helped Steven with his.

Steven showed more energy than I had seen from him, so far. He clearly was enjoying himself, especially considering Pam and Will and I were not much more than strangers. He was one of the guys, okay, but Mary was his security blanket too.

16

Pam and I stayed in town and went to a couple parties, while Will and Mary went in her car with Steven to Newport News, back to the hospital, where his mother and siblings waited. The kid was asleep long before arrival and looked dead to Mrs. Harnley. and the nurse.

"He's fine," the nurse said, this one a younger woman. In the room she checked his vitals. "Worn out, but okay."

Mary conferred with Linda Harnley and assured her of Steven's good care during the day, the fun time he had, and his attack on the pizza he ate. "He's invited back in two weeks for the next home game. If he's still strong enough, and it's okay with you and his doctor."

Will could swear she was doing a selling job, paving the way. Maybe there was hope. Maybe her shield was cracking.

It was well after dark when they were back on the road to Williamsburg, traveling up two-lane Route 60 through the woods most of the way, with Mary driving.

Will said, "Well, how did you like it today? Was it that bad, wallowing in the gutter with the cretins?"

She remained silent a moment, then said, "No comment. And nobody said cretins. Pam and Doc seem to be nice enough folks. Don't speak for me."

Will let it slide for a few seconds, then said, "You know, you're not fooling anybody with that scholar-versus-cretin act. I know more about you than you think."

"Oh, so you are spying on me."

"I wouldn't call it spying, exactly. I'd say it's more like *imparting and interest* in the people I meet. My natural curiosity in my fellow man, you might say. You could use some of that." He thought that was cute.

She didn't. "You don't know crap about me."

"Really? I know you act like you're ignorant about sports, but you're not. You played tennis at that fancy private school you went to down there," he said, meaning Charleston. "And you were one of the best players in the state. And that your boyfriend played football and ran track at the Citadel, and he goes to law school now. I know *that*. So you know what a first down is."

"So you are spying on me."

"No, I just happen to have a friend who hates not knowing everything in the world, and he told me." He meant Kenny Miklos.

"So what's going on here?" She was a bit put off.

"Nothing bad, I assure you. I just think there's more to you than you want people to know. Or me to know. And that bothers me, the most trusting, concerned and considerate person in the world." He smiled. Another slick line.

She had to smile at that too. "You know," she said, "a graduate student in abnormal psychology might find you a fascinating subject, a thesis project or something."

"I'd just confuse her and make her quit."

"I can see that."

"Since you're such an intelligent, educated scholar type, so loaded with wisdom and all, and quick to judge others, I'd like to ask your advice on something."

"You can't afford my fees."

"I need a woman's advice."

"With what?"

"I met this girl recently. I've never met anyone like her—"

Mary seemed confused by that.

"You listening?" Will said.

'Sure."

"I think she's really special, not like any girl I've ever met. I'd like to go out with her, but I don't know."

"Then go out with her. What's so complicated about that? I'm sure you've gone out with the rest of them. What's one more?"

"No, that's Doc's job. He's the hound in this operation."

"And your problem is?"

"I don't know, exactly. I just don't know. Maybe a little afraid."

Mary tried suppressing a laugh, her hand over her mouth, the other steering the car. "Oh, god. Bring back the rubber boots. It's high tide in the sewer." She laughed, swerving her Mercedes across the center line an instant.

Will was having a problem suppressing his own laugh.

"I'll drop you off at the dorm," Mary said, when they were back in town.

Lights shown and flickered around the campus and the colonial district up and down Duke of Gloucester Street and the adjacent neighborhood. Noise from fraternity row, behind the stadium, was still evident, as usual.

"No, I'll walk. It's only up the street."

They parked in front of her house. A single, dim light was on in the living room. Shelley was still out, apparently. But it was still early as parties went.

"I'll walk you to the door."

"Not necessary, but thanks anyway."

"It is necessary. I'm a gentleman. My mother would shoot me if I didn't."

"Then don't tell her."

"You keep saying that."

"Suit yourself, but I don't need company, if that's what you're thinking."

"Never entered my mind. I just keep thinking about that girl I met, and how you're not helping with it, like I asked."

She didn't respond.

They reached the porch and she opened the screen door.

"No kiss goodnight?" he said.

"Go ask the girl you just met."

"See you in class." Damn.

He turned to walk away, then stopped halfway down the short walk as she opened her door. "Hey, listen. How about we grab a bite to eat tomorrow night, after your hospital stuff. You know, just a sandwich or something down on the corner, shoot the bull."

"Sorry, can't. Too busy." She closed the door behind her.

He turned back toward the street. "Figures. Damn."

Then her door flew back open. "Hey." She walked quickly back to him. "Alright. Maybe a few minutes, but it'll have to be quick. I'll have work to do."

"Oh, okay. Great. It's on me. How about six o'clock?"

"There's just this one thing, though, that's been bothering me, "she said. "Just this one thing I need to get out of the way first, if you don't mind. Just something nagging at me, bothering me, since we met the other day in registration. If that's okay. Won't take but a second to explain."

"Sure. Fine." Hell, yeah, it was okay.

Just then she slapped him across his face, not that hard, but enough to send the message.

"Good god. What the hell? You're violent."

"No, I've never done that to anyone before. I just made an exception for you this one time." She pointed her finger gently in his face. "Don't ever play with me like that again, like a child. I don't like it."

"I can tell."

"And this is just a little bite to eat thing, not a date we're talking about here. So don't get any ideas floating around in that vacuous brain of yours, with all that extra space you have in there, growing like a cancer. I'm not on the make." She turned back toward her door.

He felt his face again, to make sure it was still there. "Wouldn't think of it. I don't even like cancer." Grief.

Mary grabbed her door knob. "Seven o'clock, not six," she said. "And don't be late. I don't wait for people."

"Neither do I. So keep that in mind when seven o'clock comes." Then he added, unable to resist, "Hugo."

She went inside. And Will walked away with a grin on his face wide enough to scrape the cars on both sides of the street.

17

Early the next morning, around seven-thirty, Sunday, Kenny Miklos knocked on Will's door, waking him with a message to call Mary Poythress at her house by eight. She'd left the number. Will used the dorm phone. The hospital lab would be closed to work that morning, she said, and suggested they meet for breakfast instead at the local diner across from campus. That would have to do.

"And use mouthwash," Mary said.

"Gee, thanks for the little life tip, Hugo. It never would occur to me. I suppose you could call this a planning session for taking Steven to the next home game. Right? This way, you don't have to admit you like my company."

Mary rolled her eyes on her end of the line. "You're the most conceited person I've ever met in my life."

"Thank you."

But she was right about the breath. Athletes were mostly night people who hated to get up in the morning, so tired from the previous day, and so groggy. Except Miklos. For him, to sleep was to miss something important that might happen.

The diner was on Richmond Road, only a block up from the corner restaurant by the stadium, where they had been that night he'd seen her there alone with the half-eaten sandwich. It was a white building, low ceiling, wrapped in windows and green awnings, very quaint. People could sit in the shade there and look out and watch the few other early risers who were not having breakfast but had things to do and places to go. It was busy but quiet. Well, it was Sunday morning and the church skippers in this part of the country kept a low profile during such hours.

They took the only table open, a two-seater next to a window overlooking the road and the campus beyond. They chatted in short sentences, a little awkward, trying to find a comfortable place in the meeting that wasn't loaded with one-upmanship. They ordered toast, orange juice and coffee.

"So tell me about your boyfriend," Will said. "How serious is it?"

"Tell me about the girl you met."

Will chewed on his toast and thought about that. "Well, she's the most beautiful girl I've ever seen in my life, that's for sure. And smart. She could hold her own against Shelley Michaels in the brain department any day."

"So brains come in departments now?"

"Cute. You know what I mean."

"What does she do? She go to school here? Would or do I know her? Who is she?"

"So you're interested."

"It's your subject. I'm just a happy listener."

"I can't tell you too much. You might run your mouth and she might be put off by it, if it gets back to her, ruin my chances."

"You don't lie well," Mary said.

"I don't lie at all. One of my faults, I guess, being so honest."

She chuckled at that.

"You trying to avoid talking about your boyfriend?"

"I don't have a boyfriend, as such."

"Except the Citadel grad law student guy."

Will couldn't imagine a guy not being serious about Mary Poythress.

"It's not serious with me. Giles Collier(Coll-yeh) is an old friend I've known all my life. Our families are close. We've dated off and on, but it's not serious. For me anyway. Besides, he has enough girl-friends."

"But he wants you."

"Life is too short and serious for such as that."

"You'll break his heart."

"He'll do fine," she said. "He'll marry rich to someone South of Broad who travels and entertains and chairs charity fundraisers. He'll be successful in his father's and grandfather's two-hundred-year-old law office, and drink happily ever after."

"South of Broad?"

"The part of town in Charleston where we come from, at the end of the peninsula, overlooking the harbor and Fort Sumpter, where the old families and money live."

"And interbreed."

"Kind of. But not like you'd think. We do spread our wings. It is the nineteen-sixties, you know."

"Tell me, how does a guy live with a name like that, without shooting himself? *Giles.*"

"You make fun of people's religions and names, too."

"I don't like to leave anybody out."

"You're a prince," she said. "The football team is lucky to have you. You'd be a big hit in prison, I bet. If you weren't majoring in football."

"Like to get your opinion on something," Will said. "What would you recommend as a first date. If I can get one with her?"

"You're asking me what to do on a date?"

"She's special."

"Bet you say that to all of them."

"I don't want to screw it up. A girl's opinion can't hurt."

"I don't know anything about her, so I wouldn't know where to start. Wing it."

"I thought about the bridge," Will said, gazing out the window in the direction of it.

"Bridge? What bridge?"

"On campus here, over the pond."

"Oh, that one. Isn't that a little serious for a first date?"

Will nodded that he didn't know.

"Got a clue for you," Mary said. "Don't move too fast. She's not going to know what you're thinking. Might frighten her off. Remember the number one rule of dating: never propose marriage on the first date."

"Let's walk over there," he said. "Get a closer look. I'll show you what I mean. Eat up."

"I don't have the time."

"Only take a minute or two."

She relented, ready to get it over with. "When we finish eating," she said. "Now I'm a dating counselor. Make it quick, please."

"Quit complaining. Look at all the valuable life experience you're getting for free, hanging around with me on the wild side, not to mention a free breakfast."

"I need to keep those rubber boots handy."

They crossed the road and took the shortcut between the administration buildings and around the Sunken Garden, a recessed field for marching and parades during the colonial period, now a tourist site. They went into the edge of the woods to the arched bridge that spanned the pond, where water drained in from all over campus to form a creek. There had been an older pier-like structure there for decades prior to this newer one, put up recently. It was of Oriental style, reddish-green and gray, with the arch humping over the center of it, kind of storybook-like, like curious, grinning little forest creatures might jump out of the bushes any moment.

"Okay," Mary said, "so you bring her here, assuming she'll come. Then what?"

"Then we stand in the middle. You know about the middle, right?"

"I've heard."

"I'll show you what I mean." He put out his hand. "Come here."

She went along with it, took his hand, unsure of his motive. He pulled her along the few steps to the top of the arch. Then he let go and turned and leaned on the railing with both hands, away from her, and looked out over the pond, at the thick foliage covering the banks.,

"They say if a couple comes here and stand in this spot and kiss, then walk over to the other side, they'll be together the rest of their lives."

"That's BS. You're a faux romantic. I'd like to see the divorce rate."

"And you're not a romantic? Quit using those English Lit. words. Just say fake or something, and let it be."

She didn't answer to that.

Will said, "I think this is where the rest of my life begins." He grinned big.

"Every moment is the beginning of the rest of your life, in case you haven't noticed."

"You sound like a freshman philosophy student quoting Descartes. 'I think, therefore, I am.'"

She gave a quizzical look, probably wondering how he'd ever heard of Descartes.

"I've got to get back," she said. "Let's go."

"Stop. Please." His heart was pounding like it'd explode out of his chest. He was not smiling.

She stared back at him, like she could sense what was coming. She swallowed big. "That an order or something?" she said.

"No, an invitation. Come here," he said again, a little more confident this time, having sensed her own vulnerability. He grabbed her shoulders, not roughly but not gently either, and kissed her on the lips.

She recoiled, stared him in the eye, then grabbed the back of his head with both hands and responded even more passionately. "If you're going to do that," she said, "put something into it." And kissed him harder.

They both were speechless a long moment, embracing.

"Oh, my," she said. "What have we done? I think the world is moving way too fast right now, Will. We have to slow down."

"I think it's moving just fine," he said. He took her hand again. "Now we have to cross over."

She looked at the end of the bridge to the bank. "Don't get any big ideas. It's just a walk, some superstitious pablum."

"Not for me. I knew it right from the first second. I knew I'd have to walk across this bridge with you. It didn't mean crap to me before then. Funny how things change when it's personal."

"What if the bridge weren't here?" she said.

"Then we'd walk across the street, or the Sunken Garden. Or the football field. Or a cigarette butt on the road. Or a dead dog in the street. Who give's a rat's? What difference does it make, long as we do it together? We can call it a life walk, if you want, make it easier."

"You're nuts. My life is already planned out, and it doesn't include time for a lot of personal stuff. And you're too sure of yourself." But her voice didn't have that certainty to it.

"Maybe." He was getting a little frustrated. "I'll make a deal with you. What time do you have to be at the hospital?"

"Three o'clock or so. But I have to study till then."

"Stay with me till you have to leave. There's a special place in Jamestown I want you to see. If you don't want to see me again after that, don't want this to go any further, then I won't bother you. You'll have to make the next move, call me, if you want, and we'll just stay acquaintances. How's that?"

"Jamestown? Your circle is widening. You're a travel agent now. I don't need suggestions from you. I make my own plans."

Will was dejected, or pretending to be. "Okay, you win. I tried." He let go of her hand. "Let's go home." He turned back toward the other side.

"Why don't we just take it easy, just slow down a bit," she said. "Get to know one another before we start taking field trips together. There's a novel idea."

"We're already acquaintances."

Mary took a deep breath and blew it out. She looked at him, up and down. "Alright, alright," she finally said. "Let's go. Jamestown, here we come. I must be losing my mind. I know you've already lost yours, if you ever had one."

"You know, Hugo, to be so bright, you have a passable sense of humor." He laughed and took her hand again. A win.

"You really do have to stop the Hugo business."

"It's a term of endearment. I love you." He stopped, stunned by what he'd just said.

Mary looked shocked, paralyzed. Her mouth fell open.

Will said, "Oh. Did I just say that?"

They stared at one another a long moment.

Then she grinned, nodding. "I think you did."

He looked around for the door out of this thing, like it was in the air or something. "Well, it must be true." Then he grinned big too. "Because I don't lie."

18

They drove in Will's car the seven miles to Jamestown, to the site of the famous English Settlement, and parked in the lot just outside. It was a formal park now, had been for years, and drew tourists from all over the world. Never mind that Leif Erikson, the Scandinavian, landed on the continent long before, though didn't settle, and that the Spanish had been all over what later would become Florida, or that the natives—Pocahontas and her father Chief Powhatan—had been around for thousands of years before John Smith and John Rolfe, and Thomas Gosnold and Christopher Newport, and others. This was the touchstone of what would become the dominant culture, so it was a big deal. And protected. You couldn't just wander around any time you wanted, like you owned the place. Unless you were a college student. There was a big wrought iron gate across the entrance road, where no civilian vehicles were allowed, and a guard, fees to pay, but only during hours it was open. It was closed now, a little after ten a.m.

"Now what?" Mary said, as they got out of the car.

"We go in."

"It's closed. Sign says open at twelve o'clock."

"That's for everybody else. Not for us. When you're with me, there are no barriers. Let me show you. Rules are for fools. People do this all the time. You ought to be here at night sometime. More people than a drive-in movie."

"No, thank you. Let's go back." She turned for the car.

"Here," he said. "We'll be in and out before anybody gets here. The park staff don't start getting here till about eleven-thirty or so."

"I'm not climbing that fence."

"You don't have to." He pointed to the left side of the road, where the gate ended, attached to pillars on both sides of the entrance. On the left there was a ditch, the thick woods beyond, and you could walk around the pillar by going a few feet down into the ditch, then up and around the other side.

"That's trespassing on government property. That's a crime," Mary said.

"No, we're going to church."

"No, we're going to jail. You've lost your mind. I can't do this." Her hands were on her head when she said it.

"We do this all the time. You want to be the only student here who never did it?"

"I wouldn't mind that."

"Just follow me." He took her hand. "We'll be back out and on our way before you know it."

They got to the other side, inside the park, easier than she expected. The old fort and the reconstructed additions were within sight, a short walk, where the pavement stopped and became a wide dirt path created by years of visitor traffic. The settlement site was adjacent a swamp on the banks of the James River and you could still see poles sticking out of the water two hundred yards out, where the original fort had been before the river shifted with time.

"This is spooky," Mary said, gazing around.

"There," Will said, pointing. "That's the church." A short way an old brick building stood open to the elements, its roof lost to history and wear, a shell of its original self. "The first brick church in the colony."

She followed him in, and they entered and stood inside its dilapidated walls, looking up and around. It looked like Berlin after the war.

"So y'all come here all the time?" Mary said.

It was the first time Will had heard her say y'all.

"Frats and sororities party here sometimes. Initiations, that kind of thing. Except in summer, at night, the mosquitos and gnats will eat you alive. We have cookouts here."

"What about park rangers?"

"Not late at night. And we don't leave any messes, so they don't know beans, probably." He took her hand. He couldn't stop taking her hand. "Come here."

He led her over to a shaded corner, out of the sunlight. She kept looking around, like she expected to be caught any moment. Silence. Just the sound of her own heartbeat.

Will was hot as a firecracker, throbbing, and it must have been infectious. Within seconds, they were kissing furiously.

"You're trying to climb in my mouth," she said. "At least you could take off your shoes."

"I can do better than that."

"Not here. Let's go." This time she took his hand, out of the church, back down the ditch, then around the pillar to the car in the parking lot, where they climbed into the back seat and went at each other like savages. Fortunate creatures, like newborns witnessing life and its wonders for the first time.

"Let's go back to my house," she said. "Shelley's gone for the day. We can be alone, before I have to be at the hospital."

They got there and were hardly in the door before tearing at one another.

And nothing ever would be the same again for either of them.

19

Every moment awake they could find was spent together. That wasn't so often, what with their schedules, but was intense when they could be at Mary's house, all over the place, or in her room when Shelley was there, or in Will's dorm room, since he had the place to himself. They ate at the diner or at the grill across from campus, when pressed for time and not able to be physical. It became their special place. And Will always insisted on paying because he didn't know how to let a girl pay a bill. And that made his parents wonder where all this extra cash he begged for was going. Not that they were broke. They weren't. His father was a shop supervisor in the shipyard and made a decent living, and his mother was a part-time substitute teacher, but mostly stayed home and looked after the house and Will's younger brother Hank, or Henry, named after his mother's younger brother, the Dutch rub guy, who seemed to get more money from the family than did Will. But Will's winning argument was all the money he was saving the family by being on scholarship.

"So when do we get to meet this girl who eats so much?" his father said. "How much does she weigh?"

"Cute. About a hundred and fifteen pounds, give or take. And she'll knock your eyes out. Wait and see."

His father chuckled. "Okay, see you at the game."

Pete and Martha Lynn Wythe met Mary, and she knocked their eyes out, just like Will said. "Good god," his father said, "she's prettier than a bucket of movie stars." Then he thought about that. "After you, of course," he said to Martha Lynn.

"You're so full of it," she said back to him. "She's going to make someone some beautiful children. No doubt about that. But I'm not so sure she's right for him. I'm not so sure he can keep up with her and where she comes from."

"It's not a matter of keeping up. It's not a competition. All he has to do is be a man. That's either good enough, or it's not. Besides, it's a little too early to call."

"No, he's in it for what it's worth," Martha Lynn said. "It's a one-way street for him. Mark my word. I just hope it works out somehow, if they keep it up."

Pete and Martha Lynn were standing at the back door window after Sunday dinner, looking out at Will and Mary chasing one another around the backyard, where they lived, a few blocks from me. Leaves were falling all over the place, and Will and Mary were having a pine cone fight.

"She's beating the living hell out of him," Pete said.

Martha Lynn was looking over his shoulder. "He needs it. I think I like this girl."

"What about your mother?" Shelley said. "How's she going to take it?"

They were having coffee and toast in their kitchen, before Monday morning classes.

"The sixty-four-thousand-dollar question. We'll see when the time comes. But not too well, I imagine. Momma anyway. Daddy's kind of laid back. It's wait and see with him. He's going home with me Thanksgiving weekend," she said of Will.

"That ought to be good. Like to be a fly on the wall for that one."

"I'll give you a full report."

They laughed. Kind of.

Will, Kenny Miklos and I were in Will's room shooting the bull a couple nights before the next home game.

"She's out of your league, buddy," Kenney said of Will's plan to spend Thanksgiving with Mary in Charleston. "That girl has five names. Your old man works in the shipyard. It won't work. Those people down there have houses with names longer than yours."

"He'll knock 'em dead with his charm," I said.

"No, they'll kill him on arrival. My old man had a war buddy who lived in that neighborhood. Stopped in to see him one time on the way to Florida. Told the guy's five-year-old nephew that Santa Claus was a Yankee. Scared the hell out of the kid. Went screaming to his mother, 'Momma, momma, that man said Santa Claus is a Yankee.' She didn't take it so well."

We laughed at that one too.

Will said, "I'll win them over. I'm driving Doc's car. I'll look like a young man on his way up."

"What, with a football hanging around your neck?" Kenny said. "Wish I could be there. You're at the dinner table. It's Thanksgiving and the old man asked you what your future plans are, and you say, 'Oh, she'll be fine. I'm going to throw the football around.'" He laughed. Even Will thought it was funny.

"Then he'll say," Kenny said, 'Oh, then I know my daughter will be well taken care of.'" More laughter. "Yeah, I can see you blending right in with those bluebloods, right now. You'll be the family dog. Probably sleep in the backyard, in the utility shed, with the lawnmower.

"And by the way," Kenny said, "Humphrey says you've been ducking him, keep cancelling on him. Last time you cracked a book with him was last week. Every time I see Coach, it's the first thing he says, 'is Wythe studying?' And I keep lying for you. Maybe you ought to get Mary to help you, you spend so much time with her."

I grinned big. "Can you imagine a guy, much less Will, trying to concentrate sitting next to Mary?"

"Well, you better do something, Will. Mid-terms will be here before you know it. Warning slips come out just about the time you get back from your little Thanksgiving trip. Humphrey doesn't hand in any time sheets to get paid, Coach is going to be all over you." The athletic department paid for tutoring jocks.

"How is your average?" I said to Kenny.

"B minus, so I'm doing okay. Levitt's not doing so well, though," he said of another lineman on the team. "He's got the same problem as Will, here, thinking with the wrong head. Doesn't shape up, he'll be back home in his old man's furniture store instead of law school at Harvard. Guy had SATs over fifteen hundred, honor role in high school, accepted to the best schools, and can't keep a C average here. We're not a college football team, we're a travelling zoo. I swear, I spend half my time as a probation officer with you guys. I should be getting paid."

"You know," I said of Humphrey, for no reason at all, but changing the subject, "Dickey's not totally blind. He can actually see."

"Yeah," Miklos said, "but his glasses are big as headlights. What the hell was the purpose of that statement?"

We all laughed again.

Then a knock on the door. It was a message for Will to call Mary at the hospital in Newport News. He used the hall phone and a nurse got her on the line.

"I'm in Steven's room," she said. "I won't be back in time to see you tonight, looks like. They've got him downstairs. Doesn't look good. I love you."

"Love you, too. But what's wrong?" Will said.

"Not sure. A coma, I was told. I came up from the lab to see him. Nurse said he was convulsing. I'm staying. His mother is on her way."

"I'll be right down," Will said.

"Not necessary. Stay and study. I'll call later."

"You care enough to stay, so do I. I'll be there soon as I can. Besides, I have this chin strap to give him. It'll cheer him up when he comes to."

He explained to me what was happening and asked if I wanted to come along. "You coming, L.D.?" So I knew it was kind of serious when he switched from Doc to L.D.

"I've got a paper to write, due in the morning. Call me if I can do anything."

It was over an hour later when Will got there and to Steven's floor. Mary was at the end of the hall, sitting alone on the bench, staring at nothing, just a few feet from Steven's door. He glanced in as he passed it, and the bed was already being made up for the next patient. It did not look good. He went and sat next to her, put his arm around her shoulder. "So what happened? What's going on?"

Her eyes glistened. "He's gone."

"You mean?"

"Yes."

"I'm—I'm sorry, Mary." And as an afterthought, "His mother."

"She's down with him. She's with friends. His father is on his way home from Germany. Got sicker yesterday, went into a coma. I'm just up here putting his things together for her."

"You just found out about it? Nobody told you?"

"When I came up to visit, they told me. The nurses on shift at the time don't know me."

"I'm sorry. How lucky he was to have somebody like you to care for him." He did not know what else to say.

"It's not fair," she said.

Will looked at the chin strap from his football helmet. He had written his name and jersey number on it with a black marker so he could give it to the kid. Always a day late and a dollar short, he thought.

"You can give it to Mrs. Harnley," she said. "Go with his other stuff. His bag is in the room."

"Yeah. If you want, I can drive you back. Pam and L.D. will come down and pick up your car for you, later."

"I'll drive. I want to be alone awhile," she said, staring at the floor. "I hope you understand. I'll be fine."

"I don't know what to say."

"I'm not sure I'm cut out for all this," she said.

"Yes, you are. You're going to be the greatest doctor in the world. You're going to do exactly what you set out to do." He pulled her close to him and kissed her on the head. "I love you, Hugo. I love who you are and what you are. You need to know that. I love the way you think and what you think. I love your feelings and the way you see the world. And I want to see it with you, through your eyes, for the rest of my life. That's what I want. So stop talking like that."

She squeezed his hand and grinned through her tears. "If you'll just can the 'Hugo' business."

Will grinned back at her. "I think you're asking way too much."

20

We lost the home game to V.M.I. that Saturday. The guys felt kind of bad for Steven's passing, so they placed a wheelchair at the end of the bench, his seat, with his name on a sign hanging over the back visible to the crowd behind us but mostly unnoticed. It was the least we could have done.

Mary sat in the student section with Shelley Michaels and her date, and Dickey Humphrey and his girlfriend, Carol Foley, who was already half looped and louder than anybody from the free beer supplied by Dickey's roommate, Alvin Findley, whose old man owned the beer franchise.

But a bigger loss than the game was losing Kenny Miklos in the second quarter to a knee injury. He tore a ligament and would have to have surgery Monday, and was out for the season, something that would have a profound affect down the road and change his life forever.

The biggest thing in Will's life at the time was the Thanksgiving weekend with Mary and her family in Charleston, coming up, and how that would go. He was looking forward to it, to meeting the parents who had produced this beautiful, intelligent, and sexy human being he was so madly in love with. It would be like meeting God, in a way. Well, in a way.

That Wednesday, the day before Thanksgiving, they drove the almost five hundred miles to the end of the peninsula, to the neighborhood Mary referred to as South of Broad, on the battery, arriving before dark. They parked in the one last space remaining of the three in the driveway. The community overlooked the harbor. Houses and townhouses were cramped together on the narrow back streets with thin alleys, with little space for parking, Mary's place one of few exceptions, as most of these places were built before the automobile. Lot of brick driveways with gates and brick backyards, and rows of stately mansions facing the water, all of it worth a fortune in the real estate market, if you could find one for sale, Mary explained, and if they'd sell it to you. It depended on who you were. Almost all of them were lived in by the same families for generations going back to the colonial period. Mary's family lived in a three-story, with a widow's watch on a fourth level, brilliant white with wrap-around, colonnaded porches, dark green awnings, touches of mint green accents, palmetto trees about, and landscaping done by the hired help. It was bigger than my house, Will said. Well, my parents' house anyway. My name wasn't on the deed. Aunt Evie and I lived there like tenants, a higher class of squatters, you might say.

The weather was milder than back home in Virginia when they arrived in my Austin-Healey ragtop, which went well with the house and plant life, Will told me later. Mary's parents must have thought the new boyfriend to be normal by their standards, because of the car, and might have been crossing their fingers, since the boyfriend was from the outside world. Might as well have been from outer space.

Mary already had explained to Will briefly about her mother's obsession over her future, as kind of a warning, if for nothing else. Because nothing—absolutely *nothing* —must stand in the way of Mary's going to medical school and being the first woman physician in her family tree, something her mother had failed to do. When she had come along, few women were allowed into the profession outside nurses and orderlies. Her side of the family had lost almost its entire fortune in the Civil War, and the rest in the Great Depression. Only her pedigree had allowed her to marry rich into old money and influence. And her daughter would have what she had been denied, come hell or high water. Mary admitted to Will that she sometimes wondered whose dream she was chasing, hers or her mother's. Sure, she wanted to find a cure for the disease that killed her brother, and she did want to be a doctor, but she wasn't the only one, like the world was waiting on her for a cure.

Her mother came out onto the front porch to greet them with a smile as they walked up what seemed like a million steps. Late forties. She stood with one hand on a hip, the other puffing a lit cigarette in a filtered holder, confident, taking her measure of the boyfriend, much the queen of her domain. She was a perfect copy of Mary, erect posture, but with gray-streaked hair pulled back and tied with a black bow, and well-covered stress lines in the face and neck. She wore a plaid skirt of autumnal colors, stylish loafers, and a simple top. Her smile was conservative and practiced, and seemed to camouflage a number of impressions at once. Her voice was pleasantly southern, and slightly raspy, probably from the smoking. She hugged Mary and shook Will's hand. "Welcome, Will. It's a great pleasure to meet you. Y'all come on in."

Will had the feeling Rene Reedlaw Poythress, Bootsie to family and friends, wished he were someone else. But he would withhold judgment, and she would have to get used to him not being Giles Collier, if that was it. It was just a feeling. She seemed to avoid looking directly at him, avoiding a lot of eye contact, which some-times can imply more than staring. Or maybe it was because she did not know him, so why make him feel too welcomed.

"Your daddy is in the library, working," Rene said. "We weren't expecting you to get here this early. I'll get him. Y'all get something to drink in the kitchen. I'm so glad you're home, sweetheart. I miss you so much when you're gone. Wish you were going to school closer." She disappeared around a corner.

"Your mother is beautiful," Will said.

"She is. Thank you." She kissed him quickly and went to the kitchen.

Will looked the place over. He'd never been in anything like it. A mild breeze was wafting in the windows from the water, a faint scent of the ocean and harbor across the street. The house was like a museum, a miniature Colonial Williamsburg, but all in one room. High, coffered ceilings, papered walls, upholstered fabric and leather furniture. Oil portraits of confederate colonels, one Poythress, one Reedlaw, flanked the large fireplace in profile, looking at one another across a seascape mounted over the mantel. Portraits on other walls of Generals Wade Hampton and Johnson Hagood, state and local favorites, and Robert E. Lee. Gold leaf picture frames, some older than the country itself. A gallery of paintings and photographs of both sides of the family going back centuries. Delicate glassware and more than one photo and an oil likeness of Mary's younger, deceased brother on the mantel, a credenza, and on a coffee table. The only thing modern he could see was a T.V. set in another room across a hall. They'd call it a sitting room. Will would just call it a room, if he was put in a corner.

Mary came back in with the ice tea and handed Will his glass. "Be right back," she said, and headed for the library. He could hear her say, "Daddy," as she must have been hugging her father.

Moments later, the three of them came into the living room, her father trailing. Will stood and immediately was surprised by his appearance. He wasn't sure what he had expected, maybe a Rhett Butler match for his gorgeous wife, but what he got was a Huck Finn. Lanier Poythress—Lanny, they called him—was tall and rangy, with big hands and feet, was lean, like the defensive end Mary said he'd been at the Citadel in his day, the kind with a reach that seemed to cover half a football field, hard to get by for halfbacks and flankers like Will. You could tell he was an athlete because he had that physical something jocks have, that finished look, the something extra. He had reddish-gray hair and big ears, not unsightly but noticeable, looked fit, and had the face of a nineteen-year-old. This guy was a leader, was Will's impression, who could tear your head off in a fight or play ten guys in a game of marbles out back and win the whole thing. His clothes were casual and expensive, if a bit sloppy. Well, he was home. In a million years, Will would not have picked him out of a lineup as the husband of Rene Poythress. His family had made its earlier fortune in tea, sugar, cotton, tobacco, and wholesale hardware, and more recently in real estate development, according to Mary. Probably had no idea what rent or a mortgage payment were, except when receiving it from others. But he also was readily friendly and reached for Will's hand, without hesitation, his voice close to a baritone, maybe because it had so far to travel before getting to the mouth. His grip was firm, like making a point of who was stronger. Please, the hand, Will thought.

"Good grief, look what my daughter just dragged home," Lanny said. "You see this, Bootsie? What do you say, Will? Happy to meet you, fella. Mary tells me you play ball up that way."

"Yes, sir, I try. Happy to meet you, too."

"Best days of your life, wait and see. Come on, let's go sit in here," he said, and led them into an adjacent room that must have been the den. It wasn't much different from the one they'd just left, less formal, still lush, but not so much a museum.

Lanny talked mostly about sports and the news, this Vietnam thing, especially, while Rene was more concerned about Mary's experience and performance at school and, secondarily, about Will's future plans, since he was important enough to bring home.

Lanny got up and went to the bar. "Join us in a drink, Will?"

"No, sir. Thanks anyway. Not much for it, especially during the season. Maybe a beer or two off -season." Will would have liked nothing better than to down several, but his parents had told him never to accept a drink of booze when first meeting a girl's family, never leave a first impression as a drinker.

Lanny handed Rene her glass and sat back down. They got the initial chit chat out of the way.

Then Rene said, "So, what does your father do, Will?"

"He works in the shipyard, ma'am."

"That's wonderful. What's his position there?"

"He's a shop supervisor."

"Oh."

There it was, the first arrow.

Lanny looked at her, likely not surprised, then to Will for his reaction, seeming more interested in that.

Mary said, as politely as possible, "His father works in the shipyard, Momma, he doesn't own the shipyard."

"I never suggested he did," Rene said. "I don't own it either."

Will smiled at that, trying to seem as friendly as possible, just having been insulted to his face, the way he read it.

Obviously, they knew enough about him to know he wasn't right for their daughter, wasn't good enough. Rene anyway. Not sure about Lanny, but if a man sits and allows his wife to insult his daughter's boyfriend on the first meeting, a guest in his home, and doesn't respond in some helpful way, then he's either a weakling or agrees with her and just lets her do the dirty work, the way Will figured it. This was going to be a fun weekend, or it was going to be hell. Mary might have been right about her father being a laid-back, wait-and-see guy, hard to tell so soon, but her mother was a kill-this-thing-before-it-grows person when it came to Will Wythe.

"There was a Wythe, a George Wythe, from the same area as you, who signed the Declaration of Independence, a commander in the Revolutionary Army," Lanny said to Will. "Any kin to him, by the way?"

"I think we were cousins way back then, have some relatives in common, as I understand, sir. But I don't keep up with it. My mother is with the D.A.R," he said, meaning the Daughters of the American Revolution. "She'd know about that."

"Lot of Wythe stuff around there, in that Williamsburg region, for sure," Lanny said. "Noticed that when we were up visiting the college last spring with Mary."

Then Mary's grandmother walked in, apparently having awakened from a nap in her room. Reinforcements, Will figured. Marie

Poythress was a petite woman in her late seventies, well dressed in dark, with a string of white pearls around her neck, and angelic, well-attended white hair. Her voice had that lilting quality of Mary's. Her demeanor was confident, and she stared a hole through you with bright blue eyes when speaking to you, to make sure her words had the affect she expected. Will was wondering how such a small woman had a large son like Lanny, and was trying to imagine the physical dynamics of the necessary mating. But he knew, too, from history class in high school, that Francis Marion, the famous "Swamp Fox," from South Carolina of Revolutionary War fame, was said to be small enough at birth to fit into a one-quart container, so what did he know.

"So this is the young man who caught the fancy of my granddaughter," she said, neither approving nor condescending, but reserved. "Well, there must be something to you. My Mary baby doesn't tolerate the trifling. Come here, young man, and shake my hand."

Will did as he was told, as she took her chair beside Rene. This was a woman you did not say no to.

"And you're the wonderful grandmother Mary talks about," Will said. He didn't know she did that, but it sounded good, and maybe scored some points. Mary's eyelids went up. She needed those rubber boots again.

"You're an awfully nice-looking young man, but I wouldn't expect anything else from my Mary baby. She's the prettiest girl in Charleston. Any boy she wants."

"She's the prettiest girl in the world," Will said. And he meant that.

"We start off with an agreement," Marie said. "Don't let me interrupt you folks. You were talking."

"You're not interrupting, Marie," Rene said. "We were just chatting. Will seems to be related to George Wythe, the one who signed the Declaration of Independence."

"Maybe, not sure," he said.

"That's wonderful. How so?" Marie said.

"Distant cousins, I believe," Will said. "Not a big deal."

"Yes, it is. And something that can be traced," Marie said. "The D.A.R. keeps records on things like that. I'm a member. Nothing is too trivial to us regarding our history."

"My mother feels the same way."

"Good. She must be a delightful person. Love to meet her someday."

Rene Poythress was leaned back with the cigarette in the holder, puffing occasionally, and taking it all in, like a strategist looking for an opportunity to advance. Will could feel the underlying hostility. It was palpable. Palpable, a word he wasn't sure he knew at the time. Well, he was flunking English again.

"Your people fought in the Revolution," Rene said.

"Yes," Will said. "My family has been in every war in our history. And lost someone in every one of them, too."

Lanny nodded his head, understanding. "And in the Civil War, I imagine."

"Yes, sir. Lost several on both sides of the family."

"Where are your folks originally from?" Marie said.

"Amherst and Buckingham Counties," Will said.

Marie nodded affirmatively. "Oh, yes. Beautiful country. Near Appomattox."

Will decided to pour it on a little. He had to talk about something. Back home in Virginia, people were nuts about history, especially the Revolution, but these people in South Carolina were obsessed with the Civil War, in particular, many still not accepting defeat, considering it more a truce. He had been told of that. "My great-grandfather, Hiram Eli Hayes, on my mother's side, was involved in a famous legal case at the time. He was a lawyer before the war and a prosecutor in headquarters, in Richmond, during the war."

Their ears perked up. Rene just stared. Lanny was casual with it, like it didn't matter. But Marie was focused.

"How so?" Rene said, blowing out a puff of smoke.

"He was a major with the judge advocate office and prosecuted the Simon Poole case." Will thought it sounded good to him. He did not know if they had ever heard of it.

But it was not unknown to Marie, who seemed to be the smarter and the best informed of the bunch in this house.

"What? Your great-grandfather prosecuted Major Simon Berkeley Poole, of South Carolina, for the charge of cowardice in the face of the enemy? That Simon Poole?"

"Yes, ma'am, it was his job."

"Simon Poole was railroaded," Marie said, angry. "He was innocent, and the charges were eventually dropped, to prove it. Did you know that?"

"I think I heard something like that, yes, ma'am. Okay by me." Sure, Will wouldn't carry a grudge.

Lanny chuckled. Rene rolled her eyes, smiling.

"He was wrongfully shamed, never got over it," Marie said. "Came home and suffered the rest of his life. So did his family. Drank himself to death, such a sensitive, decent man. It still affects them to this day."

That was the third major now in this conversation, two Confederate officers, the other a big-ass mistake.

"I bet Simon Poole's descendants would like to meet you. They live just down the street," Marie said. "Not saying any of this is your fault, young man. Of course not. You seem like a decent sort, weren't even around then, like the rest of us here, but so are the Pooles innocent, and they've paid a huge, unfair price for a malicious, wrongful prosecution by an over-zealous, egotistical young lawyer, who, by the way, as I understand it, never had to face the enemy a single time during the war, never fired a shot, nor had one fired at him. And never missed a meal the whole time."

Will did not doubt it. The second arrow. What the hell was happening here? Rene was giddy but trying to suppress it. Lanny was chuckling again, finding it funny but not important, just drew on his drink and grinned, watching the show. They knew Marie better than anyone and seemed as amused by her obsession as Will was alarmed by it. At his expense, of course. They were having such a good time with him. Will's younger brother Hank, aka Hiram Hayes Wythe, would get a kick out of this.

Get me the hell out of here, was all Will could think of at the moment, and Mary sensed it. How could she not? She said, "He also has a direct physical connection to Stonewall Jackson."

"Really?" Marie said. "And what might that be?"

"Show'em, Will," Mary said. "It's in his wallet," she told them.

"Ah, they don't want to see that." He felt like she was grabbing at straws, trying to make him seem interesting enough to tolerate.

"Yes, they do. It's his membership symbol to the Stonewall Jackson Society." She was having her own fun with it.

Will pulled out the wallet from his back pocket and opened it to the photo folder. They looked closely for something significant.

"What is it?" Marie said.

"A hair from Little Sorrell, Stonewall Jackson's horse," Will said. It was lame. Him, not the horse. "From his tail."

"How'd you get that?" Marie said. "Is it a sanctioned society? Never heard of it." She seemed disappointed at missing something.

Rene was smiling big, watching this thing go downhill.

"Took it from the museum at V.M.I., in Lexington. Reached in the back of the glass display case. It's a kind of a long story," he said, though it wasn't. "Only a few of us have one."

Lanny leaned forward, staring at it. "No kidding. I'll be damned." He laughed. "That sounds like something I'd have done when I was at the Citadel, my buddies and I."

Marie said, "Yes, it certainly does. That and more."

"What do you do with it?" Rene said, blowing out a puff of smoke.

"Put it back and get another one every year."

"I see. With the goal of what?"

"Of just having something special, feeling connected in a special way with the times, the history, the great general himself, I guess," Will said. Get this show over with.

"Come on, I'll show you your room," Mary said. "Then we'll walk the battery."

"Nice meeting you, Will. We'll talk some more," Marie said. When she thought he was out of ear shot, she said, "Virginia always did seem a little too far north for me. Lost a big chunk of its state when it went with the Yankees, you notice. Pour me a drink, Lanny. Bootsie" she said to Rene, "I don't envy you, with this relationship dumped in your lap. But I know one thing, this young man is a keeper for Mary. See the way she looks at him.? It's real. You've got your hands full. My advice, if you want it? Leave it alone. It'll work or it won't."

"Y'all be careful," Rene yelled over her shoulder as they walked out the door.

21

It was well after dark when they crossed Murray Boulevard to the seawall and started up the north side, holding hands. Cars crowded the street, two lanes with a thin island in the middle, along the walkway that rimmed the tip of the peninsula, since few properties here had enough spaces on their lots. The harbor was almost empty of traffic, just a weak light or two, probably fishermen, not like back home in Hampton Roads, which was much larger and always busy. A sprinkling of lights lit up the homes facing the water and looked like someone's idea of a post card, with just enough moonlight backdropping the scene.

"Getting chilly," Mary said. "Wish we were sleeping together tonight." She laughed at the thought of her parents agreeing to that.

"I think your mother would go along with it," Will said, "so she could walk in on us and shoot me."

"I'm sorry. She'll come around. She has no choice. And I think my daddy likes you."

"What gives you that idea?"

"He was more talkative with you. He usually isn't when he first meets my dates."

"We should make sure he never has that experience again, meeting your dates. I'm more than that."

"Got that right."

"Am I sleeping in the dog house tonight?"

"The guesthouse. You'll like it. Momma and daddy lived there after they married, until I was four years old and my granddaddy died."

"I think your grandmother would try me for treason and have me hanged, just to save a bullet, if she could. She was actually mad at me."

"She wasn't mad at you, personally. She's like that with everybody. She knows everybody around here and their business. She sees herself as a lighthouse keeper, of sorts. You'll get used to her, and you'll like her. And she'll like you. I know it. She's helped a lot of people around here, very charitable, giving person. Just no-nonsense."

"The self-appointed guardian of the city."

"Something like that. If the place fell in the sea, she'd blame herself."

"Would she shoot herself?"

"Funny. The Poole family she mentioned. They live just a few blocks up, north of Broad, where she owns some real estate. She allows the family, mother and four children, to stay in one of the houses rent free because the father died a few years ago, and the mother is blind. The kids are older, they work after school and on weekends and summers, but it's hard. She doesn't want to see them on welfare. She hates for people to go that way when others should be helping. If you get mad at her, try to keep it to yourself. It'll work out, I promise."

"I trust you," Will said, "Loud and clear. I think it's time for some serious kissing."

They stopped and embraced. "Let's stay out here all night," he said. He kissed her, holding her tight. Looking across her shoulder, back toward her house, he noticed a tiny flicker of light and the hazy figure of a person standing on the front porch. Rene seemed to be looking their way and was puffing her cigarette.

They walked a mile further, taking their time, then returned to the house and got their bags from the car, and took Will's around back to the guest house. It was a two-story half covered in ivy, the two bedrooms overhead, refrigerator well stocked. It was well furnished, like the main house, but without the importance of thickness and history; room to move around without the constant reminder of who you were and where you came from, and your obligations to posterity. The yard was shaded by a couple of large, ancient trees, oak and magnolia, was well tended, as was the entire property, plenty of light through the windows. Will felt he could stay here the rest of his life, if it didn't belong to someone else and have to sleep with one eye open.

It was difficult tearing themselves apart, before going too far, but the phone rang and Rene asked if there was anything Will needed, like extra linen or something, her way of telling Mary not to stay too long, it wasn't a lovers nest.

When she got to her room upstairs in the main house, preparing to shower, her mother came in wearing a house coat, having already bathed, and sat on the edge of her bed. "We need to talk," Rene said.

"I think so. You could have been a little more welcoming, Momma. I knew it wasn't going to go over that well, but you didn't have to be that cold and unfriendly. It's not right. Daddy seemed to be okay with him. I don't like him being treated like that."

"Well, I'm sorry if my concerns for you are that transparent, or seem unfriendly, but I don't apologize either. You're my daughter, our daughter and granddaughter, and you're the only thing that's important here. You and your future."

"Sometimes I wonder."

"About what?"

"About whose future you're most concerned about, mine or the one you lost." As soon as she said it, she regretted it. "I don't mean it that way. Really. You know what I mean."

Rene seemed hurt by the remark, but not stopped by it. "I will not let life deal you a dirty hand, Mary. Not in a million years. You have too much going for you, too much promise to be lost by these little distractions. You're too young, it's too early to be sidetracked. You have an important goal to achieve, a reason and purpose for living, an accomplishment waiting for you out there. Your ticket is punched, as the saying goes, the doors open already. You know that. We've talked about it for years, your goal of being a doctor, of doing important work. And you have every opportunity to have it all. Not many kids have that kind of advantage. You're so lucky you were born into this family. Look around. We've talked about this before, a hundred times. You can have love and marriage and children, and all that comes with it. In time. But you have to keep your eye on the prize or it'll slip away. For God's sake, Mary, you're only twenty years old, is all I'm saying. Give it a chance. You've always been very intelligent. Things come easy for you. But you don't have the wisdom that comes only from experience and time. Until then, you have to rely on the judgment and advice of the adults in your life who have your best interests in mind. Is that asking so much, just to let us have a part of your decisions? We've never let you down before."

"Will is the most supportive person I've ever known, besides you and daddy and grandma. He wants the same thing for me as you and I want. You should have seen what he did for Steven." She had told Rene about Steven's situation, her time with him, and his recent death. "He made that boy's last days in this world the best he'd seen in years. You should have been there, the light he brought into that boy's life. It's the way he is, how happy his mother was to see it. So positive."

"But what does he want for himself? To be a football coach? Football is a game, Mary, not a goal. You could end up barefoot and pregnant, as the saying goes, while he's out after dark playing games with kids. Just look around and see what's happened to a couple of your friends who had everything and blew it. Do I have to go into details here?"

"Would you be all that against it if it was Giles, and not Will?"

Rene seemed stunned. "Apples and oranges," was her comeback. "You'd never be barefoot. That's for sure."

"I have a trust fund from granddaddy. I'll never be broke, even if you and daddy and grandma cut me off. Your argument is dead on arrival."

"Nice medical expression. You sure this boy isn't a gold digger? It happens, you know."

"Will is not interested in wealth or being rich. He's never talked money or said a single thing about it."

"That can be troubling. You say it like it's a virtue or something. He might not want to work for wealth, but he might be attracted to marrying it. Some men do that, target women that way."

"So do some women," Mary said. She gave a brief glance at her mother.

"I can see this little discussion is not going anywhere much. We can talk about it again, before you go back. Please tell Will we were not trying to be snobby or unfriendly to him, if it seemed that way. He does seem like a nice enough young man."

"Or you could tell him yourself, Momma, because it seemed that way."

"I'll make a point of it. And, by the way, Giles called and said he and Nell are having breakfast at the café on King Street in the morning, and asked you and Will to join them around ten o'clock," she said. Nell was Giles Collier's younger sister, Mary's age. "So please call him first thing. Also, forgot to mention it, Charles has been promoted to managing editor at the paper." Charles being Rene's younger brother and Mary's favorite uncle. "Be sure and congratulate him. He and Kate and the kids are having dinner with us tomorrow."

"Oh, that's great. I will. Good for him. He deserves it. I mean that."

"Who knows, maybe publisher isn't far behind."

"Or part owner, when his in-laws pass away." She smiled and gave another sideway glance that Rene let go by.

"He's done very well. I'm proud of him." Rene said.

Mary was getting all her toiletry items together for the shower. Women have so much stuff. "Not bad for a lowly newspaper reporter working for slave wages, wasting all that ability and talent, like you always said about it. Who would've guessed, a man being successful at what he loves, despite his family's disappointment at his doing something he wants to do, especially so young, just thirty-seven now."

"It's what happens when you marry well," Rene said, trying to resist arguing further. "Is that something to be ashamed of? So what's your point?"

"But it's not okay with you if someone like Will does the same thing?"

"Sometimes it's what else you bring to the table."

"You've both done quite well," she said of Rene and Charles, "for two people who had little to trade on but an old name, Momma. And I don't mean that disrespectfully. It just happens to be true. I'm not blind. I didn't just fall off a turnip truck."

"It's what happens when you marry well. The alternative is not to marry well. At least we have a name, and an important history in this town. That's something. I would have married your father if he hadn't had a nickel to his name."

Mary let that one slide by herself.

"Like I said, we can discuss it more, later. But I—we all—want nothing but the best for you, and that's not going to change, no matter what it takes or whose feelings we hurt, or how we have to cull off the chaff."

"So he's chaff now. I resent that."

"Come here and give me a hug. We're not going to bed fighting." She reached for her.

Mary rolled her eyes and returned the hug, but not with the same enthusiasm.

"Will and I are going to spend the rest of our lives together," Mary said. "And that's a fact. And nothing will change that, either. You might as well get used to it."

"Little early to be making that kind of prediction. You wouldn't be—you're not, uh—."

"No, of course not. Think I'm crazy, and stupid too? Think we're crazy?"

Rene seemed relieved. "Goodnight, sweetheart. See you in the morning."

22

The weather was still mild the next morning, light jackets only. Will and Mary walked to meet Giles and Nell at the café on King Street at ten a.m., across from the movie theater. The street was narrow, as most were in the old downtown, and was the main commercial stretch going back to the early days of the city. Most businesses were closed, the exception being the eating places and coffee shops, a couple hotels further up. The café was quaint, booths and tables, short French curtains over the windows with a view outside. Locals and tourists enjoying the casual atmosphere and being waited on by others.

For most, this was the practice run for the more serious eating later in the day, when families across America would gather to, what else, eat and remind themselves how fortunate they were to be eating so well. Will said it occurred to him at the moment that all of life seemed to revolve around the mouth. The good parts anyway.

Giles was about Will's height, maybe an inch taller, and leaner, and had the preppy look of a real frat brother, not a fake one, like the rag-tag SPD, though the Sigma Phi guys were clean-cut. He wore shined beef roll loafers, no socks, khakis, and a lavender cashmere V-neck sweater that must have cost more than everything Will had on at the time. His eyes were bloodshot, like he'd driven all night from school to get home late the previous night, or had been out partying, or maybe both. Mary did infer he was a drinker. Nell was not quite as tall as Mary, and was very pretty; brown eyes, dark hair to the shoulders, wore a skirt over her gymnast's figure, and carried herself with the confidence of an alpha female. She smiled big and was having trouble not staring at Will.

They ordered coffee or hot tea, toast and sweet rolls. The brother and sister seemed genuinely friendly, like it was their nature and not an act for appearances, not stuffy at all. Giles had the air of the more mature of them, as he was over two years older, a first-year law student, and was comfortable with it, and with having breakfast with his sister away from home. Will didn't know anybody that age who was that friendly with his sister. It was an observation, not a judgment. But he knew if I'd been there, I'd have been all over Nell. They caught up on the latest and talked about school, the colleges they were attending, their mutual friends, one thing or another, and Will mostly listened. He and Giles talked sports a little, of course, while the girls gossiped.

Then Mary and Nell went to the restroom. Women were always going to the restroom, and always doing it together.

"My gawd," Nell said, when they got there. "How did you find this guy? Does he have a twin brother, or a close second?"

Back at the table, Giles grinned and said to Will, "So how did you like her parents?" Getting to the point.

"You mean, how do they like me, is what you're saying."

Giles nodded.

"I don't think they like me." He gave a grin of his own.

Giles chuckled. "You're not the only one. Mary has a heart of gold. She loves everybody. But her parents aren't like that, especially with Mrs. Poythress, Bootsie. Rene. She's the griffin when it comes to Mary. Marie is okay, her grandmother. Not a better woman in this town, but very critical. Just telling you. And her daddy, Lanny, is a good guy. One of the old school Citadel crowd around here. Silver Star in the war, very well respected, all that jazz.

Just letting you know. Don't want you to think everybody here are in-breeding assholes. They're not, but it must look like it."

"You get along with them, though."

"Sure. Known them all my life. Mary and I were pretty serious, until recently, just before she left for school in Virginia. Well, kind of, me anyway. In fact, if I thought she'd ever marry me, I'd ask her to today. But it's not going to happen, and I know it. So if she's serious about you, and I hear she is, you're the luckiest guy in the world, in my opinion. And I hope it goes well for you. She deserves it."

"So how did you know she was serious with someone?" Will said.

"When her mother called me last night and said to make sure I saw Mary this weekend. She's always liked the idea of Mary and me together. And so do my parents. And I'd like this to stay between us, if that's okay. I have to live here."

Will nodded his agreement. There it was, Arrow Number Three. All he could say at the moment was, "I see," and nod his head and try not to look like it surprised or offended him further.

But Giles could tell it did bother Will. "All I'm saying is, you could be the richest person in the world, or a Kennedy, or a Rockefeller, or a Nobel Prize recipient, or discover a cure for cancer, but you'd still be an outsider, far as folks around here are concerned, just another Geechee. Nothing to do with you, personally. You know what I'm talking about. People up where you're from are the same way, only it's a whole state and not just a town. I know, I've been there a couple times and have relatives there. Snootiest people I've ever met."

"Geechee," Will said. "What's that?"

"An expression, kind of a term of endearment down here. Could be good, bad, or nothing. Refers to the early Gullah, the Africans who lived here in the low country, on the coast, from the colonial period."

"Working class."

"Yep. Something like that. Don't feel bad. We call each other that sometimes."

Will nodded his understanding. He felt like he was one of the variables in a Sociology One-0-Two study.

Mary and Nell returned from the restroom, and they chatted a while longer.

"Nell wants to come up for a weekend sometime," Mary said.

Great, Will thought. The SPD will be all over her like stink on a zoo.

The four of them walked back to the neighborhood together, since Giles and Nell lived just three blocks over from the Poythress home. They stopped to chat briefly with a couple of people all but Will knew who were also out walking themselves or their dogs. Giles and Nell split at their street and said their goodbyes, and Will and Mary continued toward the battery.

Will was thinking how great it must be live in a place like this, where there seemed to be no sense of urgency or things to worry about coming at you tomorrow, visualizing Mary growing up here and how he wished he could have grown up with her, like Giles did. On the other hand, what would he do with all the time to keep from going stark-raving nuts from boredom. He could walk the riverfront at home. He lived just a block from it. And the beach was just a couple blocks down. In some respects, the folks here really didn't have more than he and his friends and neighbors. Though he had been here less than a full day, he could already tell that Mary was the most energetic and focused person he'd met. He also knew he never could live here, not that he ever considered it, and that he'd never see the museums and churches and other sites of historical importance Mary had planned on showing him over the weekend. Not this time. He was going home today.

"Hugo, I can't stay here. I'm leaving." Will said.

"What?"

"I stayed awake for hours last night thinking about it. It won't work. I don't belong here."

"Yes, you do. Give it time, like I said."

"No. You're asking too much. I thought I'd come here with you and they'd all be nice and chummy to my face, then work on you after I left. But that's not what happened. That mother of yours came right at me before I could get in the door, and you know it. Your father seems like a nice guy on the outside, but he's actually the sneakiest one. Sorry to have to say that, but I won't lie to you."

"Why don't you stay, just for dinner at least, meet Charles and Kate. You'll like them, and they'll like you. Then you can say you called home and something came up and you have to leave early.

"Lie to them? They didn't lie to me. They let me know right up front what they thought of me."

"Will, I'm so sorry."

"You don't have to be. I'm the odd person out here, not you or your family. You have no apologies to make. You could never offend anybody. You're too good for that."

"What do I say to them? This puts me in a difficult spot. Puts both of us in one."

"You don't say anything. I put my stuff in the car, and you tell your father that I want to talk with him outside, before I leave."

"I hope you're not going to start something with my daddy."

"Of course not. I just want to have a little talk with him, make him feel better about things, is all. And, by the way, I take back what I said about Giles, making fun of his name that time. He seems like a nice guy. And Nell is nice too."

"Yes, they are."

They were silent the rest of the way, until crossing the boulevard and walking up to the porch.

"I'll get my bags and put them in the car," Will said. "Ask your father to meet me out here in a couple minutes, if you will."

"If you're going, I'm going," Mary said.

"No, Hugo, you stay. It's your family. It's Thanksgiving. This is where you belong. I can drive back down here Saturday and pick you up, or you can fly back and I'll meet you at Patrick Henry," he said, referring to the airport in Newport News.

"I said I'm going. I belong with you as much as I belong here. So it's my choice."

He blew out a puff of air. "Your head is getting harder than mine, hanging around with me so much." He grinned.

She kissed him quickly. "Go get your bags. I'll get mine." She went up the steps.

When Mary came down, Rene said, "What's going on here? What are you doing?"

"We're going back early, Momma. I think you know why. I don't want to get into it now. I'll call when I get there."

"Just stop right there and tell me what's going on."

"No. I'm leaving. Will is leaving and I'm going with him." She stopped for an instant. "Frankly, I can't blame him."

"This is the kind of thing I tried to warn you about when you left for school up there. What can happen when you get involved with the unknown."

"So he's unknown now."

"See the trouble it's already causing? Please, sweetheart, think about this. We're the ones who're going to be here for you and pick up the pieces when it all goes bad. We're the ones who love you."

"Not the only ones, Momma. I'll be home Christmas. If you'll have me." Couldn't resist that little jab on the end. "Where's Daddy?"

"Back there," she said, indicating the library.

Will was putting his bags in the trunk when Lanny came out onto the porch. "What's this all about?" he said. "Mary said y'all are leaving. What for?"

Mary came down the steps with her bags and put them in the car.

Will walked over to the foot of the steps to meet him as Lanny came down.

"Just want to speak to you a second, sir."

"Sure, but what's this all about, y'all leaving like this?"

"You say it like you don't know, Mr. Poythress. First of all, I appreciate your hospitality, what there was of it. Second, and I want you to listen to me very carefully. I'm going to make you a promise, and you can hold me to it, because I don't break promises. I love Mary, and I'm going to spend the rest of my life with her proving it. And as long as I live, I will never come to your house again. No matter what." He turned around and went and got into the car.

Mary hugged her mother and father quickly. "See you Christmas. Everything is going to be fine. Tell Grandma I love her."

Lanny looked at Rene with a what-the-hell expression. Rene stared a hole through Will as the car pulled off. If looks could have killed.

23

Will and Mary took two-lane Route 17 over the Cooper River bridge leaving Charleston, heading north. As they got into Mt. Pleasant on the other side, Mary said, "Take a right here."

"What for?"

"The beach house. Sullivan's Island. We have a place there."

"I don't want to be on your family's property, Hugo, and they don't want me here. The reason we're leaving."

"It's not just theirs, it's ours. My granddaddy left it, and my name is on the deed too."

They drove down the dirt road and reached the coastal drive along the oceanfront. Houses and cottages, old and newer, overlooked the beach. Mary's was an older but large house of weathered gray cedar shingles and wrap-around porches, up and down. A hammock and several rockers were still out. Not a busy place, just a few people around, most likely full-time residents. Hearty palmetto trees and tropical greenery were dominant on the island, and old oaks with Spanish moss dripped like witches' hair almost to the ground.

They drove up the sandy driveway, parking in the back, or front, depending on one's reference. Inside was well furnished in bright and tropical colors of florals and stripes. The theme here was maritime and nautical, though still somewhat historical; ship wheel and brass instruments, seascape oils, models of ships large and small, in and out of glass cases, and dark woods. It resembled a captain's cabin on a galleon, but much larger. Wrap-around windows framed a panoramic view of the beach, and harbor to the right, Ft. Sumpter farther out, and the Atlantic Ocean forever.

"Get undressed, Will. We're taking a shower," she said.

Will didn't think he had ever seen her so eager. And that drove up his adrenaline to an explosive level. They did not wash, as showers go, just let the water fall over them as they hungered for and at one another, and went at it like beasts in a mating rage, like there wouldn't be a tomorrow, so get it all now. Afterward, they lay naked and wet on the bed, without speaking for several minutes, catching their breath.

"You're not ever going anywhere without me," Mary said. "You understand that? Not ever."

"I don't think there is anywhere to go that I'd want to be without you, Hugo. So that's not a problem."

And Mary would make good on that promise down the road.

They locked the beach house and drove up the highway past sugarcane fields and forests, and tiny towns and tourist stops, and signage hawking candy, figurines, hot dogs, cigarettes, peanuts and pecans, cheap clothing, and gasoline, and a lot of wilderness as well.

After leaving Georgetown, the first place of any size since Charleston, and the smell of pulp and paper still in the air from before the holiday, they soon were in Myrtle Beach, a long strip of motels and restaurants, a pier, amusement park and a Ferris wheel, among other attractions closed for the season. They checked into a motel room with some of the money his parents gave him for the trip. They ate at a seafood and steakhouse, then walked the beach and surf line, near dark. It was all but deserted, but the lonely feeling of isolation couldn't have touched them with a ten-foot pole.

"Tomorrow, when we get back," Will said, "I want us to go over to the bridge, at the pond. Something I want to show you."

They got up at four a.m. and drove the almost four hundred miles back, arriving just after noon. Will had wanted to stop first at his house to see his parents and brother, and to explain things, then to mine to swap back cars, but didn't want to do it in Mary's presence and make her uncomfortable. I wasn't home at the time, Aunt Evie told him, so they went to Mary's house in Williamsburg. Shelley had gone home to Hampton for the weekend, and they had the place to themselves. Mary called her and told her she was back, would explain later.

"Uh-oh," Shelley said. "I smell a rat."

"Afraid so," Mary said. "But all is well. Later."

It was Friday, the day after Thanksgiving, so people were out like crazy, tourists all over the place, but few students, so it wasn't so bad at their favorite diner. Most locals were out and about in Richmond and Newport News shopping, preparing for the massive assault on Christmas, a month away. And the end of the semester.

They left the diner and walked across the road to the campus, and through the patch of trees, around the Sunken Garden, to the top of the bridge over the pond.

"Okay, now what? Show me," Mary said, looking around.

Will pointed to a spot in the brush on the far bank. "There. See it?" he said.

"No. What?"

He pointed again. "There, that thing sticking out of the ground."

"Oh, yeah," she said, maybe seeing it, maybe not.

"My oar, the paddle end of it. The one I keep on the wall in the dorm. It's to my row boat I keep at the boat basin down the street from my house. The other is home on my bedroom wall. I cut it off the other day, before we left, drove it down in the ground. To mark this spot. Our spot. This is our special place, Hugo. It belongs to us. The whole world can use it, but it's ours."

"That's so sweet."

"Don't get mushy on me."

"You're such a romantic. "

"Not so loud, Hugo. People might hear."

She laughed. "You're an idiot."

"I know. But I'm not really a romantic. I'm only like this with you."

"Liar. You're a secret romantic." She laughed and hugged him.

Will dug in his pocket and felt the ring. Just a small diamond, nothing fancy, just what he could afford. He brought it out and held it up. "I want to make it official. I want us to get married someday, when the time is right for both of us. No hurry, but this seals it for us."

"I'll have to think it over for a few years."

"Smart aleck already."

She laughed again. "Yes, we will marry. It's official, from this point forward."

He put it on her finger and she admired it. Well, women do that.

"This is our place, Mary. We have to come here and pay homage from time to time, to revere the marker and its meaning. It is us together as one, our symbol. And we have to make sure nobody moves it. That's why I put it where it's hard to see."

"You're so good at hiding things. Maybe you should be a professional hider. Open up your own office or something."

"You're getting the hang of the wisenheimer thing."

"Let's go back to my house and celebrate."

24

It was Saturday and the campus was still vacant of most students, just a few around who lived too far away to go home for just a long weekend. But tourists and other locals would have made an aerial view of the town look like an ant colony, very busy. The weather was tolerable but not as mild as Charleston. Charleston. There was a memory for the books, far as Will was concerned.

Will and Mary drove down to my house to switch cars and hang out awhile with Pam and me. Ken Miklos was limping around from the surgery on his knee and using a cane. He drove his car and brought Dickey Humphrey with him. Miklos had to see his doctor Monday so he'd stayed at school.

"Next time I'm driving, blind or not," Dickey said. "You ever ride with this guy? Imagine it with one leg and no brake."

Miklos laughed. "Scared the crap out of him."

Aunt Evie had gone shopping with a couple of her lady friends and left some food for us to eat, so we sat around the dining room table doing our part. After that, we went into the living room where it was more comfortable for lounging around. My mother, back in the day when she actually stayed home, maintained a semi-formal though traditional décor with lots of fabrics and upholstery, casual pieces of very little historical significance, more Chippendale and New England than Queen Anne, if that makes sense.

Mary and Pam went shopping, so we guys were alone.

"Where's Carol?" I said to Dickey.

"With her mother in Norfolk, trying to lose weight or something. Going to Virginia Beach to walk the boardwalk later. Have to have exotic venues to do it, you know."

"She's not overweight," I said. "Why don't they go to Buckroe?" It was a beach right down the road, much closer.

"Not as many nice restaurants."

Miklos said, "Tell her to eat all she wants, just do it in the dark, a closet or something. If you eat in the dark, you don't gain weight because the calories can't see where they're going."

We had a big laugh at that.

"Mid-semester reports coming out Monday," Dickey said. "How you think you're going to do, Will?" Mid-semesters were the unofficial way professors let students know exactly where they stood at the time regarding grades.

"Have to wait and see. Antise is the one I'm worried about. The others I can slide by with a C, maybe one B minus in Art History."

"Antise likes to flunk people," Miklos said. "He's the school's number one hatchet man, the Grand Protector of the Queen's English. Maintain the grading curve, the reputation, all that. Kill 'em early so they can't become full-fledged juniors."

"Well, he's got easy pickings with Will here," Dickey said. "A junior still taking English Two-0-Two, not an official junior. Make a D or F and you're on condition, can't play ball, and lose your scholarship."

"All those damn books," Will said. "And reports and term paper. Not enough time for just one class. You'd think we were grad students or something, like there was only one class that mattered, his."

Kenny Miklos switched subjects, asking Will how it went down in Charleston. Will already had told me about it earlier, when Mary and Pam weren't close by.

"Not good," Will said. "Why we came back early. And don't say anything to her."

"Sorry to hear it, but I tried to tell you. You went down there thinking everything would be hunky dory and they handed you your ass in a hat, is what happened."

"That's about it. But I handed it back to them."

"Good for you. Next time you go there they'll have a machine gun emplacement ready for you."

"Won't be a next time."

"Then they'll save on ammunition. What's Mary say about it?"

"She came back with me, didn't she?"

Then Will switched subjects. "What about your knee? Be ready for spring practice?"

"I don't know, tell you the truth. It's not looking good. It'll heal okay, but the doctor says I won't be ready for spring. Might not be able to play next year, if at all. Says if I get a similar injury, I could have a stiff leg the rest of my life, or even lose it below the knee. I'll know more Tuesday. But I'll tell you one thing, if I can't play ball, I'm not staying in school. It's the only reason I'm here."

"And do what?" I said.

"Get a job as a reporter, a correspondent. This Vietnam thing is heating up like crazy, lasting a lot longer than predicted."

"You drop out of school," Dickey said, "you better get married quick, or be picked up by the draft."

"Never happen. I'm not getting married now. And I'm not going in the army or anything else either. I'll go to Canada, what some guys are doing, if I have to."

"Great. Be a draft dodger and on the run the rest of your life," Dickey said.

"Look on the brighter side. I'll be alive."

"As a war reporter? Where you going to report from, Disney-land?"

"As a reporter in the field, I can move around, chase the story. As a soldier, the story chases me, trying to kill me."

"Exactly where is Vietnam anyway?" Will said.

"Southeast Asia. Used to be called Indochina," Miklos said.

"Next to Outdochina," I said.

"You're a wiseass, Doc," Miklos said, and we all laughed. Sure, it was funny. "I can see you shit birds are lost in this world."

"We're having a party for Findley next Saturday," Dickey said of his roommate. "Guy's been furnishing us beer the whole semester. Time to pay back. He drinks and eats for free. It's only right."

"Any excuse to drink beer is fine with me," Miklos said.

"Party where?" I said. "We don't have a house, like normal people."

"Well, it won't be at Bowman's," Will said. "His old man will kill us all." Rick Bowman's home had been thoroughly trashed the week of registration, as mentioned.

Dickey said, "If the weather is right, we can do it at the bridge, or in the Sunken Garden, that little patch of woods there."

"If we don't get chased out," Will said.

"What about tourists?" Miklos said.

"What about them?" Dickey said. "Invite them."

"You got that much beer?" Miklos said.

"We take up a collection."

"And girls," I said. "Invite lots of girls."

"But I'm not kidding, Will," Dickey said. "You better get on that English Lit. Semester will be over second week of January. It's make-or-break time for you. I can help you with it, but I can't write your paper or take your exam."

"You screw it up, you'll be in the shipyard and coaching rec league instead of college," Miklos said.

"Or in the service, if he doesn't get married," Dickey said.

"I'll get it done," Will said. "Just so hard to concentrate these days, is all."

We sat around talking another couple hours or so, even raided Aunt Evie's stash of booze for a drink or two. I looked out the window a lot, to the river and the ships and small craft moving about or at anchor, the very same view I'd had almost every day of my life growing up, except when away at military school. The view was always captivating, especially the horizon, where my thoughts drifted to faraway places I would travel to someday, adventures I would experience with excitement, challenge, and maybe a little fear too. Not sure if I was chasing a dream or running away from something. What happens when you lose yourself in your imagination, all kinds of crap shows up in your head.

Mary and Pam got back from shopping, and Kenny Miklos and Dickey left for Williamsburg. "You drive like you did coming down here," Dickey said, "and I'm jumping out and taking a cab."

Pam and I went upstairs to one of the spare bedrooms to be alone awhile. Will and Mary could wait, since they'd have Mary's house in Williamsburg to themselves later. She sat in his lap on the sofa.

"I'll be in the hospital all morning tomorrow," Mary said. "Studying after that. Please get with Dickey and study. Then study some more. You have to get by this course, Will. You know that."

"I know. It's hard keeping my mind on anything but you." He hugged her tight.

"But there's more to life than love and lust, you big dummy."

"You're sounding like your mother."

"She's not wrong about everything, just about you. Staying focused is important. We want to get through this together. We don't want anything separating us. I couldn't take that."

"You keep talking like that, I'll drag you upstairs to my bedroom, like a caveman, and ravage you."

"Promises, promises. But not now. Here comes Aunt Evie. Down, boy."

25

Pam and I stayed home with Aunt Evie until after dark, then I took Pam home and came back. Aunt Evie and I sat in the living room talking a bit and watching TV.

"Your mother called today, L.D. You weren't here. She really wanted to speak with you." I noticed she waited that long to tell me.

"Where are they now, in Egypt?"

"Cape Town, South Africa. But here's the good part. They want both of us to join them for Christmas vacation in Switzerland. Isn't that great? They'll send the tickets. We'll have so much fun. Just think, Switzerland, the Alps, skiing. Well, you skiing, me watching the views." I could see her skiing down the slopes with a gin and tonic in her hand.

"I think it will do you good to go, Aunt Evie. You deserve a vacation. I don't want one, and I don't need one. That's just their way of saying they're not coming home for the holidays, just like I told you. Which is okay with me because my social calendar is too busy for things like Christmas with family. If you don't go, I'll stay and spend it with you, but I'm not traveling half way around the world to be with them so they can spend all their time partying with their friends while I stay in a hotel room. We don't have that much in common. But I think you should go. Really, you should."

"It's you they want to see, L.D."

"I don't want to get into it, Aunt Evie." Just for a second I re-membered Stevie being in the hospital dying, while his father was in Germany, a half a world away. So it was impossible to feel sorry for myself. How could I? I just rolled with it. It was getting easier with time. What else was new.

The next afternoon, Sunday, Pam and I took Aunt Evie and Will and Mary to dinner at Chowning's Tavern in Williamsburg, my treat. Will was newly broke anyway from his trip to Charleston, and I had more spending money than brains, thanks to my mother's guilt payments.

Chowning's was on Duke of Gloucester Street a few short blocks up from Jockstrap Corner. Well, "the corner," more appro-priately. The place, Josiah Chowning's, had been around since the colonial days, before the revolution, and it's said that Thomas Jef-ferson and his buddies drank ale there when they were students in town. In warmer weather you could eat outside in the fenced-in backyard, under the trellis and vines. The building, itself, was a two-story old house-like structure, with a cellar for supplies. Res-ervations were important, the food always good.

Aunt Evie at first declined a drink, but relented after I insisted. She was dying for one anyway, I could tell. "If you insist," she said. We didn't have one because it would have felt uncomfortable in her presence. Sneak her booze at home, but not drink it in front of her. Sure, noble us. The men in the place were having a ball sneak-ing looks at Mary and Pam. And Mary looked so much more mature than her almost twenty-one.

Later, I took Aunt Evie back home and returned to the dorm, since I had an early class the next morning. I was getting to the point lately of feeling guilty about leaving her in the big house alone, especially at night, all the loneliness she must have felt. Why she filled her life with booze and mostly women friends, I guess. I knew the feeling, though I don't drink much. Her predicament made me wonder how somebody could be totally destroyed by the death of someone close to you, like she was by her husband's death in the war over twenty years before, and never again allowing herself to have that feeling or experience with another man. That was hard to grasp. She was extremely sensitive and humane, and at times I wondered how she and my father could have been born of and raised by the same parents in the same house.

Shelley wasn't coming back to town until the next morning, Monday, because she had a late class, so Mary could study alone, and Will stopped by my dorm room, before calling it a day.

"You're suppose to be working on your paper," I said.

He flopped down on the adjacent bunk. "Screw it. I'll get on it tomorrow. More time, now that the season's over. I'm finding it hard to concentrate, L.D." He said L.D. instead of Doc, so I knew it was kind of serious.

"That was your excuse during the season. Not the case now."

"It's Mary."

"So it's Mary's fault."

"No. I just can't think about anything else. I just want to crawl up inside her and spend the rest of my life there and never come out. Can't stand to be away from her."

"Well, you better stand it. For your sake and hers."

"Antise is going to crap on me tomorrow," he said, referring to the mid-semester progress reports coming out. "I don't think he likes jocks anyway. You know how some of these professors are. They pick the B students and the F students the first day of class, then stick to it, no matter how well you do. No A students, of course. They've all been stuffed and put in museums. He knows your record all the way back to high school. Tells his freshmen students the first day of class that they've spent the last twelve years mastering the English language, they're in college now, not remedial training, time to learn the true meaning of the English language, the great literature of the culture, all that crap. Read books, write papers. And listen to his stupid lectures."

"I think he's on to something," I said.

He laughed. "That's because you got a C, asshole. And didn't have Antise. You're a brilliant scholar."

Then I laughed. The great C student.

"You know," he said out of nowhere, "I think Mary's grandmother was the only honest person I met in her family, though I met just three of them. Looks you in the face and tells you what she thinks. I could get used to her, even if she doesn't like me."

"You going to make another run at them?"

"Hell, no. I said it and I meant it."

"Not even if Mary asks you to?"

"No. Probably the only thing I could ever deny her."

"But it might be the only important thing she wants."

"Cross that bridge when we get to it."

"You better think about it because it'll come to it."

Will grinned. "You writing for Dear Abby now or something? Where you getting all this wisdom from? A girl like Pam worships you and you're all over the place. Don't know what's good for you."

"Exactly where you were couple months ago."

"Ancient history. You know, I think her hard-ass parents make me love her more, if that's possible.

"If they knew that, they'd be a hell of a lot nicer to you."

We both laughed again.

The next day Doctor Antise posted the progress reports on the bulletin board outside his classroom, a list with the current grades and the last four digits of students' Social Security numbers, for privacy. Will got a C and it was like he'd been nominated for that Nobel Mary ridiculed him about when they first met.

"We'll have to make it a double celebration Saturday," I said. "Findley and Will."

We were sitting around in Will's dorm room.

"Hell, no," Miklos said. "A separate party, so we can drink beer twice. Besides, we don't want to water down Findley's day in the sunshine. It wouldn't be right."

It was unanimous, of course.

"Might have been a B if you'd studied," Dickey said.

"I don't trust him," Will said. He was having second thoughts about his sudden rise in scholarship. "These grades aren't official. He can call them any way he wants, doesn't mean crap. End of the semester comes and he can switch on you. He doesn't flunk or give D's to twenty-to-twenty-five percent of the class, he loses his job. That's the system. Maintain the curve, the almighty standards. You remember what happened to Alice Sawyer. Refused to fail students who met course requirements, but didn't honor the percentages, so they let her go. First time I ever felt sorry for an English prof. She was a Phi Beta Kappa, for crap sake, students loved her. My freshman teacher, made English interesting. Nobody skipped her classes."

"In the Ivy League they give everybody A's," Miklos said. "I have friends there."

Dickey said, "I hear those A's are paid for by rich alumni parents."

"You survived to flunk another day," Miklos said. "Drink all the beer you can now. Lean times are coming after you check out."

Mary was excited by Will's C and the prospect of his getting by the semester and staying in school for one more in the spring. After the next spring semester she'd have the summer and fall sessions, then graduate mid-term with her double major and be off to med school after sitting out one while waiting for the next class to start. She'd stay in town so she and Will could remain together, no matter what her parents wanted. Once she started to med school, Will could find a job coaching or teaching and, with luck, maybe even a college coaching position, even if she had to go to her father for help. He had friends all over the place, some of them football coaches, fellow teammates. It's how she was getting into medical school when others weren't, no matter how smart.

26

Will and I spent our spare time at school working out at the gym with the team. When Christmas and New Year's break came, Mary went home to Charleston and Will and I went home to Newport News. He spent some time with his younger brother and Pam and I hung out some that first couple days. Then Will and I met with some old friends from high school, including a few of the original SPD frat members, and threw the football around and played a couple games of touch, because we didn't know how to live without doing it.

Mary's mother was not pleased when she saw the engagement ring, though she had to have expected it sooner or later. "Isn't that pushing it a bit?" she said. They were sitting alone in the living room.

"We're not in a hurry, Momma. Neither of us."

"You think you're planning to marry somebody who says he'll never set foot in this house again. How's that going to work?"

"It'll work."

"What's your wedding going to look like? I can just imagine that. A can of worms."

"Plenty of time for that. A wedding is just a ceremony. The commitment is what counts."

"The daughter lecturing the mother," Rene said. "Well, your daddy and grandmother will have opinions, for certain."

"I think they and you already stated those to his face, as a matter of fact, when he was here, as you remember."

"Let me ask you this one little favor. A consideration, if you will. Would you consider putting the ring away for the holidays, then telling them when you're back at school?"

If looks could have killed.

"What I thought," Rene said. "I had to ask. Just mediating here. Anyway, we're glad to have you home. We love you, no matter what. But it's not going to go over well, and you know it. I only ask you not to rush. To slow down. It's not just the immediate future you're dealing with here, sweetheart, it's your entire life on this earth. Decisions have consequences. All decisions, large or small, have consequences, good or bad."

"And Will and I will be in love with one another the rest of our lives, Momma. It doesn't get any better than that. That's the consequence of our decision."

Rene blew out a puff of air but said nothing further of it, but did say, "I knew you should have gone up to Clemson."

Mary said, "I'm meeting some of the girls at the beach house for a couple nights, day after tomorrow. Don't suppose you and daddy are using it then. Are you?"

"You and who?"

"Old friends from school. You know, Lauren, Eileen, Barb, that bunch. Haven't seen them in so long. A Christmas get together."

"Long as you're back Christmas Eve."

"Of course."

Mary reached her old friends and swore them to secrecy about staying at the beach house on Sullivan's Island with Will. She would get together with them the week after Christmas, closer to New Year's Eve. Hopefully, no one in her family would run into one of them till after them.

Will drove down to Sullivan's Island four days before Christmas, arriving at dark. Mary was waiting for him with a fire in the fireplace. They went at and clung to one another like they'd been apart for months and not days. He said when they held one another, they didn't want to let go, the oddest feeling he'd ever had, like they were the only two people in the world, a couple of Siamese twins or something. I remember envying him, wishing I could be that way with Pam, when Pam was always exactly that way with me. They stayed inside most of the time, an occasional walk on the beach. Will worried her parents might drop by, since they were only minutes away and practically in sight of the place, or a neighbor might tip them off, not knowing what was going on. Luckily, it didn't happen.

But Mary's Uncle Charles, her mother's younger brother, the newspaper managing editor, did stop in, a surprise. And he looked like an editor, or somebody who did a lot of reading. Kind of skinny, average height, not an athlete, wore khakis and loafers, a starched shirt with button-down collar, windbreaker jacket, and wire rim glasses he kept adjusting, until letting them hang down on the cord around his neck. The kind of guy, Mary said, who, if locked in a room, would read the paint on the wall, never miss a drop. But he also seemed good natured and greeted Will with a big smile and a firm hand shake, after hugging Mary.

"Missed you two at Thanksgiving," Charles said.

"You heard," Mary said.

"Yes, how could I not."

"And what's your thoughts on it?" Mary said.

"I'm an editor, not a judge," Charles said. "But I know your mother, so I know what this is all about. I'm on your side, if it means anything."

"It does, Charles. Thank you. I suppose Momma asked you to come by here."

"Yes and no. Not directly, but she asked me to check on the house if I were over this way this week checking on our place, which I had every intention of doing today anyway.

"Sorry about Thanksgiving," Mary said. "I'll make it up to Kate and the kids this time."

"All is well with us. You know that. We're your biggest cheer-leaders. My Mary can do no wrong." They hugged again. No wonder he was Mary's favorite uncle.

They sat around the bar drinking coffee and talking, then walked out onto the porch and sat and looked at the ocean. It was cool, but nothing like back home.

"Lanny was saying to me the other day," Charles said of Mary's father, "that if you two are still together when you get out of school in Williamsburg, he might be able to help you, Will, find a coaching job, while you're in med school, Mary. He has old Citadel buddies all over the place. Just something to consider."

Mary was encouraged to hear that. So was Will. In a way. In spite of their obvious disapproval of him, Lanny and his mother seemed able to deal with reality, when necessary, while her mother would rather determine it. But it also made him feel like a charity case, all this influence, theirs, not his, these friends here and friends there, all this networking. It seemed to invade his sense of self-re-liance, self-determination, his self-respect.

When Charles left, Mary sat in Will's lap. Will told her, "I'm not interested in any help from your family, Hugo. I'll do whatever I need to support us when you're in medical school. Get a job teaching and coaching high school, if I have to. Work in a store, a factory, drive a truck, whatever it takes. I don't care. I won't eat out of their hands."

"You'll never have to, Will. I have a trust. We'll never have to worry about money, thanks to my granddaddy."

"I guess I should have expected that, but I didn't. Save it for our children. Because we will have them." He grinned big.

"Don't be ridiculous. William. We'll use what we need of it." She grinned back at him.

"Let's go back inside and practice having children," Will said. "I'm a little slow catching on."

"Liar."

27

While Will was in Charleston with Mary, I was heading to the mountains of Virginia to spend a couple of days with some old friends I'd known since military school, back when my mother dumped me there so she could chase my father around the world. I told Pam and Aunt Evie I'd be back by Christmas Eve, or a day sooner, that I needed to hang out with the Smiths a little bit, a couple friends, and catch up, you know. What they didn't know was that the Smiths weren't guys. They were twin sisters, Annie and Audrey, a year older than I, two pretty and intelligent girls with almost no inhibitions, especially about sex. In fact, they had introduced me to it at thirteen. Where I lost my virginity.

Annie and Audrey were seniors in college now, of course, and had lived a lot like I had lived, alone but with a relative or two close by. Their father was a circuit court judge in the mountainous western part of the state who spent more time on the circuit than at home. And when there, he and his wife stayed away as much as possible, partying and traveling with friends, while the girls were sentenced to private schools or looked after by grandparents too old to keep up with them. We had stayed in touch by calling or writing a few times since I'd started high school back home, exchanged a couple of recent photos, and I looked forward to being cooped up in that hilltop mansion with them a few days and seeing what they were like now as grown women. Their parents were gone again, always dependable. There would be eight or ten of us there, they said, an equal number of guys and girls. The place would be like a popcorn machine. I couldn't wait.

It was on a two-lane highway in Rockbridge County near Lexington, still daylight, when the accident happened. It had snowed a little two days before and there were still patches of ice on the road. My Austin-Healey sat too low to the ground to avoid a lump of ice that jerked me just enough to spin the car to the roadside and into a pile of snow that had been pushed up there by the road crew. The car flipped. I remember that much. All else was a bright blur and bubbling sounds. And a hell of a lot of pain in the neck. Fortunately, I was told later, there had been a car behind me and the driver went for help, while another person stayed with me there. The car was destroyed, and I was stuck in it. I remember people talking around me.

Then I woke up in a hospital with Aunt Evie and Pam beside me. Pam stood from her chair and kissed me on the cheek and held my hand. Aunt Evie sat next to the bed, patting me on the shoulder, a hand on my forearm.

"What in the world," Aunt Evie said. "I told you it was too dangerous to be on those roads. You're lucky you weren't killed."

"You mean, I wasn't killed?" I said. "Feels like it."

"Funny, L.D.," Pam said. "We could have lost you." And she said it like she was about to lose it herself. She was always so emotionally and openly honest.

"What's wrong with me?" I said.

"Your neck. Hairline fracture, the doctor said," Pam told me. "No nerve damage, but a fractured cervical vertebra. It'll heal. You'll make a complete recovery, he said, but you'll be in traction a few days here, then have to wear a neck brace a while."

"Can I drive home when I get out?"

"Are you nuts," Pam said. "You'll be transported home, L.D. Besides, your car is totaled."

Aunt Evie said, "The doctor gave me instructions and an appointment with the doctor back home for next week. And I called your mother soon as I got the call. She's leaving Switzerland today to be with you. Be here tomorrow."

"Can she find her way? I thought she only knew how to leave."

"Like a homing pigeon when it comes to your well-being," Aunt Evie said.

Sure, now read me a nursery rhyme.

"I called Will, too, at Mary's place at the beach. They're on their way up," Pam said.

"They don't have to come up here," I said. "It'll ruin their holiday. The roads are dangerous."

"They're clear now," Aunt Evie said. "It's how we got here."

"Want me to call the Smith brothers and tell them what happened, so they won't expect you?" Pam said. "They might be worried and want to visit you."

Might as well call the Smith Brothers of cough drop fame. "No," I said, thinking fast. "They know I might be late, like I told them. I'll call them later."

"What can we get you, L.D.?" Aunt Evie said.

"I don't need anything. I'm happy y'all came, but it's not necessary. You should go home before any more bad weather moves in. We don't need more of us hurt. This is not a Hollywood production, anyway, just an accident."

"Sure it's a Hollywood production," Pam said, grinning big. "Envelope, please. And the Oscar goes to—the idiot who drives through the mountains in the snow."

It was funny. And it hurt my neck.

"You know," I said, managing a grin of my own, "you really are growing into a very fine standup comedienne." I squeezed her hand. "I'm calling Ed Sullivan when I get back."

"You're a nobody. He won't take your call."

Then the nurse came in to give me a little something for comfort, and I was out like a light.

When I awoke hours later, Pam was curled up and sleeping in a chair beside me. I swear, that girl. Aunt Evie, she told me when she woke up, had called a cab and checked into a Holiday Inn there in town. It was close to noon, so the bar would be open for lunch. She wouldn't dare go there, but she'd order up something to her room before taking a cab back to the hospital, where her car was in the parking lot. Pam had done the driving.

Pam woke up when I started getting calls from people like frat and team members, Miklos and Humphrey, Turnbull, our quarterback, and Coach O'Neal. Will's parents also called, since they were my unofficial backup parents.

That evening my mother, Ava Dockery Cavanaugh, arrived like a diva, having gotten as far as Richmond by air, then by car with one of her old girlfriends from home who met and drove her to the hospital, a drive of several hours. We were left alone awhile and she did the requisite hugs and kisses and good-griefs and you-could-have-been-killeds, which Aunt Evie had already covered, and the what-was-going-on-in-your-mind thing, the old standby, as she stood over me dressed to kill, her perfume still alive. Well, she had traveled and freshened up.

"Where's Dad? Did he come?" I said, but I knew better.

"He couldn't. He has responsibilities and couldn't get away. He says to tell you he misses and loves you, and he'll see you soon."

"I thought y'all were on vacation."

"We are, but the people with us are company people, and he's in charge of the trip. It's a company-paid thing. He has to be there. I was lucky to get the flight and be here so quickly."

"So what was your reason for leaving to come here."

She reacted like she'd been stung. "Don't be ridiculous. You know why I'm here. You're my son and you need me."

"Really? I couldn't tell."

"Please, don't talk like that, L.D. You know better. I'm your mother, for crying out loud. I'm here, where and when it counts. Can't you see that?"

"How long you staying?" I said.

She did a little humph and head move, like dodging a stone. "Till I talk with your doctor and feel confident you're in good hands and being cared for properly. Whatever it takes."

"I think the doctor and Aunt Evie and Pam can handle anything I might need. I just don't want to impose on you."

"That's enough, L.D. Stop the sarcasm. Please. It's unbecoming of you. You're not a child any longer."

"You used to call me Layton, the name you gave me."

"I—I, Yes, I did. We all did. But you got older and L.D. was more suitable. Did I come this far to argue semantics with you?"

"Only you know why you came this far, mother." That slipped. It felt so odd calling her mother, like I was a stranger invading her private life, an interloper.

She was exasperated. And I did feel a little impish for poking at her. But not too much.

All through this uneasy exchange I was hiding my joy of having her there with me, coming that far to be by my bedside. I wanted to jump up from the bed and hug her neck and never let her go back to Switzerland or South Africa, or wherever the hell else she went. But I didn't dare. It wouldn't do any good.

After an odd moment of silence she said, "I know what you're thinking, L.D. That I'm a lousy mother and don't love you enough to stay home. But that's not true. I also love your father, so I have two men in my life to look after. And at the risk of sounding cruel and unfair, your father actually needs more of my time and care than you do. He always has. The two of you are different kinds of people, L.D. You've always functioned well by yourself, been well grounded, independent. You're stronger. I knew that when you were a child.

"But your father is not like that," she said further. "He's a loose cannon. He can't live alone, like you and Evie. He's a responsible and successful man with a lot on his shoulders that he manages very well on the job, but off the job he falls apart. He's helpless and reckless.

He drinks too much, gets in fights, plays at dangerous sports and gets hurt. When I'm there, all that goes away. I dread the day when he retires, frankly. I'm trying to talk him into coming back home to live and work, but it's early.

"I'm not saying that's a good excuse for my being away all the time, but it's why I'm gone all the time. And it'll be that way until we both come back home together to stay. I'm living two lives, you're living one. I have too much in mine, and you don't have enough in yours. Life is unfair and unbalanced, but that's the way it is."

I guess nobody could accuse my mother of not getting to the point.

"Every day I think of you, Layton." Her eyes were moist now. "I loved being at home with you, and I loved teaching. But I had to give it up. I think all the time about the two of us having breakfast together at home in that big house, and looking out the window every morning at the river and the boats and ships, and the fishermen and the seagulls in the water. Then driving or walking down the street to the school, and coming home together in the afternoon. And I remember having to tell Mrs. Wheeler," she said, meaning her boss, our principal, "that I was resigning in order to go and care for your father in Puerto Rico, where he almost killed himself in that stupid boat accident. And the day I drove you up here to military school, and the sense of hurt and shame and fear of dropping you off and leaving without you, that look on your face. I can always teach again, but we can never go back to grammar school together. That's something we've both lost, and it hurts, still.

"And I'll tell you something else," she added, since she was on a roll, I guess. "That girl out there," meaning Pam, "is the best thing that'll ever happen to you from this point on in your life. If you know what's good for you, you'll keep it that way and never let her go. She worships you. You're so lucky you don't have to chase her around the world to keep her from killing herself." Then she said, "And the Smiths are not brothers, they're sisters. I met them when

I visited you at school once, you might remember. So can the bull-shit and be the man you are. Your secret is safe with me, but don't push it.

"Now, Evie and Pam and I are going to dinner in town," she said, "if we can find a place still open at this hour. If you want something, we can bring it back. Then Evie's going back home with Marge," meaning the friend who drove her up, "and Pam and I are staying at my motel tonight."

I was kind of stunned, but managed to say, "I'd kill for a cheese-burger and fries. Or die for a pizza and beer."

She leaned over and kissed me on the forehead and rubbed her hands through my hair. Just like a mother, then left the room.

The nurse came in immediately, a different one this time.

"I don't want any pain killers," I said.

"Sorry, doctor's orders."

"Then let him take them. I don't need them." I said it politely.

"Well, okay, if you wish. Let me know if you change your mind." She left.

Truth was, I was afraid to fall asleep and miss something. Afraid to wake up and my mother be gone again to someplace on the other side of the earth.

28

My mother stayed in town, like she said she would, and was in and out of the room when not at the motel at nights, said she would be there until I was back home. Then she would rejoin my father in Zurich for a day or so before they returned to Cape Town. I think her story of my father's recklessness off the job was a bit melodramatic, self-defensive, but it was the only one I'd get, since it was hers, and she was sticking to it.

But Pam hardly ever left the room, even spent the night there once, though she had a motel room to go to. You'd think she was the mother, the way she stayed close and looked after every detail of my care and needs, like some quality control agent. At one point, we even managed to sneak in a little sex episode late at night, when my mother was downstairs at the coffee shop. Pam was voracious and I thought nothing would be left of me when she finished but a pile of crumbs to take home. Well, it was therapy, I tell you. Normally, visitors were not allowed in the rooms so often, but I guess their being present saved the staff some work too, except when changing sheets, doing tests, and so forth. But these were the same people who didn't allow flowers in the rooms, but let folks smoke in them. The place often looked like a pool hall.

Will and Mary got there. Mary had become good friends with Pam and me over the last few months, and the four of us had spent a lot of time together, what there was of it. Mary still went to the hospital and did lab work, and studied often. She also entertained and looked after a couple of kids who were patients, like she had with Stevie. She was such a giving person. Will and Pam and I all agreed she'd be a great pediatric specialist, after med school and a Ph.D. in biochemistry, her plans for a career in research. She'd make Phi Beta Kappa in grad school, for sure, just like she'd said she would.

"Y'all should go back home," I said. "You're missing the holidays with your families. I'll be out of here in a day or two anyway."

"Don't tell me what to do, Doc." Will said. "You didn't tell me to come here. You don't tell me to leave."

"Agreed," Mary said. "You mustn't be alone too long."

"You know better, L.D.," Pam said. "I'm staying till you leave, so drop the subject."

Will said, "Can you eat pizza, without a neck? I'll order one. Do these hillbillies up here in these mountains eat pizza?"

"There are more colleges and students up here than trees," Pam said. "Of course they do."

"Long as I can do it without head moves," I said.

"Miklos is quitting school after the semester," Will said.

"He's nuts," I said.

"Says he's going to try to find a reporting job so he can go to Vietnam. Big-time war correspondent."

"What's the team going to do next year if half of it's gone?"

"Normal attrition. We'll manage."

"Coach must be loving this."

"Coach is leaving too, according to Miklos."

"You're kidding."

"Nope."

Pam said to Mary, "Let's go down to the coffee shop. You can meet L.D.'s mother."

They left us and I said, "Where's he going?" referring to Coach O'Neal.

"Got an offer in Florida somewhere, small college."

"Damn. The whole world is falling apart. Who's taking his place?"

"Bear Bryant," he said, and we both laughed. And my neck hurt from it. Bryant was the famous national championship coach at Alabama. Fat chance he would come to Williamsburg as anything but a tourist or a paid speaker.

When Pam stayed at the motel with my mother and I as alone in my room, I managed to call Annie and Audrey Smith and explain the situation, and took a rain check.

Aunt Evie had left for home with Marge, my mother's friend, and my mother went out to a local dealer and bought a new dark green Mustang convertible for me so she could drive me home the next day, Christmas eve, while Pam followed in Aunt Evie's car.

The doctor had reviewed my x-rays and said a hospital transport wouldn't be necessary, long as I wore the neck brace and followed his orders.

Will and Mary had left the previous day, after being with me over twenty-four hours. They went out of the way to Williamsburg first to pick up Mary's car, but he followed her to there and home and would be pushing it to get her back to Charleston for the remainder of the holidays, and he could get back and be with his. Tell you, these little incidents disrupt a lot of lives. I felt like an idiot. Mr. Wonderful. Mr. Everything. Mr. Important rearranging other people's worlds with his sneaky behavior, while they dealt with real problems. Maybe my mother had been right about that much anyway, about being a man, while she kept my dirty little secret.

Ava Dockery Cavanaugh, better known as my mother, and my father's wife, left the morning after Christmas the same way she'd arrived, dressed to kill, like it was a show as much as a flight. She was in first class on the first plane out of Patrick Henry to catch the tail end of the Switzerland trip. Pam and I took her to the airport for the connection to Washington, D.C., for Zurich, Pam driving the new Mustang. It was like my mother couldn't leave fast enough, but kind of hated to go, too. I could tell that by the way she had often gazed out the window, while home, to the river and the Chesapeake Bay and ocean beyond, the very same way I did, maybe looking for something but not sure what. She promised to come home more often, and bring my father, but I wasn't holding my breath. Somehow, the screaming need to have her and my father there with me was diminishing.

"Let's drive over to Virginia Beach," I said to Pam, before the turnoff back home.

"Really? In this cold?"

"Yes, I just want to go there."

So we got on I-64, what we locals called the tunnel road that led to the two-mile bridge-tunnel over to the Norfolk side of the James River. Then we drove through the Ocean View community, a residential-commercial complex at the beach there, with the amusement park and roller coaster and all that, then down Shore Drive past the naval amphibious base. After a few short miles through the woods past parks and an army facility, we were in the old North End of Virginia Beach, peaceful and pricey, beach homes. A mile or so further we were in the commercial district, almost completely closed then, except for a few hotels and restaurants. It was sunny and chilly and breezy, light sparkled off the water green as a spillage of emeralds. We parked and went to the boardwalk and strolled hand-in-hand. I loved it here in winter as much as in summer, and always came over at least once or twice in the off season. In summer I was doing it, living it. In winter I was remembering it, so I experienced it twice. Some others were also here for similar reasons, to hold onto something special that made them alive. You could tell, they had the look, the view of the past, good or bad.

I loved the violence of the choppy Atlantic, nothing to the horizon but water and the occasional ship, and all the dreams and the memories that could swim in your head. The sea didn't know that, of course, it had no feelings. All the feelings were in your head. Here was a place where young people, among others, congregated in summer to be young people. Yearlings, often the first venture from the nests. First sex, first drunk and hangover. First freedom from all but self-restraint. First romance. The joy and comfort of being together like a species unto itself inhabiting some exotic island where no one ever said no or stop, but innocent, too, like in some Disney movie or something. A sense of family, of belonging, but something short-lived, though forever felt and remembered with yearning as the years passed, before life was dulled by all the baggage of reality.

We sat alone at a table on the patio of a coffee shop and looked out at the ocean. My neck was a little stiff and sore.

"It's cold, L.D.," Pam said. "It's bad for your neck. Why don't we go inside. It's warm and nice. We can eat something too."

"Do something stupid in life, Pammie. Be dumb for a change, like me. Let's sit here and catch pneumonia and freeze to death. Life is all about risks." Pammie was what her family called her.

She laughed and patted my hand.

"You win," I said. "Let's eat, then drive over to Croatan."

Croatan Beach was popular with kids and those who wanted to avoid the business of the main drag. It was a mile or so down, over the Rudee Inlet via a short bridge, then down a side road on the left. Nothing commercial, strictly residential with sparse housing. On the beach road were no more than eight or ten homes, maybe a dozen, two or three with year-round residents, the others rentals, and most not occupied until spring break and summer when it was stuffed with college and high school kids making asses of themselves, with pride—they'd brag about the stupid crap they did—while piling up memories. Our frats in high school and college had stayed here immediately after semester's end each year.

We parked on the sandy roadside and walked the shoreline.

"Mary liked your mother," Pam said. "Very impressed by her. Said she seems to have an exciting life."

"That's one of us. Two if you include my father. They're such a fun couple."

"But she did get the feeling, and I agree, that the reason she stays gone all the time is more about not letting your father get away from her than about saving him from himself. Just a woman's intuition. Tell me if I'm being too personal."

"I agree. And I don't see how you and I could be more personal than we are. Have we left anything out or untried?" I chuckled at that.

"You told me before that her father left the family when she was in the fifth grade. That must have been devastating."

"Abandonment seems to run in my family. It's a tradition. People are always running away somewhere, leaving somebody else."

"Her father leaves her, she leaves you. Maybe that's why she taught elementary school, to stay in the fifth grade, before all the leaving started."

"I never thought about it that way. Maybe you're right. We're such psychoanalysts."

"We should charge."

"If we could find a patient dumb enough to pay us." We both laughed.

I looked out and up over the ocean, trying to visualize where my mother's plane might be at that moment, and how her feelings of leaving one more time squared with her excitement and anxiety of getting back to my father, which was stronger, the need to stay or the need to go. "Yeah, we should charge."

"Let's go back to Atlantic Avenue, to the hotel," I said, "and check out a room for a while. Then we can go home, and I want to take Aunt Evie out to dinner. She deserves special attention. Both of you. I'm tired of all this crap about my missing people. Would have been better if she hadn't come home at all. Then I wouldn't have been surprised and disappointed at her hauling ass again."

"But she is your mother, L.D."

"Of sorts, yes. But like she said, I'm a big boy now."

We checked into a room on the third floor and opened the curtains wide to a panoramic view of the ocean, the water sparkling green, choppy. We stripped and had sex, taking in the whole thing, our eyes wide open the whole time, like we were the only people seeing it, like it was ours, something no one could take away from us. I swear, that Pam.

29

It was the first week of January and the holidays were over. We were back in school with a week to go before exams. And it was snowing like crazy. Williamsburg was covered in white and intoxicating at night, with the place lit up like a greeting card scene, particularly Duke of Gloucester Street, all the lamp posts and colorful window displays and tourists and locals about.

Will and Mary were at their favorite diner having coffee and sweet rolls and watching the activity on the street while discussing the near future, among other things. Mary's was all mapped out, of course, every step of her life the next decade at least. Will's could take a wrong turn in the next couple of weeks, all of it hanging on that damn English Lit course in Dr. Antise's class. Until this point he'd never considered something as strange as failure or the remote possibility of it. Life was a football, you played with it, and as long as you held onto it all would be well. Maybe not the case now.

Mary said, "You can't fail. We depend on it. We must stay together here."

"It's the curve," he said. "No matter how well I do on the paper and the exam, I'm still in the bottom twenty percent of the class. I don't think I'll make the cut, Hugo. To this place it's not good enough to do well in the course. You have to do better than seventy-five-to-eighty percent of the class or you're done. I'm marked. I know it. That D last time that put me on condition was like the Scarlet Letter. Does that sound intelligent and English Lit-like?"

"We have to start thinking about options, Will. I don't want you losing your scholarship and leaving school. You'll be drafted. I just know it. Don't even want to think about it."

He gazed out the window. "I knew I should have gone to V.M.I. or Tech."

"Then we wouldn't have met."

"And you'd be a lost soul floating around space like a free radical?" He grinned.

"Something like that." She grinned back, biting down on her lower lip.

"You know, maybe your mother isn't all that wrong about us. Or me, I should say. Maybe she deserves more credit. I'm beginning to understand her situation better. You're the one taking all the risks here."

"No. Stop. This has nothing to do with my mother. Cut the bullshit. We'll get past this together."

He smiled back at her, biting his own lip. He could almost see a halo around her. "Yes, we will. Let's walk the street and freeze to death, like a couple of idiots," meaning Duke of Gloucester. "You know, Hugo, I could come over this table and take you right now and get arrested."

"Dare you, you rat." They laughed. "You're such a romantic."

"My grandfather said once that all men are romantics. Some just hide it better. You know how he knew that?"

"Your grandmother, the smart one." They laughed again.

"You don't miss much. Do you?"

"No, I don't."

Later that month Will got a C on his term paper in Dr. Antise's English Literature 202 class. But he got the expected D in the course, so it wasn't like he was ambushed. He'd known it was coming. He was staring at his grade posted on the wall outside the classroom. The Berlin Wall, as some students referred to it; shot going in, shot going out. He glanced at his watch and wondered if he could turn it back four-and-a-half months and start all over. Sure. But it might make a good fantasy movie. He went into the classroom and got his exam paper from a graduate assistant who was passing them out. He had missed only two questions, the difference between a C and a D. He went to the commons to meet Mary.

"You have to talk to him," Mary said of Dr. Antise. "You have to try. Beg for a re-exam, with different questions, of course. Whatever it takes. We don't quit now."

"It's the curve, Mary, like I said. You know that."

"We bombard him, wear him down, make him die to give you a second chance so he can get you out of his mangy-looking hair." Antise had wild hair, like the guy didn't own a comb or brush or a mirror, or hardly ever looked into one, though his clothes were impeccable. The faculty club would never tolerate a slob, but screwy hair was always welcomed in academia, long as it was clean, because it was Einstein-ish, and some of these folks adopted the look for that reason, apparently.

"I don't want to crawl to that sonofabitch."

She blew out a breath of air, exasperated. "Male pride. Don't be dumb. We're not quitting, so get it out of your head." He liked the way she said we. "And he's not a sonofabitch just because he flunked you. But he will be if he doesn't give you a re-take."

Will said, "I guess I could tell him I didn't do so well on the exam because I couldn't study much, since I spent half the holidays in England at Stratford-Upon-Avon studying Shakespeare's life and work, and the other half in Africa with the Peace Corps feeding the hungry."

"Your humor is a coping mechanism, not a solution to the problem. Think about something besides a ball with two points on it. *William*." She accented that. "Get your head straight." But she said it with sympathy, kind of.

"I've got to go see Coach, tell him what happened, before he finds out first."

"Meet me at the diner at four."

Will went over to the lecture hall to check on his Art History grade. He got a B. Yea. It wasn't hard academics, but it was something, and everything was hard here for all but the top students.

Dr. Sandridge was alone in his office, at his desk. Will poked his head in and said, "Doctor Sandridge. Thanks for the grade. I really appreciate it."

"You earned it. What else could I do? If I could have flunked you, I would have." He grinned big. "What's this I hear about Miklos and Levitt?"

"Miklos is dropping out and Levitt's flunking out," Will said.

"That's a big hit for the team, with Coach O'Neal leaving, too, and others graduating. What's your situation?"

"I'm out. Off the team anyway." He looked at his watch. "In about fifteen minutes, after I see Coach and tell him about my D in Dr. Antise's class."

Dr. Sandridge nodded his understanding. "You staying in school here?"

"I doubt it."

"Financial?"

"No, sir. My family can afford it, but I'm not going to burden them with it. I'll try to get a scholarship to play next year at Tech or somewhere, maybe East Carolina or Hampden-Sydney. Maybe even V.M.I. They offered me a full scholarship before."

Sandridge smiled. "And you scored on them a couple times too. Won't hurt your hopes. I hate to see you go, though. Wish there was something I could do. I'll talk with Dr. Antise. It won't do any good, I'm sure. But I'll do that much, let you know how it goes, either way."

"Appreciate it very much, sir. Anything you could do."

"You know, he's taking over as Provost next year." Provost is a college's equivalent of an academic top cop who insures a school's academic standards and rules and regulations regarding research, et cetera, are met. Antise's promotion, far as Will was concerned, was like Hitler being promoted from head of the Nazi Party to Fuhrer of the Third Reich. No mercy for the weak and enemies of the standards.

"And the young lady you're going with, I understand, Miss Poythress. Will she be leaving with you?"

"No, sir."

"She's a brilliant student, a very sharp mind. One of the best I've seen here." Then he grinned. "How'd she get hooked up with you?"

They both laughed.

"We all makes mistakes, I guess," Will said.

"Anyway, I wish you luck. And keep me posted. And if you play against us next year, we can conspire to throw the game, or at least cheat a little."

They laughed again. But Will felt bad inside. This was one of the people he would miss most, a serious academic with a great sense of humor, as well as a football fan. Very rare here.

Will went to the coach's office under the football stadium, where he sat a few minutes waiting, shifting back and forth in the squeaky swivel chair, gazing around, wondering how it would be now, no longer sharing this part of his life with the team and the whole thing about playing the sport here, the tradition.

Coach O'Neal came in and dropped his ball cap on his desk and plopped down in his own squeaky swivel chair. "So what's the news, good or bad?" he said.

"Bad. At least for now."

"What does that mean, for now?"

He told him. "I'll ask for a re-exam, since I only missed two questions, and got a C on my paper."

Coach was already moving his head no. "You know where that's going. He'll never do it. And your scholarship is safe if you're injured on the playing field, but not if you flunk or drop below twelve credits, full-time. You know that. The most you can be next semester is part-time, and part-timers can't play varsity. It'd be a year before you could even be considered, and only if you overcame the deficiency. Your best shot is going to another school."

"Yes, sir. Assuming it doesn't work out, I was going to ask you if you could help me get on a team close by, in the state even."

"See what I can do, but with the time lapse before you could suit up again, most coaches, if any, won't be interested when they have eighteen-and nineteen-year-olds coming in. You'd be twenty-two, a little old for starting over. That's the way it is. A.D.s make those final decisions on transfers, not coaches, usually." A.D.s, of course, were athletic directors in charge of all sports programs.

"How about an assistant coaching position somewhere?" Will said.

"I'll ask around, Will, but you know those positions go to guys with years of experience. Get a couple years under your belt, high school or college, then get in touch, if I'm still around. But you won't coach high school in this state without a teacher's certificate, and you have to have the degree for that. So you're screwed in that respect. The short cut is to get in school somewhere as a player or not, and hang out with the team, volunteer, if not playing. That'll give you the in you need. That I can help you with."

"Well, I had to ask."

"So what are you going to do if none of this works out? If you don't stay in school, you're eligible for the draft. You better get a student deferment or get married, one or the other, if you're looking to stay out of the service."

They talked a few minutes longer and Will thanked him for the scholarship out of high school, the chance to play at this great school, with all its history and reputation for scholarship, and the times on the team. And he apologized for not holding up his end of the contract, of letting down the team.

"You'd likely have been on the Dean's List somewhere else," Coach said. "So don't feel so down about it. You're not nearly the only one. It's a crapshoot with half the kids who come here. Like Tim Davis and Levitt. It's an academic shock. You'll do well, whatever you do."

Will thanked him again and left.

30

They were at their favorite table in the diner.

"It's not an option," Mary said. "We wouldn't see each other. Wouldn't be together. Besides, it's too late to apply anywhere else for spring semester. It'd be the summer before you got in someplace."

"Longer than that to play ball. Transfers have to sit out a season."

"Why?"

"It's a rule to help keep coaches from recruiting other schools' players, make it harder."

"And we'd still be apart. So the better option is for you to stay here three-quarter-time in spring and summer till next year. At least we're together that way, and you're still in school, still moving toward your degree."

"And still facing that damn English Two-0-Two course and eligible for the draft. D's count against you in your GPA here, you know, but not toward requirements. I'd still have to try one more time for a C in the course, and also beat the curve. No way. That's not going to happen while Antise is in charge of not only the department but the whole thing as provost. He'll make sure I don't get by."

"I believe Antise will have more on his mind than just you, in spite of your male ego importance. Another professor could make all the difference. It's the only way."

"I could go to O.D.U. this summer," he said, meaning Old Dominion University in Norfolk, "maybe pass it there and transfer the credit back here in the fall."

"Now you're starting to think. How about Christopher Newport? It's right there in town."

"But it's still this school, just a satellite campus., like O.D.U. used to be until 1961. And I'd still be less than full-time till then. And easy pickings for the draft."

"Gawd. I don't even want to think about it. Don't talk like that."

"It'll happen. They already have my number out. One slip, I'm gone. I've already filled out the form for them."

"So has every other young male over eighteen. If worse comes to worst, we get married early. Then they can't draft you."

"Get married if I'm not in school and don't have a job? No way. I think we're running out of the options you mentioned," Will said.

"Girls are marrying guys they don't know all over the country, just to keep them out of service so they don't get killed. It would be easy for us, and the right thing, because we do know and love one another. The service is not getting you, Will, except over my dead body. So drop it."

"My priority right now is finding a job and getting by Two-0-Two, so I can work and coach and support us while you're in med school. The least I have to do is work at something."

"We'll work it out. We're never going to be broke. Remember that. I have a trust."

"Save it for the house full of children we're going to have because I can't keep my hands off you and screwing your brains out."

"You rat. I could drag you back to my house now and make you prove it."

"Dare you."

Mary took her morning exam the next day, then went to the English Department faculty offices and asked for a meeting with its head, Dr. Anthony Antise, Mister B.A. here in Williamsburg—

where else?—M.A. and Ph.D. Harvard, Mister Doctor-Who-Never-Had-A-Problem-Making-A-Good-Grade-In-College.

Dr. Antise rose from behind his large, ancient wooden desk when Mary walked in. His clothes were expensive browns and blues, wools and cotton, a vest, season appropriate. Tortoise shell horn rim glasses. His hair looked like it might have been caught at the intersection of four wind tunnels at nearby NASA Langley Research Center in Hampton. Guy should have been an engineer, a mad scientist or something helping us beat the Russians to the moon. He motioned for her to sit, and re-took his regal high back.

"And what is it I can do for you, Miss Poythress? You're a student here, I presume."

"Yes, sir, I am. Pre-Med. I'm here on behalf of my fiancé, who doesn't know I'm here, and wouldn't approve if he knew it. But I'm here anyway."

"Then maybe we shouldn't be discussing his private business."

"I assure you it's important enough, and he'll never know we spoke. That's a promise."

Antise nodded, cautious. "Then we're speaking unofficially." He glanced at her ring finger. "Who is he?"

"William Wythe, sir. Will Wythe. He had your Two-0-Two class this semester."

He nodded again, but stronger, and gave the faintest smile, in the eyes only. "And your purpose on his behalf?" But he knew.

"I came here to ask you to allow him a re-take on the final, on which he made a D by only two points. I ask because he won't."

"Then it's not important to him?"

"No, it's his pride."

Antise looked away, then back at her, fiddling with a cigarette lighter in his hand. She could see the no in his expression. "Miss Poythress, specific identities aside, a student has an entire semester to meet the qualifications of a course, just like every other student. And, say, one might be passing halfway through the semester. I shouldn't get involved with this at all, frankly. But since you two are that close, you say, I will discuss it only superficially, and briefly. But first, let me tell you this, maybe save us both some time. Re-exams are not offered, except in rare cases of accidents, illnesses, or verified family tragedies where exams are missed. If a student shows up for and takes an exam, it is obvious one of those exceptions does not apply to him."

"Let me ask you this, sir," Mary said. "If he'd gotten those two answers correct and made a C, would it have made a difference?"

"No, frankly, it would not have. Grades on papers and exams are only two of the course criteria, the others being class participation, comprehension and appreciation of subject matter, earnestness of effort, and the professor's judgement. This last one most important. Taking the course seriously and not just looking for a passing grade. It's why a high number of students in that class are English majors and not people looking for an easy three credits."

"I wonder why a History and Phys. Ed. major would be routed into such a class?" Mary said.

"Routed is a correct term, I think. The Athletic Department handles a lot of scheduling for athletes. I know that. You might ask them. But I assure you the standards are applied equally in all courses. It's just that some courses are less demanding than others."

"Meaning meeting the standards of the curve, the twenty-to-twenty-five-percent failure requirement."

"Not a requirement at all. That's a misperception, and unfair. Failing that many students in a course is a natural result of that many not meeting requirements. It's not by design. There are no percentages to meet. Our standards are high, yes, probably the highest in the country. We're here to teach. Students are here to learn, presumably. Some aren't, obviously. They misjudge us, so they fail."

It was a lie, Mary knew, a line of BS a mile long.

"I think the misperception," Dr. Antise said, "is on the expectation that a seventy on a test is a C, therefore, passing. It is not. Some courses require a seventy-five or eighty or higher for a C, so the A's and B's are fewer in number. People making seventies think they've been misled. Students coming here already should know this."

Sure, like I'm an idiot, Mary thought.

"Look," Antise said, "we get students here from all over the place. And they're all bright, just like your fiancé. Doesn't mean all of them are guaranteed success, or that they'll take things seriously. Kids come here because it's a beautiful place to be. All the history, the ambiance. The romance, the quaintness. Or maybe it's the only place they can come and play sports. Or it's close to home. Or their parents send them here. Some come here thinking that's more important than the academics, a common mistake. Truth is, a lot of these students should have gone somewhere else."

"The shock factor," Mary said.

"Yes, sadly."

"So my plea is pointless?"

"No, it's admirable, but it's useless. And I don't mean for that to sound harsh. We have our standards. And we're not bending them for one student, nor for a hundred and one students. Sorry." He did seem genuine about it.

"He'll be drafted. He might end up in Vietnam. All because of being in this one course and failing it. Does that seem right?"

He leaned back and opened his hands, running out of patience. "We're a college, Miss Poythress. We're here to teach people who want to learn. There are tens of thousands of young men his age in Vietnam now for a variety of reasons, as you must know. It is not our mission to save them, nor to put them in harm's way. I don't know what else I can say, except that I certainly hope nothing bad happens to him. I'm afraid another exam is not possible, in any event. Sorry." He opened his hands again.

Mary was stunned. She was just shot down like an enemy aircraft. The argument she was prepared to give was null and void, killed almost before takeoff. But she wasn't finished.

"But isn't there another way of looking at something like this, Dr. Antise? A positive alternative, an opportunity to be pro-active, make a difference in a person's life? Maybe save a life? I mean, if he's out of school, he'll be drafted, probably be sent to Vietnam, maybe die there." Her eyes were watering slightly. The thought of her last question frightened her.

"It's not a situation peculiar to him alone."

"But I'm not here for the others, sir. I'm here only for him."

"And I say again, such a student would not pass the course if he'd gotten ten more questions correct on the exam. It's about more than that, as I've explained.

"Let me ask you something," he said. "Since draftees are drawn in lotteries based on quotas of specific numbers being called at a given time, and, say, he got out of it by passing a particular course based on special consideration, can you give me the name of the young man who would have to go in his place, the one who got no special consideration? And would you be willing to be the one who explains it all to his mother, his family? Why Student A was given the benefit of influence over Student B, theirs, who paid the ultimate price for it? You know, in the big war, some draftees escaped service by paying large sums of money to the federal government for others to take their places. Was that fair?" He knew he had her.

"I think I get your point," Mary said. "But I don't see it as an either or, one student or another. I see it in its simplest form, the opportunity to make a difference in one student's life. Or not to. But I had to ask." She stood. "Thank you for your time."

"You're welcome, Miss Poythress. Sorry I couldn't be more helpful."

"No, you're not. Deny me, but do not lie to me, sir." She turned to leave, then stopped a moment. "I suspect when this Vietnam thing is over with, and the graveyards are full of young men who didn't catch a break, you folks here and your precious standards will still be around. But I have the feeling no one will give a crap by then, that it'll all seem so unimportant and you'll have to beg people to come to school here."

"This school has been here since colonial days, Miss Poythress. It'll be here a lot longer. It'll survive. Good day."

But she wasn't finished. "You know, since being here," she said, "I've overheard students say, even tell me, that you're a SOB. I never believed that because I didn't know you. Now I do. Don't mean to be harsh. Good day to you too."

She felt like an idiot insulting him at the end, unable to control her emotions. He probably thought of her the way he likely thought of Will, not very well. But it was done, and she couldn't take it back.

31

Mary couldn't keep it a secret from Will about going to Dr. Antise. She didn't want him surprised or embarrassed if he and the great professor happened to cross paths and he got a funny look. And Will was okay with it.

"I would've done the same thing for you, Hugo. Which I won't ever have to think about because you're never going to make a bad grade."

They were at Mary's house. Shelley went home to Hampton for a day or two after her final exam, so they had the place to themselves and were lying in bed. Will still had one more exam to take, which would not be a problem.

"You have to register early as possible," Mary said. "I'd take Two-0-Two with someone else, like we talked about. Or take it at O.D.U. in the summer."

"Already filled up here, I'm told."

"Then try. See for yourself. Don't believe everything you hear. I think I did us both a disservice by going to Antise. Now he'll think we're both idiots."

"Right. Before that I was the only idiot."

"Thanks."

"You know what I mean."

"Yes, I do." She rolled over and kissed him, her leg across his waist.

"Not so fast with the registration thing," Will said. "Let's think this over." His arm was hugging her neck as he nuzzled and kissed at her hair. "Take stock of our situation here. Get our bearings straight."

"The Bearing Strait."

"Funny. You're coming around," he said." She laughed.

"So here it is," he said. "Fact Number One, I'm madly in love with the most beautiful and intelligent young woman in the world whose whole life has been anointed by God. That's indisputable. Fact Number Two, you, on the other hand, are equally in love with the dumbest bat brain who ever lived. An insult to bats. A guy with SAT's

of fourteen ten who can't get past the same English course, twice. Who just lost his scholarship, causing his financial burden to fall on the shoulders of his working class parents, and who refuses to let it happen. Fact Number Three, therefore, an alternative plan is required, one that makes the most sense, with less stress on everybody."

"Will, I have enough in my checking account to pay your semester bills, then some. Stop worrying."

"You're wonderful, but I will not start our life together by taking your money. I said it, and I meant it."

"You can consider it a loan, if it makes you feel better about it."

"No. It would be a fake loan. How does a guy repay a loan with no income?"

"Men are so damn hardheaded."

"It's not just the money, Mary. It's the whole thing. Somebody else's money is not going to solve my problem. I screwed up royally. I had the world in my hands. I was playing football, which I love and want to be my life's work. I had a free ride at one of the finest colleges in this country to do it, one with a revered history second to none. And I blew it. I let down my parents, my little brother. They just don't know it yet. My coach and my teammates. The school and you. Tell you what, if it weren't for you, I'd be a lost soul, for sure. Maybe Antise had it right.

"But I do have you," he said, "and I'm not lost. And I know exactly what I have to do to make this work, to put it all back together. A different route, but I'll get there. Number one objective is not be a burden to others, to carry my own weight. Get a job."

"Am I in there somewhere?" Mary said.

"The whole thing is about you, us."

"And just what might that job be without your degree?"

"A temporary thing." He was hesitant about telling her, but there was no choice. "I talked with Major McHugh, our ROTC commander, and the Army recruiter yesterday, when I went home to take my laundry."

Mary was startled. She sat up. "What? You did what?"

"No, no. Listen. Hear me out. I didn't volunteer to get shot. Just laying down a plan to get us through this."

She flopped back down and looked at the ceiling. "Oh, gawd."

"Don't overreact. Listen. It's not as bad as you think. Lots of guys are doing it."

"And a lot of guys are getting shot,"

"Not me, I'm bullet proof."

"Cut the joking, Will. I'm not buying it."

"Here's what happens. I enlist. I stay home for two or three weeks till my paperwork is processed. Meanwhile, I'm on the payroll. Not much but something. Paperwork comes back and my enlistment is flipped to a commission. I've already had my officer basic in ROTC. I'm a second lieutenant. Now I have a living salary and benefits. I can support us the next three years, while you finish here and start med school."

"Three years?" Mary said. "Where will you be the whole time?"

"Maybe right here, Fort Eustice. Or Fort Bragg, down in Carolina a short drive. I can request a specific field or station, though there is no guarantee I'll get it. But no matter where I am, or we are, you'll be able to continue school, and I'll be supporting us. Then, when I'm out, I can go back to school on the G.I. Bill and work, while you finish med school and your doctoral work."

"We'll be apart. I don't like it."

"I don't either, Hugo, but there is no better option. We will be together on weekends and holidays. And if I'm close, we'll be together all the time. I'll have to go somewhere for a couple or three months for training, then a permanent assignment till I'm out. It's not so bad. We can be married when I'm commissioned and have that first check in my hand."

"They'll send you to Vietnam. I know it. Or some other place overseas."

"Everybody can't go to Vietnam. Most don't. And the ones who do, most serve in the rear or support areas and don't even see the enemy."

"And the others do."

"They're going to get me anyway, is what I'm saying, Mary. I might as well make the most of it. Hunker down and do it, and get it behind us. Maybe they'll put me in an office and I can staple papers, sign stuff. Lot of signing stuff in the service."

"Sure, maybe station you as a reviewer at the local drive-in movie."

She was right, of course. A sugar-coated line of BS a mile long was still a mile-long line of BS. He knew there was a better-than-even chance of his being put in the infantry, where so many were going in the huge build up in Vietnam. Where else? But if he was going to be the man he needed to be for this wonderful girl in his life who changed him so much lately for the better, he'd have to measure up, be the man she deserved and not abdicate his first real challenge, his responsibility of providing for this woman he would marry. He already had screwed up the scholarship. He'd be damned if she would pay the price for that miserable failure. Not to mention that hard-ass mother of hers who would gloat for years to come. "I told you so." He could hear it now.

"Baby," Mary said, "I've already told you that you'd never go anywhere in this life or world without me. And I meant that. I hope you're taking me seriously about it."

Her chin was resting on her hands, which were on his chest, faces almost touching. His eyes looked over her face and hair. He settled on her lips and licked his own. "Hugo," he said, "I'll take you any way and anywhere I can get you."

"Now you're talking. But it better not be somewhere I can't go. I don't like the risk here. Once you put on that uniform, you're not in charge any more. They are."

The next day Will took his last exam and hung out at his dorm room for the last time, with some frat brothers and teammates. They all promised to stay in touch, and he lived just twenty-five miles down the road, so he'd be up there a lot anyway with Mary. Then he went home with his clothes and other stuff packed in his car. Mary had flown home to Charleston for a couple days to be with her family, before starting the spring semester. I was already home playing pick-up sandlot football games at the local school athletic field and hanging out with Pam.

Martha Lynn, Will's mother, had worried all along about his grades, and was devastated to hear he'd lost his scholarship, of course. What else would she be? She immediately started helping him design his future with the aid of her motherly sage advice.

"There is just one way to stay out of that stupid thing over in Vietnam," Martha Lynn said. They were at the kitchen table. Martha Lynn was cleaning up, doing make-work, agitated, and Will was scarfing lunch. "They damn well will not get you. That's a filthy quagmire the government has gotten us into over there."

"It's an obligation based on a treaty and agreement. It's perfectly legal and legitimate," Will said. Because he took history and political science. "A member nation asks for help against aggression, and all signatories are obliged to come to its aid. Just like in Korea. It's a conflict, Momma, not a war as such. It's suppose to be over by the end of the year."

"That's what they were saying from the start. Out in a month, then six months. Then by the end of a year. Now it's been almost two years and we don't know when it'll end, keeps getting bigger. And the obituaries keep coming in. It's the first thing people around here read in the paper every day. See who they know who was killed or wounded. It's disgusting. They're not getting you. They keep saying it's a conflict, not a war, but it's a damned war. Killing is killing, and dying is dying.

"If you and Mary are that serious about things, then you should get married now. Your daddy can help get you into the apprentice school or in another job in the shipyard. They're hiring like crazy."

"Yes, because of the buildup in Vietnam. Everybody's hiring." Will took economics and international relations too.

She ignored the remark. "Y'all can live somewhere between here and Williamsburg, maybe Lee Hall or Denbigh," she said, meaning the areas of town between Newport News and the college, "and she can finish her schooling. Or y'all can stay with us. We can fix up the garage up top to an apartment. You can go to school at nights. You're not quitting."

That's when Will dropped it on her about his already considering signing on with the Army.

"Oh, my god. Don't you dare. I'll kill you myself. You hear me?"

"Her parents will be happy to hear that."

"I don't give a damn what makes her parents happy. They don't have a child that'll ever happen to. Get married, stay in school. We can pay your bills while you finish and get a teaching and coaching job. You won't be a burden on Mary, either. You can not do anything to disrupt her plans. You hear me? If you do, I'll help her mother kill you."

"She's not changing her plans. We want to do it on our own, Momma. And we can. I never would have gone to college if I hadn't gotten the grant-in-aid. And I won't let you and daddy pay for it."

"Really? What does she think of this, you going into the Army? Bet she doesn't like it."

"She doesn't. But we'll work it out."

"Famous last words."

Will changed the subject, or tried to, but Martha Lynn prattled on like a mother hen. Well, she had a reason and a right.

In Charleston, Mary's mother, Rene, met her at the airport in North Charleston and headed with her the ten miles back downtown to South of Broad. Mary could sense an interrogation coming on, and their somewhat happy—somewhat because there was tension, you know— loving welcome was waning before they left the parking lot.

"You're suddenly quiet, Mary. What is it?"

"Nothing. I'm fine, just tired."

"Not so. What is it?" Rene was puffing a cigarette in her holder and blowing smoke out the crack in the window. As they pulled onto the highway, she said, "How's Will doing?"

"You're asking about Will, or investigating him? He's fine."

"Wasn't called for. Can't I ask?"

They'd know soon enough, so she let her have it. "Will lost his football scholarship. Not the end of the world, though."

"Oh, you don't say. So how does a football player lose a football scholarship?"

Mary hesitated.

"I asked you a question, sweetheart. Is it so hard to answer?"

"He flunked English. Well, he made a D. Dropped below full-time passing, put on condition, so he can't play till next year or later, after summer school. He'll miss spring practice. Not good."

Rene looked over at Mary's ring finger. She couldn't help slipping in a subtle jab. "So how does one fail a language course in his native language?"

"It was a literature course, Momma, not grammar. You went to college."

"But it was in English. Right? Does he read anything?"

"Would you please?"

They were silent a long moment, then Rene said, "Well. What are your thoughts on that?"

"We'll get around it."

"We. That's a nice, tight little plural pronoun, long as we're talking English here. But my concern is with you. I like that singular pronoun most."

"Yes, I know. You've made yourself clear on that. You all have."

"So what's he going to do now, work in the shipyard, like his father? Some sweaty shop job?"

"He'll finish his education. Please don't snipe at me."

"I'm not sniping, shoog."

"Yes, you are. I didn't come home for this."

"You're my daughter. You're engaged to marry someone who seems to be a college dropout. And assuming you actually go through with it—I mean, things can happen— I have a right and a responsibility to know what my future son-in-law will do because it directly affects you. You are still thinking of marriage. Right?"

"Yes, we are. What makes you think we might not be?"

"Getting married is easy. It's staying that way that's tougher. For one, both of you are very attractive people, Mary. You know that. You know how it is. It's going to be a constant challenge for the two for you to remain faithful to one another, especially him. Most men are weak that way by nature. You could wake up one day and your marriage could be over, your heart broken because he came home and told you he was leaving you for Susie Q. That's all I'm saying. Happens all the time to couples who thought they were madly in love forever."

"Not our problem."

"So what's he going to do? And how is he going to do it? Support you? I hope you're not going to dip into your trust fund first thing. You're twenty-one now. You have access to part of it. The rest when you're twenty-five and thirty-five. Allotted in increments, all for good reason. Moments like this, you know, when you might be vulnerable. Your granddaddy was a smart man, no fool when it came to money."

"Of course not. Will wouldn't accept that anyway. He's already said so. I offered, but not with my trust, and he refused help. He's also refusing help from his parents."

"Oh, already offered. See why your granddaddy did your trust like that?"

Mary just blew out a breath of air, exasperated.

"So he now knows you have a trust," Rene said.

"And I know he doesn't. So what?"

"Let's don't argue."

"Especially about what we have and don't have. I won't if you won't. You keep bringing it up."

"How is he going to support you, I asked. You didn't bother to answer that."

"We've discussed an option that's reasonable. It's not the best, and not one I particularly like, but it's workable. We'll be fine."

"Like what?"

"He's been offered a commission in the Army for three years. Then back to school on the GI. Bill. Meanwhile, he takes courses along the way, when he can, to build up credits. He might do that. Not certain yet."

"And you do what in the meantime? Drop out of school to follow him all over the world, or stay home alone? Maybe get widowed?"

"You make it sound like a prison or death sentence. He'll be a second lieutenant, not a private. We'll get by. It's only for three years."

"Still not much money, a second lieutenant."

"The same rank Daddy started at in the war."

"But money was never a concern for him. And he rose to lieutenant colonel on Mark Clark's staff by the end of the war." She was referring to General Mark Clark of World War Two fame, who later became president of The Citadel, Lanny Poythress's alma mater, there in town. "Does Will have that kind of future?"

Mary said nothing to that.

Rene said, "Then there's that attitude about his saying he'll never set foot in our house again. I don't see how that can work out well. Ask me, it's a horrible way to begin a relationship with your future wife's family."

"I think you can blame yourself for that, Momma. You left him nothing else to say."

"Please be careful and don't let yourself get pregnant, is all I ask. Gawd, that would just be so unfortunate. Your opportunity for med school isn't indefinite, you know. You miss it and it's gone. Lot of girls would die for your good fortune."

"But it would've been okay with Giles?"

"I wish you would quit harping about Giles."

"Likewise."

"Okay, let's don't argue. We're so happy you're here and that your grades were excellent, as usual. Keep up the good work. Although the B in biophysics was unexpected. What happened there? Not that I'm complaining. Too much romance, not enough studying?"

"No. There is never too much romance between us." She smiled privately at that gotcha little ditty. "There are very few A's given out there, Momma. It's not like other places. There was only one A in the class, a Biophysics major who's brilliant and deserved it. Mine was the second highest grade, a B plus, and I was lucky to get it. It would have been an A plus anywhere else."

Mary let a second or two go by, then said, "And I'm not pregnant. And I'm not going to get pregnant. And we're getting married soon as he gets his commission, or another job, and starts getting paid, if he goes that route. You see, he insists on supporting me, not the other way around."

"So noble of him. But there's a long way to go. We'll see. So when will this be, the wedding?"

"Within a month. We'll know by then if he goes in the army. But it won't be long, even if he doesn't."

"A month? How are we going to plan and conduct a wedding in

a month? Are you getting married by a justice of the peace or something? You're not eloping. Are you?"

"No, Momma. We're getting married on campus, at the bridge. It's already decided."

"Well, we're going to need to talk about this. Who gets married on bridges?"

"The one over the pond we saw when we visited the campus last year, you remember. In the woods."

"Oh, that beautiful little place I liked so much. The one on the poster I bought at the bookstore. That one."

"Yes. We'll have a local pastor officiate. No big show, just a little ceremony."

"Well, I'm not sure I care for that as the mother of the bride. Won't go over big with your grandmother, either, I tell you. I can see Marie now when she hears this. Not to mention your daddy. It just seems to me that you're shutting us out, going off in a whole different direction in your life. I knew you should have gone to Clemson or Duke." Which meant she wished to hell Mary never had met Will Wythe.

"So you've said."

"Would you consider having the wedding here, at our church? Like you would have had ordinarily? This is your home. You're on the register. It's important here."

"It would depend on how Will felt about it. So I doubt it. He's not on the register, you know. He won't enter our house again. You made sure of that. So what's the point?"

"He'll be on the register if he marries you. We can talk more about it later. Things are moving too fast for me in your world."

"Talk all you want, Momma. You've made it impossible for us to have a normal wedding or life here. Because you've planned out my whole future and left me no decisions of my own to make. Not to mention poisoning the well for Will, rejecting my choice for a husband. I'm an adult now, been an adult for years, and I have a voice in my own plans."

Thinking quickly, Rene said, "What about this. What if we have the wedding here, then a repeat back in Williamsburg? Or vice versa? That way, you and Will can do your quaint little thing at the bridge, and you can remain a part of this community and family?"

"Our quaint little thing? So I wouldn't be a part of this family any longer?"

"I didn't mean for it to sound like that."

"You said it."

"We're having dinner at the club tonight. You and I and your daddy and grandma can talk about it then. Okay?"

"Talk all you want."

32

It was a couple days before classes resumed. Will and Kenny Miklos and I were lounging around my house in Newport News eating lunch. Nothing prepared, just what we could find in the kitchen. Kenny was staying in town a day or two over before going back home to Pennsylvania to break the news to his family about dropping out of school and becoming the big deal war correspondent. It would not go over big, so he was not in a hurry. Aunt Evie was out with her church friends, some kind of luncheon, planning another luncheon.

"You're nuts if you do that army crap," Kenny was telling Will. "You know what's going on over there?"

"What's in the news."

"Tim Davis. Remember what happened to him. I wouldn't do it, not as a soldier."

"The atrocities," I said.

"That too," Kenny said.

"We're suppose to be fighting communism," Will said.

"But it's over there, not here," Kenny said. "You sound like you're trying to talk yourself into it."

"Not sure I can avoid it, since I'm officially out of school. One of my mother's friends is a member of the local draft board, and they have my number loaded and ready to fire. Nothing she can do about it. I'll know in a couple of weeks, if not sooner."

"Remember Brame and Wilson," I said to Will. Then to Kenny, "They're guys we know from high school. Itinerate football players. They'll go anywhere and try to make a team. They were up in Blacksburg, at V.P.I., between quarters last fall, in the registrar's office trying to get registered for spring semester so they could try out for the team at spring practice. Said they seemed to be the only guys on campus in suits and ties, so everybody thought they were officials. Never mind they looked sixteen between the two of them, if you added their ages. Even the admin people were casual.

"So the students, the guys, are coming into the office scared to death because they don't have enough passing credits to get a deferment. They're all ragged and hippy-looking. Army field jackets, shaggy hair, the works. They're begging for somebody, anybody, to sign their student deferment forms, give them C's at least, so they don't get drafted, even though some had flunked and were easy pickings. They head right to Brame and Wilson, begging for help, since they had on coats and ties. So they start signing the forms, giving them passing grades, forging the registrar's signature, signing their own names too. And these guys are running back down the stairs giggling, happy as hell. They'll live another quarter. Brame says they must have saved twenty lives that day."

"Now they're real American heroes," Kenny said. "They could have gotten in a lot of trouble, but did it anyway. Give them the Medal of Honor. Just think, life or death could mean a signed piece of paper. Something to think about, Will."

"I'm not breaking the law to stay out of service," Will said. "Besides, I need a job. I'm getting married."

Just then, Pam and Shelley Michaels came in. Shelley lived only a few blocks away, in Hampton, in the Wythe neighborhood, when not in school. More Wythe stuff. Kenny had the hots for Shelley and was always a little shy around her. He couldn't keep his eyes off her, the petite, brainy little girl who'd spend her life at some remote archaeological dig somewhere a million miles away, while he romped all over the globe chasing news stories. Kenny wished opposites attracted in his case, as they often did. I mean, look at Will and Mary. But not in a million years in this one. Kenny was afraid to even ask her out. Only sign of fear I'd ever seen from him. And she'd said he talked like he had a wood rasp in his throat, like he was fifty years old and a heavy smoker. No way she'd go out with a tank like him.

Shelley said Mary called her, since she couldn't reach Will at his house. She was getting the pressure from her mother. Rene was trying to convince Mary it would be better if Will was in the army for a year or two before they got married. Give him a chance to get lost or get killed, probably, so Mary could resume her normal life without the distractions of outside influence. "Tell him I love him. And I'll see him tomorrow when he picks me up at the airport," she'd said.

We hit Aunt Evie's stash and poured a couple drinks, except Pam and Shelley. They weren't big drinkers. We went out onto the front porch and sat around. It was cool but not cold, kind of mild for this time of year, and the sun was shining. The water glistened, and the ships and boats came and went and worked, immune to the season.

Birds were all over the front yard and the seawall across the boulevard. I envied them, in a way, their togetherness, sense of community, no matter their squabbling and competing for food. They were family. Pam mentioned how beautiful they were, a few cardinals mixed in, but all getting along, sharing.

Then Kenny said, "Sure, but keep in mind, if they were four feet tall, they'd kill you and eat you."

Will and Pam and I laughed. Shelley rolled her eyes.

It was just after school and the paperboy threw the folded afternoon edition on the porch and waved as he went by on his bike. I set it on the window sill to read later. Kenny reached for it. Papers were his world, you know.

"You don't mind if I look at it," Kenny said.

"Help yourself," I said.

"I'll put it back the way I found it."

"Knock yourself out."

We talked about one thing or another, while Kenny went through the paper like a kid goes through a new comic book, glued to the page, afraid to miss something. After a couple minutes he turned the paper to Will and said, "You know any of these guys?" It was the obituaries, and two photos and names stood out. Cecil Blantz and Delman Kemper. Grief.

We all looked, and we all but Kenny knew them one way or one degree or another. Blantz we'd known since grammar school, was our age, and had lived four blocks over. He was a marine, now killed in action near Danang. Kemper had been from the same neighborhood as Shelley, a grade behind her, and was now missing in action in the army. It was stunning.

"This is the kind of crap I'm trying to tell you about," Kenny said. He ranted his distaste of the whole subject of our government's involvement in Vietnam, while we sat in silence, stunned by the reality of something like this being so close to home. Just down the street.

"Makes you want to go to colleges all over the country and sign those deferment forms," Kenny said. "Damn these people."

Aunt Evie pulled into the driveway and looked surprisingly sober. I guess the church crowd can do that to you. Between drinks. We went back inside and chatted with her, to be sociable, and to warm up a bit. She took off her coat and hat and checked the kitchen. "If I'd known y'all would be here," she called out, "I'd have fixed something for you." Coming out of the kitchen, she said, kind of smiling, "L.D., have you been in my stuff?" meaning her liquor.

Will and Kenny and I said no too quickly, even though our boozy breath must have stunk like dogs.

"Have you read the paper?" Aunt Evie said.

"Yeah. Just did. Blantz and Kemper," I said.

"Cecil's aunt was with us at lunch today, telling us about it. I swear, it's a shame. His mother is a wreck."

"It's more than a shame, if you ask me," Kenny said. "They're not getting me. They're just not."

"And they're not getting you, L.D.," Pam said.

Will remained silent. He was starting to feel different.

The phone rang. Aunt Evie said, "Will, it's for you. Mary."

"I'm coming back early," Mary said. "Can you pick me up tonight at the airport at nine o'clock?"

"I'll stop the plane in mid-air and snatch you off of it, if you want."

33

Will signed on with the army. He took the deal offered and was biding his time till the paperwork came back in a couple weeks or so making him a brand new second lieutenant, or butter bar as the army called them, referring to the gold color of the rank insignia. In the corps we called them boot lieutenants, or boot-ass lieutenants, though not to their faces. Well, marines and sailors talked dirtier. He didn't want to go in the shipyard. Those who did didn't want to go into the service, or were eager to get away from their parents' homes and buy that new car, or get married early, or both, and were looking for the steady Friday paycheck, with no particular aspirations in life. It wouldn't get him closer to coaching college football. Even though the shipyard had a good athletic program competing against small colleges—I mean, who else would they play?—it wouldn't put him on the right path.

Mary continued with her new classes and doing her volunteer work at the hospital, working in the lab and playing surrogate mother with one or two juvenile patients as she had with Stevie. She and I and Pam saw one another almost daily. So did she and Will, when he wasn't home in Newport News. He tried not to impose on Shelley's space and act like a fungus, since she was Mary's roommate and paid half the rent and utilities, and needed time and solitude for studying. So he and Mary met at the diner often, a couple times with me and Pam most mornings during this period. They couldn't stay away from one another. He also felt guilty for failing and dropping out of school, a new experience in life, before going away for a couple months of training at Fort Benning, Georgia.

Infantry. Not the pie shop job he'd wanted and asked for in an office and eating at the officers club when not golfing or coaching a base football team somewhere for Special Services, the recreational arm of the military. Besides, many bases had cancelled their sports programs in deference to the conflict in Vietnam, where every available body was needed. When not eating lunch at the officers club or playing golf, that is.

During this same period, Miklos finally had gone home to Pennsylvania. Good luck with that. He'd promised to stay in touch, maybe even drop in on us in a few weeks or months. So Dickey Humphrey had lost his best buddy and dependable ride, and his second set of eyes. Dickey's roommate, Alvin Findley, assumed the responsibilities and was now doing the driving and seeing for him.

Findley, the beer god, was quiet and unassuming, a small guy, as his name would suggest, a low-key guy who might make a great dentist one day. Unlike his older brother David, who'd been a well-known track star in college and an Olympic contender, having been the national indoor sixty-yard-dash champion. He was now a flamboyant trial attorney and politician in Richmond, where his family bought up real estate faster than God could make it. It made their beer and wine business look like a hobby. So they didn't miss a case or two, is what it meant to us. They stopped by my house one afternoon, while Will was in Williamsburg with Mary. It was a Friday, so classes were over for the week, and we team guys had worked out at the gym before leaving campus, a requirement.

Aunt Evie was out again with friends, and we were sitting around in my living room having a drink or two from her latest trip to the ABC store. Family connections, you know. I didn't drink much, but had a few in the off season.

Findley said, "So Will is giving up college for being a grunt. That's crazy as hell."

"It's crazier than that," Dickey said.

"Shelly Michaels got accepted in grad school in Montreal, starting this summer," I said. "Our football team is in shreds now. Kenny and Will out, couple others injured and won't play. Couple more transferring."

"Things sure do change fast," Findley said.

"I think adulthood is overrated," I said.

"One day you're in this bucolic setting of Williamsburg, having the greatest time of your life. Then you're snapped up and dropped in a hell hole and getting your ass shot off," Dickey said. "Things are moving too fast for me. My friends are disappearing. And I don't like it."

"You know," Findley said, "there's an anti-war demonstration scheduled for next week on campus. I might go."

"We don't have those kind of students here. They'll be lucky to draw twelve people," I said. "These folks around here don't understand anti-government behavior. The government owns this place. If it closed down, the place would starve to death. All these hillbillies and Carolinians would have to go back home. Tidewater, Virginia, would look like a prune."

"Yeah, and the girls wouldn't know what to wear to a demonstration anyway," Dickey said. "Carol would buy new clothes and tear them up trying to look like a hippie."

Will knocked on the door and came in. Mary went to the hospital for a few hours, he said, to check on her wee patients. They'd meet later and he'd go back to Williamsburg with her and spend the night, since Shelley was also back this way staying in Hampton with her parents the weekend.

"Well, I got my orders," Will said. "Stopped by the house and my mother gave me the letter. After Benning, I'm going overseas with the air cavalry, and they're not in Hawaii."

"Vietnam," I said.

"'fraid so," he said.

"You told Mary yet?"

"No. I'll wait till tonight. Or tomorrow. Don't say anything, if you see her."

Findley said, "My cousin beat the system. He said if you're drafted, when you have the induction physical there at McGuire Army Hospital in Richmond, just go to the bathroom a few minutes before it's your turn to be looked at by the doctors. Pop two or three packs or more of BC Powders in your mouth, and your blood pressure will go sky high, and they'll send you home for a month. Go back again next month, do the same thing. They'll dismiss you permanently. It works. They don't want anybody with a chronic medical problem to take care of."

"They didn't believe me at my local draft board, when I first registered" Dickey said. "I had to go in there with my brother and a doctor's statement saying I was legally blind. They even tried to get my brother. I was lucky to get the hell out of there with him."

"You must have flunked the eye test," I said.

"Can't get anything by you." It was funny.

Will wasn't drinking anything because he had to follow Mary back to Williamsburg later. After a couple hours Dickey and Findley left ahead of him so they could make the rounds of parties on frat row for the almost-free booze. One of the advantages of being a maverick fraternity like us was not having to throw parties every weekend and clean up the mess, or do maintenance or pay bills or worry about campus authorities. You just made a small donation and drank your face off, then left. Our SPD didn't even have initiations or hazing, much less dues. Too much involvement. We were more an ad hoc hit-and-run operation, a laid-back bunch, so we didn't cause any trouble. To be so young and free of serious matters. So halcyon of us.

When they got back to Mary's, she and Will went at one another with their usual passion, trying to defy a law of physics by attempting to prove that two things could occupy the same space at the same time, and succeeding. I never knew two people in my life, before or since, who were so crazy about one another. Even rabbits took breaks.

When finished, they lay back breathing and sweating.

And that's when he told her.

"After Benning, I'll be going to Vietnam with the air cavalry. Just found that out today."

It wasn't like she was surprised. She was silent a long moment.

"I just knew it," she said.

"It's a year tour."

"Unless something happens, you mean."

"It won't. I promise."

"You can't make those kinds of promises. Stop the bullshit."

"Who knows, I might get there and be put in an office, maybe in supply or something, never go to the field. Not everybody goes to the field."

"Sure. That's why they're sending you to infantry officers training school, so you can be in an office. I don't like it."

"I don't either. It'll be over before you know it. By time I get back, you'll be in med school. You'll get an allotment every month to pay the bills. You can stay here with Shelley till she graduates, then get a roommate here, or another place. It'll work out. But if we get married now, before I leave, we'll need our own place so we don't impose on Shelley."

"How about the National Guard?"

"They're full up, not taking any more at the moment."

"You're laying out these plans like you're writing your own script or something. My mother has already written out my plans. Now you're writing out ours. Well, I'm not having it. And I'm going to make you a promise. I told you and I meant it. You don't go anywhere in this world without me. If you go to Vietnam, so do I."

"Uh, that's not how it works, Hugo. That's not possible." It was funny, so he chuckled.

"Really? We'll see. You think I'm not capable of it? You think I won't?"

"I don't doubt anything you say you can do. I just don't think it's the right way to think about it. Besides, there won't be a med school to go to there."

"Med school can wait. It's not everything. But you and I are."

"You're sounding reckless."

"No. I'm just making a promise I can keep, William." She accented the William again. "Now stay put, while I show you what I can do."

He lay there and she went at him like he was leaving today, like there was a truck outside the door waiting to carry him away for the last time.

34

It was for Mary's benefit that Will agreed to a wedding ceremony in Charleston, with the usual hoopla for her family and the registry thing. They were, after all, her family and community and church, the people she grew up around. Her friends. People like Giles and his sister Nell, among many others. It was only right. How could he deny her. But he would not set foot in her parents' house or yard. So if there were any plans that included that, he'd skip that part. And his parents would not accept any accommodations from her family, like lodging, no matter tradition. They would pay their own way. The wedding wherein Rene could play her mother-of-the-bride role, even though she didn't care for the groom or his family, wished the whole thing would go away with Will when he left for the army. For months after she could play the wounded mother whose brilliant, beautiful but young and naïve daughter took up with the tramp from nowhere heading to the same place. The good-looking devil who stole her heart and left town with it. Poisoning the well, Mary had said.

The show ceremony, that is.

The real ceremony, the legal one, would be on campus, at the bridge over the pond. Their bridge, their pond, after he got back from training. It would be a simple, informal affair, close friends and Will's family, his frat brothers and former teammates, although they might have to offer free booze and food to get some of them to show up in the woods. Well, everybody wants something. And Mary's parents would know nothing of this first, official, wedding until later, when it would have the most impact on their feelings, when they came in second in something, maybe for the first time in their lives.

Will got his orders to report to Fort Benning at the end of February. The wedding was then scheduled for a Saturday, the first week of his return from training and ten days before reporting for transfer overseas. The exact date to be determined. They did it that way so Shelley wouldn't be without a paying roommate so quickly, or have to deal with a married couple crashing in on her and all the fallout it would bring. It all would work out better that way.

During Will's training, Mary kept busy as usual with school work and the hospital. They called one another two or three times a week and managed to meet twice in Myrtle Beach on weekends at the same place as before after leaving Charleston. It was so painful for them to be apart, but so pleasurable, so indelible when they met like that. Will questioned his own sanity for ever choosing this route and leaving in the first place. Could an alternative really have been all that bad? They spent almost as much time saying goodbye on these occasions as saying hello, having to tear themselves apart. Good practice for the big separation coming later.

Martha Lynn didn't like the idea of Mary's family, especially her mother, not being invited or even informed of their little wedding in the woods. "It's just not right. She's her mother. It's so unnatural." She'd been tempted more than once to pick up the phone and call Rene and introduce herself and tell her, but had second thoughts. Better not start a relationship with her soon-to-be daughter-in-law by breaking a trust.

Will's father didn't care one way or another, all this wedding stuff. He was like Will that way, both in temperament and looks, carbon copies but with a tinge of gray in his hair. He'd been one of those apprentice school football players in his day, before the war, and still could get by without getting killed in a sandlot touch game.

The wedding would be like a pickup game. Come if you want, pass if you want. No formal invitations, no hard feelings. And no wedding gifts, please. They wouldn't have a place to put anything anyway.

The first night home from training, a Friday in late April, Will took Mary and Shelley out to dinner at a nice little restaurant in Hilton Village, mid-town Newport News in the residential-commercial historic district. Then Shelley left for home for the weekend, leaving the house back in Williamsburg to Will and Mary who made marvelous use of every square inch of it, the floors, the walls, making it all work for them. You'd have thought they were interior designers, but their animations resembled a carnival menagerie in heat. I only surmised that from their looks and condition when I saw them later. I wasn't there.

The wedding would be the following weekend, around mid-day Saturday. No big- deal planning this time around. That would be the province of Rene Poythress and company later in Charleston. There they would go through the big production at Mary's Huguenot church. Then they'd meet discreetly with the pastor immediately after the rites, to sign the state-required papers but inform him it would not be necessary, had all been done in Virginia, and accept his promise to say nothing. Not that they really cared. Just watering down the dust before it got all over everything. Mary would tell her folks later, when she felt like it.

It was warm and sunny that Saturday in Williamsburg, the day they got married. Tourists and local folks were all over the place, including a few at the bridge over the pond when we all arrived. The temperature was close to perfect, humidity low, which was a blessing because this place, any place in tidewater could be stuffy and stifling, with mosquitos and gnats all over you, eating at you. In fact, I'd wondered, especially when younger, how Captain John Smith and Pocahontas and Chief Powhatan and that bunch survived having their heinies bitten off living around here, particularly down the road seven miles in Jamestown, in those marshes by the river. The history books don't tell you about that part.

Will wore khakis and shined loafers, and a colorful shirt that made him look like one of the Beach Boys. His Kennedy-like hair had been cut to army regulation length. Mary, her hair in a ponytail, with a band of flowers around her head, dressed in a simple, ankle-length cotton peasant dress, like she might be leaving later for her honeymoon on a wagon train. Well, it was the sixties, and you knew it was the sixties. She was gorgeous, as usual. She couldn't be otherwise.

So the wedding party gathered on the bridge, where the minister waited for them in the middle. Pam and I, Aunt Evie, and Shelley, and about fifty others we knew gathered. Not bad for no official announcement. Friends and former teammates, SPD brothers, and a gaggle of curious tourists. Will's father was best man, and his kid brother Hank was the ring bearer. Pam was maid of honor, and I and Shelley were backups of some kind, filler guys, I guess, so we wouldn't feel left out, and neither of us was expected to be married anytime soon ourselves. Sure.

Will had the impulse to do something special for Mary, even though it felt kind of cornball-ish. He'd asked me about it earlier, should he do it, but what did I know. He drew on the memory of his grandfather, the romantic in the family, for strength to pull it off. I mean, Will wasn't a poet. He was dumb as I was at that stuff. He passed over the bridge by the minister, to the other side, and turned right and walked through the gathering to the bank of the pond and to the oar paddle marker he'd driven into the ground months earlier, now partially covered by bushes. He bent and touched it and turned to Mary, who was still atop the bridge, and said, "This is our symbol. It represents the love we have for one another and the place we first expressed it. It is our shrine, and we will pay homage to it each time we come here."

If Dr. Antise had been present, he might have been proud and changed Will's grade in English Two-0-Two.

On second thought, nah.

Mary then broke away and hurried to Will's side, stopping first to ask Pam for a tube of her lipstick. She bent and put a single large dot of lipstick on the marker and said aloud to him, "And this is evidence of my vow to you and to our union. This marks our spot, and we will honor it on every visit to this place. We will preserve it and insure it is sanctified forever."

It must have been contagious because Pam then left my side and went to them. She took the lipstick from Mary and put her own dot on the marker, looking directly at me, and said, "And I vow the same to the one I love."

The three of them returned to the center of the bridge. And over the course of the ceremony several woman, and a couple men, walked to the spot and put their own marks on the oar paddle. Well, people do copy one another.

All got quiet. The minister quoted the requisite Biblical verses and traditional vows for them to repeat, which they did, holding hands. Then they spoke their own simple, brief message to one another.

"Always in love," Mary said.

"Together in life," Will said.

"Together in death," she said.

"Together in eternity," they said together.

That was it. The crowd cheered. Some took pictures, including a few tourists.

Pam wept and squeezed my hand. In fact, many of the women teared up, including Martha Lynn and Aunt Evie.

I watched Aunt Evie, maybe a little differently this time, for what reason I don't know. It was ironic. I wondered if she might be revisiting the feelings and memories of her own marriage to the man she loved and who gave her so much joy, as I understood it, until he was shipped overseas to die in the war, the love of her own life. How happy she might have been then, so briefly, like Will and Mary were now. Then how she came to be so alone and suffer the loss in her drink, spending so many nights in the dark, in that big house, while I spent an equal number at Will's or in military school, or somewhere else lost in my own loneliness as a parentless kid. People sure do leave one another in so many different ways.

A conference room had been rented at the premier inn in town for those who wished to stop by for some food and booze, and commiserate, thanks to Will and Mary, his family, and the SPD, including Findley, the beer god, who showed up with a cache of wine.

Mary's feelings were mixed, not all happy ones. She was hurt that her family wouldn't share this with her, the real moment, not the fake repeat. But it had been their fault, not hers, and they'd get the consolation prize, for what it was worth.

And Will felt her sorrow too, he said to her later, when they were alone. "We can't let this ruin it for us, Hugo. We have to look at it positively. Maybe someday they'll come around enough to make it tolerable. But you have to know, too, that as long as they live, they'll never accept the fact that you married wrong. That'll always be in the room with us. And I'll never set foot in their house, like I said. I'll do anything for you but that."

"Every room we'll ever be in will be our room, Will. Makes no difference what others think. We're the ones who count here. We won't let anyone ruin it for us. And when we have children, I don't want them having to deal with those kinds of feelings. I won't have it."

Later, when they were alone in their room there, spending the night before driving off a few days to wherever caught their fancy, they couldn't shake the coming reality of their impending separation, just days away.

"But it'll go by quicker than you think," Will said. "We'll both be so busy the time will fly. Wait and see."

"I don't like it, like I said. And I won't tolerate it," Mary said. "It's not right for us to be married and be apart. It's unnatural. I won't accept it. I've told you that."

"We don't have a choice."

"Yes, we do."

"I'd like to know what it is. This whole thing here is carved in stone, my new bride. My beautiful, wonderful, brilliant Mary Collette Rene Reedlaw Poythress Wythe. What a sound, but let's give our kids shorter names. I love you so much, Hugo. I don't deserve you. But we're now controlled by forces stronger than us for the next year. We have to hunker down and do it."

"That's what you think, William Longman Wythe, the man I love so much. The man I'll be with forever, who'll father my children and rock my grandchildren in his lap. You haven't seen anything yet."

35

Will had several more days left with Mary, before leaving for overseas.

Overseas. Now there was a familiar term in the American lexicon. American G.I.s were always going overseas somewhere, like some rite of passage for every generation. It was like it was expected. *So where's Billy? Oh, he's overseas.*

They had enough money to stay on the road at least five of those days. Then they'd come back and Will would have a couple days with the folks, while Mary jumped back on the books. In fact, she took her work with her in Will's car, reading along the way to sneak in a little studying in those rare moments when they weren't screwing their brains out or exploring the countryside.

They went to the mountains first. They'd come back to the beach later, but it was late April now and there was nothing like it when spring warmed and lit up the Blue Ridge.

In Lexington they stopped in at V.M.I. Mary never had been there, and Will wanted to share some of his experiences and memories with her of his track meets in the old fieldhouse. And the Stonewall Jackson Society. The museum was open, only three or four others inside at the time. The same attractive woman who'd been attending it in the earlier years was still in charge from her little desk in the lobby. Something familiar and comfortable about that.

They went into the room where Little Sorrell was mounted and on display in the glass case.

"Should've come here," Will said. "Should've taken the scholarship. I'd still be in school."

"But you didn't."

He made sure no one was looking. "You're about to become a member of the Stonewall Jackson Society," he said. "A very rare honor, indeed. Even all the SPD and team guys are not members. So you're special."

"Pays to know people, I guess" she said, and grinned. "You're nuts."

"Yes, I know. But also the luckiest nutcase in the world. Because with this honor I'm about to bestow upon you, I get a big, fat, juicy kiss as an initiation fee."

"Did y'all kiss one another?" She giggled..

"Don't be cute."

"Then I guess I am special. You're certifiable. We're going to get arrested."

"Life is all about risks," he said. He reached in and plucked a single hair from the horse's tail and handed it to her. She held it between her fingers and looked around like she'd robbed a bank.

They were in a long kiss when an elderly couple walked in. "Oh, excuse us," the lady said. "Is this part open?" She was a slender woman, gray hair, stress lines in her face. He was tall and serious looking.

They broke their embrace. "Oh, yes, it is," Will said. "Come on in. We don't work here. Just visiting."

The lady smiled. "I see that."

The man with her said, "So this is General Jackson's horse. I'll be." He looked it over with fascination.

"You go here?" the woman said to Will, meaning V.M.I. Probably the haircut.

"No, ma'am, just visiting."

"Our grandson aways wanted to come here," she said, looking over the room. "But he never made it. That's why we came to visit. We raised him."

"So where does your grandson go?" Mary said, being cordial.

"Unfortunately, he died four months ago," she said, her voice breaking a little.

"We're so sorry," Mary said, and Will concurred with a head nod.

"So are we. What a waste. He was such a wonderful boy. He was only nineteen. He was a marine."

"You mean, in Vietnam?" Will said.

"Yes."

They didn't know what else to say, except another sorry.

"Your hair is short," the woman said to Will, matter of fact. "You in the service?"

"Yes, ma'am, the army. Just went in."

"You be careful. This is a bad time for a young man in this country."

Will nodded. "I will." Mary didn't know what else to say.

The woman said, "He told us that the marines have a saying over there. 'Keep your head down, your eyes up, and don't walk back on the same trail.' They came back on the same trail, his buddy told us in a letter. You watch yourself, if they send you there. You hear me? You remember that."

"Yes, ma'am. Loud and clear."

The couple started to walk away.

"Wait," Will said. He reached back into the glass case and extracted another hair from Little Sorrell's tail and handed it to the man, who looked at it, then around for any sign of trouble, not understanding.

"In memory of your grandson," Will said. "It's unofficial, so we keep it to ourselves. But nothing is more important here than General Jackson, who taught school here before the Civil War, as you probably know. And there aren't but a few of us who know and appreciate this. This makes you a member of the Stonewall Jackson Society. We're happy to have you share the spirit of this place with us."

The man looked around again. "We're not going to get in trouble with this. Are we?" But he was also smiling.

Will put a finger to his lips. "No. It's our private thing. Keep it to yourself."

The man chuckled. "Well, thank you. I accept it in that spirit." His wife squeezed Will's arm, and gave Mary a quick little hug, and they left.

Will looked down at the hair in Mary's fingers. Small consolation for losing a grandson. Such kid stuff.

They spent the time driving up and down Skyline Drive to one site or another, then returned to Williamsburg so Mary could unload and reload for their stay at Will's parents' house in Newport News. They'd be there a couple nights in Will's now old room next to Hank's, when not out and about. They stopped by my house. Pam came over. And Aunt Evie made us all a nice dinner, before joining some of her friends for an outing.

"Miklos is back," I told them. "He's on his way down now, he and Dickey."

"Back in school?" Will said.

"No, just stopping by on his way back home from Atlanta. Had a job interview or something. Didn't go well. Said his parents didn't take it well, either, his dropping out. He's staying here tonight, leaving tomorrow. And Findley was accepted to law school for his senior year. Wants to practice with his brother when he graduates. So much for the botany major."

Pam and Mary went out onto the front porch and sat in the rocking chairs and looked out at the river.

Mary said, "After Will leaves you'll have to go home with me to Charleston one weekend. Show you around. You'll love it."

"Maybe when school's out would be great." After a moment she said, "You're worried. Aren't you?"

"Darn right I am. The whole situation worries me. We should have found another way."

"Just stay close to me and L.D. as much as you want while he's gone. You can stay at my house as much as you want. We have plenty of room, and my parents would love to have you."

"Thanks. I'll take you up on that a time or two. Until I leave after finals next month."

"Leave to where? You're going to summer school. Aren't you?"

"No, I'm going to Vietnam," Mary said, serious as could be.

"What? You're kidding me? You can't do that. Can you?"

"Watch me. I told him he'd never go anywhere in this world without me, and I meant it. Literally."

"Does he know that?"

"No."

"But you can't be with the army."

"Not exactly. I have something else in mind. I'll tell you about it later. But you have to promise me you won't say a word to anybody, especially Will. Okay? Not a soul."

"I won't. I promise."

Miklos and Humphrey arrived and got some leftovers from the kitchen. We were in the living room.

"How'd it go in Atlanta?" I said to Kenny.

"Not well. No relevant experience, they told me."

"You went to the biggest paper in the South, the Journal and Constitution," I said. "What'd you expect?"

"Smaller papers can't afford to send people overseas to report."

"So what do you do now?" Will said.

"Go home and finish the big blow-out with my family, then haul ass to Canada. I have an old buddy from high school there, in Montreal, who works for an advertising paper, said he could get me on. I'll have to sell ads, too, but it's a start. Can't stay home."

"So what happened?" Will said.

"My old man kicked me out, is what happened."

"You're kidding," I said.

"Hell, no, I'm not kidding. My father is a hard-ass. His way is the only way."

"So what happened?" I said.

Kenny was temporarily stuffing a sandwich in his mouth. So Dickey said, "He refused to go in the draft."

Kenny was nodding yes while finishing his bite, then said, "I'm working in the family business, taking orders over the phone, driving the forklift and loading trucks, whatever is needed. So I get a notice to report, and I don't go. I get another notice and a phone call last week, and I still don't go. So my father asks me, 'What the hell gives? What're you doing here?' And I tell him straight up I'm not going in no service, but I'm going to find a job reporting the war. Do it my way, not the government's way."

"Didn't go over big," Dickey said.

Kenny said, "Said he could help me get in the Pennsylvania National Guard. The commanding general of it is a member of his country club or something. I tell him no, it's still the service, and I can't report the war in Vietnam from Pennsylvania."

"And he didn't like it," Dickey said, always happy to help.

Kenny said, "So my father gives me the old story of how we owe this great country of ours anything it asks of us, it's been so good to us, like family. How my grandfather, who was right there and heard all this, by the way, came over from the old country with six dollars in his pockets and one change of clothes, only to be drafted in the army and put on a boat and sent right back over to Europe to the war. And how he, my father himself, served in World War Two. And my Uncle Nick, who got his ass shot up in Korea—God bless him, he's a great guy. And that it was my duty to be a man and an American and answer the call. Et cetera, et cetera. And in my family, when my father speaks, everybody listens. And when my grandfather speaks, everybody drops to their knees and listens."

"Tell 'em what he said then," Dickey said.

"He told me to pack my bags and get the hell out. And don't come back through his door again without a military uniform on.

"I told him," Kenny said further, "that I loved this country, too, as much as anybody, as much as him, but that I also knew why I did, and this wasn't it."

"Wow," Will said. "So you can't go back home?"

"To get my stuff, is all. My mother slipped me a little money. Said she and my sister would wire me a little money each month, if I needed it."

"You got enough to get out of the country?" I said.

"Barely. But I can't take my car. The government could maybe track me that way. And I'm not a Canadian citizen, so I couldn't re-register it without a formal passport, which I can't get because I'll be an illegal. I'll be okay once I get to my buddy's place. Lot of guys are going there."

"Then we take up a collection for you, right now," Will said. "Let's dig in. I'll be first, a U.S. Army officer aiding and abetting a draft dodger. I'd be court-martialed and shot as a traitor."

We all thought that was funny. But kind of not.

"Can't take your money." Kenny said. "I'll make it okay."

"Yes, hell, you will." Dickey said. "The Sigma Phi dollars go with you."

"You don't have a choice," I said. "You're out-numbered. Now shut up and stick out your hand. Your frat brothers have spoken. This isn't Mickey Mouse college boy stuff. This is the real and deadly world we're dealing with. And we have to help one another."

"Besides," Will said, "you're not running out on anyone. You're trying to go to

the same place I am. Just doing it your own way, on your own terms. We have to respect that."

Kenny was somewhat embarrassed by it, but managed to lighten up the moment. "I don't want to hear any of this corny brothers-for-life crap. We're the SPD. We don't operate like that."

But we kind of did.

That night Will, Mary, Pam and I, with Kenny and Dickey following in Kenny's car, drove over to Virginia Beach, first to the Surf Rider Restaurant on Rudee's Inlet, at the end of Atlantic Avenue. It was a popular place, built like a lodge, high ceiling, big windows, a long bar in the front, with a mixed-age crowd, civil, and always busy place at the end of the strip. The food was good and there was usually some form of entertainment. This night, as with most, it was a combo playing folk songs—what else, it was the sixties— in front of the fireplace at the far end. We sat outside on the long wooden deck and ate with a view of the ocean. It was dusk. The sound of the surf and smell of the water and residual aroma of suntan lotions, and a twinkling of lights now coming on up and down the strip was soothing.

I asked Mary about Shelley, for Kenny's benefit.

"Went to the Original Club with her date," she said. That was a live-band dancing place downtown Newport News on a side street off West Avenue, near the shipyard. Industrial strength recreation, but a neat place, as we said then. Kenny liked the idea of Shelley Michaels or any discussion of her. Just hearing her name got his attention.

"Maybe you and Shelley can meet up in Montreal, since you'll both be there this summer," I said.

"It's a big town, but, yeah, that'd be nice. If she didn't mind," Kenny said.

"Mind? Why would she mind?" Will said. "She won't know anybody there. Write down the name of where you'll be working. Mary can give it to her. At least the two of you will know somebody there, in case you want to get together, or need help or something."

Kenny wrote it down on a napkin and gave it to Mary.

The sun sat and we decided to go back up the Avenue to the Peppermint Beach Club, another dance spot that played mostly rock music, with a little folk mixed in. Bill Deal and the Rhondels were the favorite there. They were local recording artists who'd been playing there for a few years, and always drew a big crowd, and you had to use your elbows a lot, especially on the dance floor. You could hear them for blocks up and down the boardwalk and Atlantic Avenue. They were a blast. No casual conversation here, except between sets, too noisy.

Will and Mary danced and sweated the rest of the night, staring at one another, absorbing the sounds and sights of others and the flashing strobe lights, making it all part of their pre-mating ritual. They would tear at one another later in their usual fashion.

For the moment, all the world was in harmony.

36

The day came. A Monday morning. Time for Will to leave. He said his goodbyes to his parents and brother, then stopped by briefly with Mary to see Aunt Evie and Pam and me, before we left for classes in Williamsburg. Mary would drive him to the airport, where he would catch his flight to California and join a planeload of other soldiers for the flight to Vietnam. He would depart to his unit in the field after orientation.

He and Mary were so anxious they were shaking, literally, like a neurosis of some kind at having to be apart after all their recent closeness. A lot of that going around in those days all over the country.

"Got your hair with you?" I said to him before he left my house. I was referring, of course, to the horse tail hair from Little Sorrell.

"Right here." He patted the hip pocket of his summer khaki uniform. "Wouldn't go without it."

"It'll give you special protection," I said.

"Didn't do Stonewall any good." The general had been shot and killed accidentally by his own men in the war, who'd thought he was the enemy.

"But it will for you because I said so. Remember, everything over there is a fourth and ten, they tell me." Nice football metaphor.

"I'll be back. You can count on it."

We shook hands and gave one another a brotherly hug.

Pam and I would have breakfast with Mary the next morning at the diner back at school. And we, especially Pam, would spend a lot of time with her so she wouldn't feel alone, except when she wanted.

Will got checked in at Patrick Henry, and they sat in the coffee shop there until flight time. It was a busy morning, and he was not the only G.I. there.

"I feel like a freak, leaving you so soon after getting married," Will said. "I'm sorry for not trying harder in school. There's something unnatural feeling about leaving home to go half way around the world to kill people, or be killed." He had a second thought on that. "Didn't mean to say that. Sorry."

"We'll get through it."

"Yes, we will, Mrs. Wythe."

"I like it when you call me that. Keep it up and you'll never make your flight." They chuckled at that. Her eyes moistened.

"That's why I said it."

"Remember what I told you more than once?" she said. "That you'd never go anywhere in this world without me?"

He nodded. "Well," she said, "you're not going there without me either. I can't let you go without telling you that."

"Meaning what?"

"Meaning I'll be over there, one way or another. And it won't take long."

"Don't talk crazy, Hugo. That's not possible. You brought that up before. What's going on in that beautiful, brilliant head of yours?"

"Wait and see, William. You haven't seen anything yet."

"We'll be able to meet in six months when I get R&R. We can go to Hawaii, meet there if you want."

"We'll be going together."

"You're losing me, Mary. You can't go to Vietnam. You'd have to be with a government agency of some kind, or in the service. You've got school and med school. We don't need two dropouts in one family of two people. Let me be the dumb one who learns the hard way. One of us has to be smart."

"We are two people but one soul, Will. That's the way it is. We don't stay apart."

"I love you so much," Will said. He looked around to see if he was overheard. It was a private thing to him. He didn't care much for public displays of affection. He was so lucky to have Mary there to see him off. He wondered what it must feel like to some of the other G.I.s there who were leaving alone. It reminded him of the first day he started school, when his mother and others dropped off their children and met the teachers, when some of the other kids were just dumped off to find their own way. There was also something particularly unnatural about that too. All of these old feelings and memories seemed to be popping up in the present reminding him how dumb this whole thing was. Funny how little things seem so important at a time like this.

"I'll write every day," Mary said.

"I don't want you here when I leave," he said. "I don't want to look out the window of that plane and see you standing there alone, watching me leave. I can't stand the thought of you being alone. It reminds me of how stupid I've been." He chuckled at that to lighten the moment.

The announcement over the P.A. speaker said the plane boards in five minutes. Will walked Mary to the terminal entrance. They hugged and kissed long and hard, and he watched her as she turned and left, heading for the parking lot. She stood next to her car for twenty minutes and watched the plane take off and disappear into the air.

Pam and I spent a lot of time with Mary the next three weeks, until after exams, when she returned to Charleston. She left school with the option of re-enrolling without having to re-apply, if she chose, depending on how things went at home. This whole thing would be over in a year and Will likely would be stationed stateside.

They could be together and she could finish her last semester and get her double degrees before starting med school. Or skip med school for the time being and begin her graduate work in her doctoral field and go to med school after that. Her mother would go nuts, but Rene's wishes were secondary now, and she was well aware of it, though she would not give up easily.

I spent my own summer partly in two classes for credits delayed taking a lighter load during football season. I also did several weeks at Quantico in the PLC officer training program with the Marine Corps, as every summer. When home I worked out several nights a week, played sandlot ball at the school with some of the guys from the neighborhood, and did errands and chores around the house for Aunt Evie. And hung out with Pam, when I wasn't hanging out with other girls. That's what hounds do.

Mary and Shelley didn't renew their lease on the little house, of course. Humphrey and Findley would pick up their lease and move out of the dorms. And Shelley was leaving in a week or so for Montreal to start graduate school. Mary was burning this bridge. They had a night out together in town, eating at Chowning's and commiserating with mutual friends. The next morning they packed up their belongings and said their goodbyes and promised to stay in touch. Mary paid her last visits, also, with her child patients at the hospital. And the staff she worked with there in the lab gave her a little going-away party.

Mary drove home to Charleston, spending the night alone in the motel in Myrtle Beach she and Will had stayed at before. She did that because she wanted to feel a closeness with him. Besides, it was very late when she got that far. In Charleston she stopped first at the newspaper building downtown, just a few blocks from home. Her mother would not know this, if it went well. She went to Uncle Charles' office and asked to see him. She chatted briefly with his secretary and others in the office.

Charles then came out of a meeting and gave her a big hug. "In here," he said. They went into his office and closed the door. She took a chair in front of his desk. He sat behind it and took off his glasses.

"So, I presume school went well," Charles said.

"Yes, swimmingly, as they say."

"How's Will? You two are still together, I'm guessing."

"Very much so. He left for Vietnam three weeks ago. I haven't bothered to tell mother yet, but she knows he was going."

"Yes, she said he joined the army. And you're going back to summer school, of course. How long you home?"

"No."

"No, what?"

"No, not going back to school."

"You going down here, in town?"

"Not going at all. Taking some time off," Mary said.

"Something I should know? I miss something?"

"Charles, I need to confide in you. And I need you to keep it to yourself, not let momma or daddy or grandma, or anybody, know we talked or what we discuss here. Is that okay?"

He was hesitant. "Well, sure. But what gives?"

"I haven't been home yet. I came here to see you first."

"That important? I'm listening."

"I need a job in the news business. In Saigon." His eyes went wide open. "Anything. Reporter, typist, research assistant. Gofer, anything. I'll volunteer, if I have to, but I have to get there."

"Saigon?" He was incredulous.

"Yes."

"You kidding?"

"Dead serious. You hear me?"

"Loud and clear. But why?"

"Because that's where Will is, in Vietnam."

"That's it? Will's there? He's in the army, Mary. He's supposed to be there." He was staring right through her, dumbfounded.

"And so am I." She was desperate, almost crying now. "Take me seriously, Charles. I need this. And I will find a way, no matter what. I'm trusting you. Need you and trusting you."

"Just what do you think I can do? Even if I tried, Charleston would be more dangerous than Saigon for me, if your mother ever discovered I tried to help you. God, can you imagine that? And she'd find out too, if you were with a news service. That wouldn't fool anybody. She'd come right for me."

"She doesn't have to know."

"We don't have a correspondent on the payroll over there. We depend on the wire services and network T.V. to feed us material. Even if you could get there, it's a war zone, Mary. Too dangerous."

"You'd have me as a resource. And it wouldn't cost the paper a cent."

He was already waving that away. "Doesn't work like that." He swiveled in his chair and thought a moment. "There's something you're not telling me."

"Is it that obvious?' Mary said.

"Yes. I've known you all your life. Did you think you could walk in here and shell out half a story and I'd buy it?" He gave a little smile.

"Will and I are already married."

Charles leaned back and held his hands over his head a moment. "Oh, great. Something else I now know that'll get me killed." He sat up straight. "You're not pregnant. Are you?"

"No, of course not. Why would I go to Vietnam pregnant?"

"Well, that's a point in your favor. What about the big wedding Rene is planning for y'all, when he gets back?"

"It'll go on as usual. We can tell her later. Nobody has to know now."

"So my favorite, lovely little niece is no longer a Poythress, but a Wythe."

"Poythress-Wythe is fine."

"You now have a name longer than a football field."

He gazed out the window. "Seems like yesterday your mother was giving me money to walk you down the street for ice cream because you were too young and small to go alone. Now look at you. All grown up and wandering all over the world by yourself."

Mary was still waiting for him to crack. "I'm sick without him, Charles. I need help. If you only knew how we feel about one another."

"What does he think? He know you're trying to go there? He approves of it?"

"I told him I was. He doesn't like the idea, to be honest. I'm not sure he even believes me. But it's also not his decision."

"Whew. What a thing to hit me in the face with at the end of the day. It's so dangerous, Mary, a place like that."

"Not that much in Saigon," Mary said. "I've done my homework. It's a big city, relatively safe. Lot of civilians and military there. Hotels, restaurants, shopping, night clubs. The war is unpopular here in the West. You know that. And the press is the best foreign friend the North Vietnamese and Viet Cong have. They don't target the press, I'm told."

"Not all westerners are against the war. And not all the press. They do get hit on occasions there, in Saigon, for opinions contrary to communist aggression."

She waited.

"I can't make any promises, except that I'll reach out to a couple people I know in New York and D.C. who're with the wire services. Maybe there's something you could do. Office help or something. But nothing that takes you in the field. That's for the hard-core guys. Don't get your hopes up. You won't be able to go to him, you know, even if you get there."

She nodded.

"I'll let you know if I hear anything. But you better not ever say anything, or we're both done. You hear me?"

"Promise. Thank you so much, Charles. I love you. You're my favorite uncle. Always were." She walked around and hugged him.

They chatted awhile longer and he walked her to the door. "Okay," he said. "I promised I'd help you with this, if I can. Now you have to promise me you'll think it over and reconsider."

"That's a promise I can not make. Ask for something else."

"That's what I'd thought you'd say. The only reason I've agreed to this is because you're determined. And I don't want you to risk getting mixed up with anybody who might not have your best interest in mind. And that'll be my only defense if Rene and Lanny find out. Last words before the firing squad."

"But you'll try."

"Yes. Because I'm certain it won't work. But I'll try. You're my favorite relative. I owe your father, and grandmother Marie, so much. They got me my first job here when I started out of college. They didn't even need or want anybody here at the paper, especially a neophyte, but they hired me anyway because of them. And I don't want to disappoint them. We carry this to our graves with us. You understand?"

"You'll never know how grateful I am, and Will, too, when he sees how it works out," she said. "We'll owe you big."

"I'm thinking maybe he'll want to kill me. I would if I were in his situation and you showed up over there."

"I'll worry about Will. One thing he respects about me, among other things, is my independent streak. "

"Just don't let this roll back on us," Charles said. "The possibilities are very ugly."

37

Miklos was now gone, presumably, to Canada. Dickey and Findley were home for the summer and would return in the fall, Findley to law school, Humphrey a senior. So they'd room together again, but in the house they took over from Mary and Shelley. Pam and I were home in Newport News. Will was in Vietnam, and Mary was trying to get there. She'd come to Williamsburg the previous summer with the single purpose of finishing her degrees in this quaint, beautiful little paradise and heading straight to medical school so she could dedicate her life to killing the kind of disease that had killed her younger brother. How things change among the young. Such a noble goal. Now she had left school without completing her studies, a drop-out, at least temporarily, was a married woman madly in love with her husband who also was a drop-out, and was dying to go to a combat zone to be with him. About half of those who went to college with big dreams came out different.

Mary left Charles' office and went to the Poythress home on the Battery and parked in the narrow lane in front of the house. She left her bags and other items in the car. Her father was out somewhere. The cook they sometimes used was preparing dinner, while Marie was napping upstairs and Rene was on the phone.

"Oh, I've got to go. Mary's home." Rene went to Mary and hugged her. "Come here, my baby. It's so good to have you back home. We don't see you as much as we used to." Meaning because you went to that faraway place and was led astray by that alley cat.

So Mary mentioned it. "Will left for Vietnam three weeks ago," she said. "I've gotten four letters from him. He's in the field a lot."

Rene hesitated. "Well, hopefully, he'll be okay." She said it like she was wishing for a flat tire on her car. "Your daddy will be home shortly. Your grandma is sleeping. We'll have dinner in about and hour. When do classes start again?"

"I just got home, Momma. I'm not going to summer school. I'm taking some time off."

"What?"

"I've been going to school all my life. I need a break."

She could see her mother's spirit die right there.

Rene was stunned. "I don't understand. You're so close. You graduate in January. You can't stop now. You'll have a semester off till you start med school the following fall. You're almost there."

"I just want to do something else for a while. I'm tired of going to classes and writing papers and taking exams. And staying up all night. I want to be able to go to work and leave it there when I come home."

"I knew damn good and well something like this would happen," Rene said.

"I don't want to hear it, Momma."

"You don't? Just wait till you tell your daddy and grandma. You'll hear it, alright."

Mary doubted that. It was always her mother who'd planned out her life, not Lanny and Marie. They weren't driven like that. They didn't have anything to prove.

"What brought all this on?" Rene said.

"I've told you."

"Your boyfriend—excuse me, fiancé—flunks out, then you drop out. See a pattern there?"

"Please, Momma. Let's don't argue."

"Agreed. We'll discuss it later. All of us together."

"No, we won't. It's my decision to make, and I've made it. You act like I'm the only college student who ever took a break from school. I'll get there, Momma. Just don't push."

Rene blew out a breath of air and dropped her tempo. "Okay, fine. You're free, white and twenty-one. Do what you want." But she didn't mean it.

Mary and her mother spent the time before dinner taking Mary's belongings from her car to her bedroom upstairs. When alone and putting her things away, Marie walked in, now dressed for dinner.

"Oh, I thought I heard you in here. My baby's back," Marie said. "Come here and give me a big hug. Let me look at you." She said it like Mary had been gone for years. She stepped back, holding Mary's hands in hers.

"My dear," Marie said, "there is a white circle around your ring finger. Has your mother seen that?" She gave a little knowing grin, not at all hostile or surprised.

Mary was momentarily speechless, thinking fast. "No, I don't think so."

"You don't have to explain," Marie said. "I won't ask or say a thing. You can do no wrong in my eyes. How is Will?"

"Thanks for asking, Grandma. He's fine. I hope so anyway. He's in Vietnam now."

Marie nodded. Mary still wasn't giving it up about being married.

"Well, we want him to do well and come home in one piece. He has your happiness in his hands. That is my concern."

"You're wonderful, Grandma. Thank you so much." She hugged her again.

"I think we might have given him the wrong impression when he was here. For my part, it wasn't intended, but must have seemed like it, on second thought. I apologize for that. Please convey that to him when you write him next."

"I will. It'd be nice if everybody felt the same way."

"Your daddy has expressed his regret as well. He hopes he can have a second chance to make a better impression. When Will gets back, you must bring him here again. We're not hostile people, not snobs, Mary, though it might seem so. As for your mother, you must understand her. She's concerned only for your success and happiness. She had a very rough time of it growing up. Charles, too. Had to fight and struggle for everything. Then your brother. It was devastating to all of us, you know. Not a stronger woman I know. Very determined. She can be tough, but she has been the best wife for your daddy. He was a wild child, indeed, until she came along and straightened him out. Not a more dedicated wife or mother I know. So keep that in mind when you feel like you could smack her silly." She grinned. "Now, let's have dinner. And get something on that finger. Anything to cover that glaring omission." She smiled again.

Lanny wasn't at all disappointed at Mary wanting a break from school. No big deal, so take off, have some fun while you're young was his attitude. Life is about working, not working yourself to death. He just had to be careful how he expressed that opinion around Rene, not push it. He winked at Mary's actions every time Rene rolled her eyes, as kind of a counter balance.

Mary insisted on getting the mail every day from the box. She also was alert to the phone ringing. Who knows, maybe Will could find a way to call. Or it might be Charles. She and Kate and the kids went over to Kate's and Charles' beach house on Sullivan's Island for a day. But no word from Charles yet. She spent time with old friends, including Nell Collier and others, but her mind was always running on that second track, wondering and worrying about Will. She also wrote Linda Harnley to let her know she hadn't forgotten her and her family and Steven. She couldn't just watch him be buried, then forget the whole experience. It wasn't right. You didn't forget people just because they died. If it was okay to revere the Stonewalls of the world, it was also right to remember and revere your friends.

Then the call came, two weeks after she was home.

"Stop by my office today, if you can," Charles said. "Late afternoon would be best. I might have something for you."

Mary was there at four o'clock.

"There's someone I know," Charles said when Mary sat down across from him again. "We've been acquaintances for years, and the paper does business with her company, News Service Daily, NSD. They're an independent agency with reporters all over the world. Low profile but a big presence in the industry. They make their money selling information and stories, reportage, to papers, magazines, TV and radio networks, and by publishing books and research papers. She's willing to talk with you. I didn't say anything about your reason for wanting to go there, about Will. You can do that yourself, if you want. I just said you wanted a break from school, some real-life experience doing something different."

"She, you said?"

"Yes. Della Myles. She runs the company from Washington, D.C., where they're headquartered. But you don't have to go there. She'll be giving a lecture at Duke, in Durham, next Wednesday. She'll meet with you there before going back to D.C. Here's the time and address. I've told her about you. It's not a shoo-in, so don't get your hopes up." He handed her the paper.

"I can go to D.C. now, if that would be better," Mary said.

"Don't push it. This is her call."

Mary thanked him profusely. That second track in her mind was now positive and energized. She barely could sit still, was almost giddy, to the point her mother noticed.

"So what's gotten into you?" Rene said. She'd come into the house from checking her plants and shrubbery after the gardener had left. "You're awfully happy-acting all of a sudden."

"I am, Momma. I guess the break is doing me some good. It's good to relax and get enough sleep."

"Yeah, well." Rene didn't know if that was good or bad, of course. "Long as you get back in the swing by the fall."

Hold your breath, Mary thought.

She told her mother she was meeting some friends next Tuesday in Raleigh for a day or two, and would fly up Tuesday night.

"Oh, that's great. You can see Jason Aulander while you're there. He's in medical school now, you know. His mother was telling me about it last week, and asked about you too. He's like you. He's always wanted to be a doctor."

"It's a girl thing, Momma. I won't have time for Jason. Besides, I never liked him that much. He's goofy."

"Goofy. Now there's a wonderful endorsement for a young man who's going to be a great surgeon in a few years. Just a suggestion."

"I can operate just fine without suggestions regarding my social life."

"Okay, okay. Not arguing. Don't be so touchy."

If you only knew.

Mary left for Raleigh-Durham Tuesday and got a room at the same hotel Della Myles was staying at in Durham, close to the university. She was taking no chances of being late or missing that interview.

Myles, Mary later told Pam, was in her late forties or early fifties, couldn't tell which, with a sprig of grayish hair falling over her forehead that she didn't seem to notice. She looked like she cared more about working and getting the job done than dressing up and looking good. A moderately attractive woman who skipped primping and left the office late. First impression.

Della welcomed Mary with a hand shake. "Well, well, Charles said you were a looker, but I had no idea."

"Thank you."

"That's a quality that can be either a distraction or an advantage, depending."

It was a suite of two rooms and they sat in chairs at the desk and small-talked briefly.

Then Della said, "So what's the attraction to Vietnam?"

"Well, you can't get away from it," Mary said. "It's all over the news every day and people are going there all the time, some even getting killed or wounded. I guess I just want to see what it's all about. Maybe some macabre curiosity. And get away from my comfortable lifestyle for a while. I feel confined. I want to be a part of something vitally important, even if just in a small way."

"Great. Now tell me the real reason."

Mary was caught by surprise. "Is it that obvious I have one?"

Della smiled. "When a young woman looks like you, there is always a young man involved. Is your boyfriend there?" She smiled again.

"You see through walls or something?" She grinned back at her.

"News is my business. And news is about people, what they do and don't do. How the world and events in it affect them. The human element is at the heart of every story. Otherwise, it's not interesting."

"Yes," Mary said, a bit subdued, like maybe she'd lost her shot.

"Where is he?"

"All over the place since getting there, seems. Last letter he was in a place called Long Binh."

"Sixteen miles from Saigon. Airborne infantry?"

"Yes, ma'am. Charles doesn't know this. I didn't tell him." She didn't want to compromise Charles.

"And you want to be as close to him as you can get." Another little smile of understanding, maybe even envy.

"You can't go to Long Binh, you know. That's for field correspondents. You'd be office help." Mary was nodding her acceptance of the fact. "So the chances of your seeing him are slim, though not impossible. G.I.s in the field do get into town on rare occasions, but it's usually work related. Most stay in the field till their R & R rolls around after the first six months in country." R & R meaning Rest and Recuperation. "Then they can go any number of places, like Japan, Manila, Hawaii, Australia, for ten days or a couple weeks." She leaned back and blew out a breath of air. "But that's really not important for working in the office. Everybody has a reason of some kind, so it doesn't matter.

"Tell me, what do you know about Vietnam?" Della then said. She wasn't smiling now.

"Not a whole lot. Just what's in the news and magazines." She went into some detail about Vietnam's history and time being a French colony, the geography, political dichotomy, and how we got involved there starting in the early nineteen fifties. She wasn't an expert, but she'd picked up a little bit.

"Now the important thing," Della said. "Can you type?"

"Yes, ma'am, I can."

"You'd be surprised how many graduates of prestigious colleges and universities can't type. The job doesn't pay much."

"I don't need much," Mary said.

Della waved a finger. "Never say that in an interview. There are people who'll work you like a mule for little or nothing if you let them. Take all you can get."

"I'll remember that." She smiled.

"The heat is stifling there."

"I'm from Charleston. I'm used to heat and humidity."

"Not this kind, you're not. It gets to a hundred and twenty in the shade there in the summer, which is now. A hundred and thirty in some places. And the humidity is equally as bad, burn the skin right off you. The woman you'd be replacing is twenty-four and quit after six weeks. Threw in the towel. Too hot, too confining."

"Why'd she go there?" Mary said.

"Entry-level job. Wanted to be a journalist, work her way up."

"How'd she come about getting the job? Just curious."

"Like you, if you take it. Knew somebody."

"Lot of that going around, I guess." Mary said.

"Way the world works."

"Doesn't seem so fair. Does it? Some get all the breaks. Privilege, I guess. I've been accused of it."

"Not about fairness. It's about reality, how the world works. Like how you're going to be able to go to medical school, when most girls of similar qualities and intelligence won't go."

Mary nodded. "Mind if I ask how you got started here?"

"Not at all. You just did. Hadn't been for the fact that my father and his partner started this agency forty years ago, I'd be home now cleaning the house and cooking my husband's dinner." She grinned. "Take your breaks where you can get them, Mary. And don't apologize for them. Especially we women."

Mary nodded again.

"So you want the job?"

"Yes, ma'am, I do."

"Good. You're hired. When can you start?"

"Yesterday."

"Next Tuesday will be fine. There'll be another employee, a woman also, experienced, going over with you. You'll meet in Atlanta for the first leg of your flight. You'll have to have the requisite inoculations before boarding for overseas. And your passport. Can you get them by then? A family doctor, maybe?"

"Yes, I can. And I already have a passport."

Della Myles gave ger the details of her job and trip to Saigon, and had her fill out the necessary forms and papers she had prepared. They small talked some, personal stuff, Mary's plans for med school, family things.

"The staff there will fill you in, get you started. Your duties, safety precautions, where you'll be staying, where you should and shouldn't go, et cetera. Pay attention to them. Your life and health will depend on it. In spite of its cosmopolitan appearance, it's still a war zone and dangerous. People are killed and disappear all the time. Monks burn themselves to death in the streets. Public places are blown up. The power goes off frequently, and you suffer for it. The phones don't always work. Two months ago two women from a European agency there ventured from the city center to the outskirts and disappeared. One turned up on the river bank a few days later, her body tortured. The other has never been found. Women are used as sex slaves for Viet Cong troops in some cases, then disposed of. It's not romantic there. It's a beautiful country and people who're caught in the middle of a hate-filled war that's turned the place into a special kind of hell.

"There are thirteen people in our Saigon bureau," Della said further. "Four are Vietnamese native interpreters. We don't go anywhere on assignment without them. Not your worry. They're considered traitors by the Viet Cong and the North, and their days are numbered. And they know it. If they live too long, it's because they're communist sympathizers and spies. Listen to your coworkers.

"Any questions? You can reach me at this number until you're out of the country. And don't be ashamed to turn down the job. It's okay to change your mind. It's not for everybody. Just call."

Mary rose from her chair. "I won't turn down the job, Mrs. Myles. Thank you so much for the opportunity."

"And it's also okay for you to resign and leave there when your boyfriend leaves. We'll get you out of there."

Mary thanked her again and left.

Wait till the family hears this.

38

They heard it Saturday night at the yacht club. Lanny was giving up his post as commander of the fleet to a younger man. An excuse for having a party and dinner, as clubs go. Semi-formal, no princesses or penguins. Summer dresses and blazers, no ties or socks. Well, it's the South. Large round tables for whole families, a view of the river and the yachts near sunset. Monogrammed polo shirts for the wait staff. Food and booze. The din of conversation and soft music by a live band. Clinking of glass, tableware and china. A happy environment. The Poythresses and Reedlaws, Charles and Kate and kids, together. The kids at their own little tables to the side. Start them early in the life.

Mary wondered if she should break the news now, with all this protection around here, or wait till later at home and suffer the full force of Rene's wrath with no cool-down time. Being in public, even private public, had its advantages, she supposed. So she went for it between the entrée and dessert, and a couple glasses of wine for a courage booster. It did not come without some feeling of guilt, some sense of betrayal, but it had to be done. And the wine made it easier.

A family friend, and older woman close to Marie and Rene, stopped by their table to chat briefly. She asked Mary how she was doing in school, how she liked Virginia. When was she coming back to Charleston, all that.

"I'm not going back, Miss Dot," Mary said. Rene's eyes popped open wide. "I've decided to take a break from school for a while, maybe a year. I have a job I'm starting next week."

"Oh, really? What will you be doing?" Dot said.

Charles froze. Oh, no.

Mary said, "I was just about to tell Momma and Daddy and Grandma. But since you asked. I have a friend at school whose father has an import-export business. She and I will be working together traveling and acquiring goods for sale for her father's company. A dream job, really. Shopping."

Charles deflated.

Rene stared.

Miss Dot said, "How exciting. Can I go too?" They laughed.

Rene and Marie looked at one another. Lanny wasn't paying attention, but was talking to someone at the next table. Charles was looking all over the place, happy to have dodged the bullet, at least for the time.

When Dot was gone, Marie leaned over to Mary and said, "You'll have to explain all this when we get home, you know. You're full of surprises these days, baby. I'm not sure if that's good or bad. But I'm with you. Till I'm not."

"Everyone will know everything before I leave," Mary said, smiling. "It's not as bad as you think, Grandma."

"We'll see," Marie said. "Every mystery is suspect until it's explained. And when will that be, your leaving?"

"Late Monday, early Tuesday. Meeting her in Atlanta." Well, it wasn't all a lie.

"My god, you just got here."

"Opportunity calls."

"Maybe it got the wrong number," Marie said.

Rene didn't want to get into all this at the club. She waited till they were home, then went into Mary's bedroom, the way she always did when wanting a private talk and others were in the house. She leaned on the doorjamb, arms crossed.

"You spend your life raising a child to do the right thing, sacrifice opportunities of your own for her benefit. Things seem to be going so well. Then she does a one-eighty on you, and your life is upside down."

"A little melodramatic, Momma. I was going to tell you tonight."

"I'm your mother. We're your family, but Dot Fowler gets the news before we do. Just what is this job thing? Who is this friend of yours? Who's her father? What's the name and location of his business? Something's not right here, Mary. What gives?"

"I do have a job I'm starting next week. And I'll be traveling to it. But it's not shopping"

"What are you talking about?" She came closer inside.

"I have a job with a company in Vietnam. Working in an office."

"What?"

"Yes. In Saigon. It's safe. I'll be coming back when Will rotates back home next year. It's just for when he's there."

"Are you crazy? What company? Who would hire a young woman like you with no experience to go to a place like that? You have school. We have a wedding to plan together. A life."

"We can do all that when I get back. But I'll tell you, Momma, that's where he is, and that's where I'm going. And nothing is going to stop me."

"What company?"

Mary lied to protect Charles. "It's a private news agency out of D.C. They were recruiting on campus this last semester. An entry-level job." Well, didn't lie much.

Rene was angry. "Charles. It's Charles. He did this."

"No, Charles doesn't know anything about this. I haven't told him and Kate."

"If I find he has anything to do with it—."

"He doesn't, Momma. I'm telling you. Don't you think I'm capable of finding a job on my own?"

"I don't believe it. People don't hire other people with no experience and send them to the other side of the world, even to a hell hole like Vietnam. You have to know somebody. Who is it you know in that business but Charles?"

"Nobody. I did it myself."

"I don't believe it."

"Your lack of belief is not stopping me."

"Vietnam, for God's sake. You have any idea what's going on over there? You read the news? You watch television?"

"Don't insult my intelligence, Momma."

Rene sat on the edge of the bed. She seemed subdued, maybe even defeated. But probably not.

"And what does Will think about all this?"

"He doesn't want me over there. And he doesn't know for sure I'm coming. But I told him I would be."

"That's the first smart thing I've heard you say about him."

"That's an insult, and you know it. I resent that. Stop, please."

"What have we done, Mary? What have I done to make you leave us like this?"

"I'm not leaving anyone, Momma. I'm going to him. I made a promise to him that he'd never go anywhere in this world without me. And I meant it. He'll be almost as surprised as you. There's no guarantee I'll even be able to see him. But just being closer is good enough for me."

"I don't quite understand that."

"Maybe your love for Daddy isn't the same as mine is for Will."

"And just what's that supposed to mean?"

"That's a question you have to answer for yourself, Momma. And if you have to ask it, you probably don't understand it."

"Oh, the child teaching the mother again."

Mary didn't respond.

Rene said, "I'll tell you, there must be something about Will besides good looks that makes you act like this. You've always had your pick of the best-looking boys in the world."

"It's called love, Momma. You should know that. He feels the same way about me. Some things are simple but unexplainable. I'm happy. I only wish you could be happy for me."

"One part of me is, Mary. The other part worries. We've worked so hard together toward your dream."

"More like your dream, my goal, Momma. And we'll both get there, like I said. I promise."

Rene stood from the bed. "I'm going downstairs, on the porch, to smoke a cigarette. You can tell your daddy and grandma all this at breakfast in the morning. Goodnight."

39

The morning Mary left home for the airport in North Charleston, Rene buckled. She could not take her there. She couldn't watch her daughter get on that plane and fly out of her life and watchful eye into a violent world and unknown fate. It was only the second time Mary had seen her that way. The first was when her younger brother had died and Rene fell to pieces like a jigsaw puzzle. She'd be damned if she'd witness another child leave her life. So Lanny would drive her there.

Marie pulled her to the side before she left the house with just one suitcase and a carryon bag. "My dear baby," she said, "write often and call when you want. Collect, day or night. I watched you take your first step. It was only this far." She held up her index finger and thumb two inches apart. "Now you're taking one to the other side of the world. I know you're following your heart, but God also gave you a brain and good sense. Don't be afraid to use them. Come back safe and sound. Both of you. We have a lot to do that requires your presence. This family is not complete without you."

At the airport Lanny was near tears but tried to hide it with light conversation. Lanny knew about war zones. And Mary also knew him.

"It's okay, Daddy. It's going to be alright." She also almost lost it. She hugged him and hurried to board. She sat and looked out the window as he waved back at her and watched the plane leave with his little girl.

Margaret Noland, Marge she was called, was Mary's travel partner for the trip over. Stops in Atlanta, where the two met. Then California, Hawaii, and Vietnam together. She was a veteran foreign correspondent returning to Saigon from vacation. Early forties, slender, pretty. Age lines around her eyes and mouth. Bright green eyes and a presence that probably got her hired by Della's father years before. She also liked a drink or two whenever she could get them, though she was no lush. She just didn't have much of a private life, married to the news. She sipped a couple one-jigger bottles with coke as they crossed the country.

"I started traveling on the job at twenty-three, shortly after college," Marge said. "Haven't stopped yet. Wouldn't know what to do. Being still kills me."

"No husband or boyfriend?" Mary said.

"Lots of boyfriends. Lots of husbands, too, but not mine. Don't be shocked. Sex and infidelity are givens in this business, you'll see. I've seen the noblest and best of them last no longer than six months, then jump in the sack. What do you expect? They're only human. Loneliness is the biggest enemy, so quench it. Nobody's hurt, nobody's the wiser. Simple as that."

"Seems so loose, so brutal. So savage."

"So human. You haven't seen savage yet. Believe me, it's different than human.

"And just a little forewarning, since we're on the subject. Alex Knight, our bureau chief and your boss, is a hound with a sense of entitlement. And when he sees you, he'll salivate. He'll be persistent, if subtle, wait for you to come around and give it up."

"He can wait till hell freezes over," Mary said. This was the first curve in an otherwise straight road. Always something.

"You'll room with me to start with. The company pays the rent. If you want a place of your own, you can pay for it, but it's not recommended. It's safer together. All the press people stay close in an enclave, a three-block radius of the office. Della fill you in on all this?"

"Some, not all. She never said anything about Alex Knight, except that he was a first-rate reporter and good person to work for. She just didn't mention the hound part."

But Mary mentioned it to Pam in a letter the following week, and for an instant I thought she might be referring to me. A little guilt slipping in, maybe.

"She might not know. Nobody has ever complained or quit because of it, that I've heard. Like I said, it's a given. But Della is a good person to work for. If she got a complaint, she'd move him out of there fast. And that would break his heart to be put in some place with no news. Vietnam is the world's biggest story now. The only story. The Cold War doesn't compare, because it has no action. The action is where we're going to be tomorrow."

"My soul purpose for going there is to be close to Will. Nothing else matters to me. I'll do anything reasonable for my job, but I will not sleep with the boss or anyone else."

Marge patted her hand. "Stay close to me when I'm in town. Stay with the other women when I'm not. There are two other American women and a local Vietnamese national who's a clerk. You'll be fine, long as you follow safety precautions and don't wonder off. We also associate closely with State Department people, who party and drink a lot. So there's plenty to do and lots of friends to do it with, if that's your cup of tea. You're not alone in this."

"Anybody you know ever get hurt?" Mary said.

"A couple from the community, not killed but injured. One from shrapnel, one from an accident. Both were in the field. You ever hear of Dickey Chapelle?"

"No."

"A photo journalist working with the marines up in Chu Lai a couple years ago. Killed on patrol. She'd been around since World War Two, covered Korea, very well- known and respected. Not something you'll worry about. You won't be going into the field, so don't get any big ideas of visiting your boyfriend. I'm sure Della told you that."

"Yes, but I'm hoping he can get into town sometime."

"Maybe, not impossible. You can send mail, just like from home. It just takes longer, if he's on the move. And our people can deliver messages for you, if they're going to be with his unit. You'll know everything that's going on in the office. But your whole life as long as you're here will take place in a radius of no more than four or five blocks. That's what drove the last girl crazy. She had wanderlust and couldn't wander, so she quit. That and the heat.

"You'll love the food here, by the way," Marge said further. "And the average Vietnamese citizen is very likeable. They're polite, sensitive people, and intelligent and highly adaptable to the horrors going on around them. The people in the countryside, especially, live the same way they've lived for the last ten thousand years. They're just farmers caught in the middle of all this and just want to be left the hell alone. They're being brutalized from both sides now. Sometimes I just want to have an assignment covering the Olympics, you know, so I can be around friendly people who're having fun and not killing one another."

40

I could have applied to law school for my senior year, like Findley did, but it would have been too hard playing ball and studying law too. I wasn't the strongest student, and I wasn't giving up my last year of eligibility. They had a saying about law school here. The first year they scare you to death. The second year they work you to death. And the third year they bore you to death. I didn't need all that while I played ball. I just needed the lighter but full-time load during the fall season. I was on schedule to graduate on time, anyway, and I could defer my Marine Corps obligation for three years while in law school, then do the JAG Corps of the Navy, the Judge Advocate-General, the legal department.

In between officer training at Quantico and summer school, I spent my time working out and playing sandlot touch football with the usual guys from around town. And dating as many girls as I could, including Pam, who was the only one I kept going back to, like some special need or something. Maybe my mother had been on to something about keeping her in my life. How noble of me. We'd been together six years, since tenth grade, like I said. Or she had, as Shelley would say, in fact, did say. Shelley was a clear thinker.

Will and Mary stayed in touch with us. Will wrote, though not often, understandably. But Mary wrote Pam and me, mostly through Pam, though. It was a girl thing. Mary explained to Pam how it was in Saigon and what she could see and learn of Vietnam, in general. The crowded city. The heat and humidity that almost stole her breath when she landed there. The cramped but adequate living conditions, no doors in the inside, just curtains in the apartment she shared with Marge Noland, who spent more time on assignments around town and in the countryside than at the office and at home.

Mary loved the job, in spite of the conditions. She and others sweated like crazy because of poor air conditioning, the only relief from the occasional breeze through the windows and the helicopter-like whooping and squeaking sound of the overhead paddle fans. She was fascinated at being in the middle of every big story going out of the war zone. Reading and sending reports via teletype and phone from the field reporters. Most of the news was sad and political. Getting it before the rest of the world, like an insider. Witnessing and transmitting interviews and photos with American and South Vietnamese officials and military leaders with names like General William Westmoreland, Nguyen Cao Ky, Nguyen Van Thieu, General Duong "Big" Minh, U.S. cabinet Secretaries McNamara and Rusk, and others.

Mary further described the city as hectic, cramped with people, almost one-point-eight-million, smells of food and sewerage, little food and bric-a-brac stalls and shops, one-food-only street vendors squatting and offering noodles, beans and rice, tents and awnings over most. Hanging laundry up and down the side streets. And the ever-present Vietnamese army police checking citizens and making arrests of V.C. suspects in some cases. And the heavy traffic of cars, trucks, motor scooters, peddle bikes, and rickshaws everywhere. It was all high drama to her, she explained, far from the tranquility and safety of Charleston and Williamsburg, or anywhere in the states. She was saying "states" a lot now in her letters, becoming more worldly. In fact, she said, Marge began taking her with her on local and nearby assignments, using her as a photographer, teaching her to take pictures and using the lenses, while Marge did the talking.

"Never surprise a subject up close, especially military and police," Marge said, "without their knowledge or permission, unless they're part of a large crowd doing the same thing in public. If they don't understand what you're doing or who you are, they might react defensively. And that means offensively. And particularly marines who're armed. They're not like most Army people who work in large groups. The Army uses intelligence reports to locate the enemy, then overwhelms them with troops and arms to destroy them. Marines work mostly in small numbers, like fire teams and squads, just a few guys, with or without intelligence reports They don't give a shit. They're used to beating the bushes, as they say, and walking into ambushes in order to make contact with the V.C. They're jumpy and trigger happy. You point something at them they don't understand, and you're going to get greased."

"Greased?" Mary had said.

"Yes. Killed. Or 'zapped' as they sometimes call it."

That was sobering.

But Mary worried about Will more than anything, even her own safety. She sought every opportunity, spoke to every contact about him, how she might reach him. He was an ordinary soldier in the scheme of things and moved around a lot, almost constantly in combat somewhere on some level, so it was difficult, and not always in Long Binh, but maybe a hundred miles or more out in the countryside.

Until one day six weeks after she arrived, when she received a hand-written message delivered by an Army Intelligence officer, a major, stationed just two blocks away from her. He'd been in the field and met Will at a unit briefing and agreed to hand-deliver his note to Mary at her office. The private, sealed message read, *I will be in the city on Army business next Thursday a.m. Staying overnight. Leaving Friday early afternoon. We can be together Thursday 2 p.m. to Friday 11 a.m. I will come by your office. You just wait, Hugo. You ain't seen nothing yet. Love. Will.*

It was all she could think about. Her job was only a side track in her mind now.

Military Intelligence had a large contingent of people in Saigon and wanted junior combat officers from nearby bases in attendance at a class in town, to learn the finer techniques of gathering and reporting information from captives and villagers while in the field. It would be like a holiday, far as these young officers were concerned, a chance to get away from the harsh conditions and have regular baths and showers, maybe even a massage, decent meals in restaurants, a little recreation, if only for a day. Training for R & R, they called it, which would come later in their tours. The military, especially the Army and Air Force, loved to take breaks as much as work. Not so much the marines, so they weren't invited. They worked differently, as Marge had said. A more hands-on approach, up close and personal. Mary mentioned this to Pam in a letter and suggested I avoid this side of the Marine Corps, if hostilities were still going on when I went in after graduation. I was ahead of her there as a future law student.

But Mary couldn't stop being Mary either. She loved children, particularly those disadvantaged in some way, like she did with Steven and others at the hospital back home in Newport News. And she found an outlet for this passion, if you could call it that, volunteering at a local orphanage three blocks from her office and apartment. Over fifty children ages new-born-to-twelve, but most on the younger side. Traumatized by war, some missing limbs, or blind, or speechless, even catatonic. But all needing the human touch, literally. And Mary was right for the job. All of this she was experiencing in just the last few weeks was a reminder of how fortunate some of us were. And she would take every opportunity presented, for the rest of her life, to enlighten the unaware and insensitive.

But on this Thursday, she sat at her desk doing her job and watched the door like a sentry. She'd already arranged to be off while Will was in town. Finally, unable to sit still, she got up and went downstairs to the main doorway of the building and waited, like a school girl waiting for the parade. She spotted him as he rounded a corner and walked her way. He was in khaki uniform, as required, was tanned and at least ten pounds lighter. She ran to him and they grabbed one another like they were melding into one body. They stood there on the street, clenched for the longest time. Then they held hands and walked to her apartment, almost speechless, just wanting to get into one another. She led him through the short alleyway and up the steps to the apartment on the second floor. The heat of Saigon in the summer was like a polar cap next to the heat they generated the next three hours.

They lay together recuperating as they usually did after these episodes. Mary told Pam in her letter, without revealing details, of course, that it was the most gratifying experience either of them had ever had in their lives, like being welcomed into Heaven from a life of hell.

When Will asked her about the job and how she liked it and got along with her coworkers, Mary left out the part of how Alex Knight, her boss, just as Marge had warned, was coming on to her like he expected her to fold any day now. How he'd asked her to dinner and a "night out, " his "apartment for drinks" only the day before. How she was feeling the pressure on her, and his not understanding why it was taking so long with her. "You have to have somebody," he'd said. "Might as well be someone close who cares about you and shares your situation." That's what he'd said. His behavior at first was understandably masculine—so what else is new—but was now bordering on sleazy as his frustration grew. But Will was not going to hear that from her. It's the last thing he'd need when he left to go back to the field. And the last thing Alex would need from Will. That wouldn't have been good at all. Men were not diplomatic that way when it came to women, she knew.

That evening, just before sunset, they went to dinner on the top floor veranda at one of the finer hotel restaurants in the city popular to foreigners, especially westerners and other English speakers. Mary wore a light skirt and sandals, sleeveless shell, a touch of jewelry only, a small purse on a chain around her waist.

No makeup. She didn't need it. They talked and ate and looked at one another as it grew darker, the lights glittering over the cityscape. They caught up on family and friends and news from home. Mary probed for details of life in the field, since she was becoming quite the reporter now, always curious. But Will was reluctant to get into details. When she brought up the matter, his face and attention went to another place, so she stopped doing it. All he would say was, "The things that go on out there. We can talk about it another time, maybe when we get back home." Then his voice would trail off.

"By the way," Mary said, "Kenny Miklos is over this way, in Australia, according to Shelley's last letter." This way," another worldly expression. "They're together now. Can you imagine that? He contacted her when he got to Montreal, with the info I gave him. They went to lunch and have been together since. Sharing an apartment near the university. Says they're practically engaged. He's about to leave there for Danang. Stop by my office here when he reaches this far."

"Grief. That is surprising. I'm trying to visualize it now. Linebacker mates with elf." He laughed.

"He got a job with a wire service, kind of like I did. On his way up here soon, she says."

Then Mary said, "My family wants a second chance with you, Will. They're so sorry for the impression they gave. They really mean it. They want to welcome you into the family, the way it's suppose to be."

"But not your mother. Tell me the truth. Not your mother."

Mary hesitated. "It was daddy and Grandma who said it. Momma never said anything. But I know she's in agreement with them. She has no choice."

Will stared back at her. "But she does have a choice. She doesn't have to like or accept me. We can't break her arm so she'll like me."

"I'm not pushing, baby. Just think about it when you're back home."

"I'll consider anything for you. But no promise of outcome."

"Good enough. I love you for it."

"You love me anyway."

"Yes, I do, you rat."

"Speaking of engagements, I'm saving up to get you another engagement ring when we get home. A better one."

"I'm never taking this ring off. There's not a better one."

"Then you'll have an extra one. Your allotment is coming to you every month, I guess."

"Yes. No problem there. We all use the bank here."

"But your coworkers don't know you're married. Do they?"

"No."

"The guys were telling me about a nightclub here in town that's civilized, a tamer crowd. State Department types and all. *Flags*, it's called," Will said. "We can go there when we're finished here. Take a cab. Ever hear of it?"

"Heard of it is all. I spend my spare time at the orphanage. I also might be able to volunteer at the hospital here that serves American civilians."

"Can't keep you out of the lab. Can we?" Will said, grinning.

Mary returned a knowing smile.

Will said, "I'll never forget how you looked from behind when I walked into Steven's room that first time. The perfect valentine." He laughed, his face a bit red.

"You rat, again. And I'll never forget that time you pushed Steven up Richmond Road to Jockstrap Corner and Duke of Gloucester, almost killing a few people. Tourist bowling, you and Doc called it. The fun Steven was having for the first time in who knows when. How breathless he was, and how he clutched that football. I knew right then you were a keeper."

"And before that how did you feel?"

"You were just another conceited, immature jock. That's still the other half of you."

"Ah. So it wasn't love at first sight, like it was with me." He was ribbing her.

"No, it wasn't."

"Couldn't have been that bad. How fast we grow up. I think."
He looked at her. "I love you so much, Hugo. Let's eat up and go
to the club."

"That's a date, William."

41

Flags was noisy but civil enough, as Will had been told. Live band of dubious pedigree. Strobe lights flashing, more people dancing than not. Drinks flying. Conversations competing with music. But people happy, it seemed. A good crowd but not jam packed. They had a small bistro table to themselves off to the side.

"This place reminds me of the Peppermint," Mary said of the Virginia Beach club.

"But without the beach out back." Will said.

All the Americans there made the place look like a college preppy party.

Within minutes they'd joined two other couples, American and Australian medical and foreign service people, by pulling their little tables together. They talked, when they could hear one another, and danced on occasions. Mary was right at home with their medical subject matter, though they were conscious to go easy on the shop talk. Will's mind seemed to drift as he drank more, though he was far from drunk. Mostly, he looked into his glass, twisting it slowly, then squeezing it hard until it broke and splattered the table. It embarrassed him. Well, they were cheap glasses.

"Sorry. Let me clean this up," Will said, but a waitress took care of it.

"Maybe we should go," Mary said. "You seem wound up tight. You're tired."

Will nodded. They said their goodbyes to the other couples and left. They caught a beat-up old taxi that sputtered and gear-ground its way along the street to Mary's place.

Will wasn't really drunk, as he explained the incident to me in a letter a while later. It's just that when he loosened up, all that bad experience in the field jumped in front of him like a drive-in movie screen, and he saw himself in it, even around camp at the club among other soldiers. He hadn't done anything in the field to be ashamed or guilty of, personally, but being in this country the way he was had its own price. And he'd be damned glad when he left for home in the "world" again.

Will and Mary showered to get the sweat and smell of the club and the city off them, then went to bed, to their own little world of comfort, closeness, passion and peace, an escape from the foreign strangeness as much as a need to be home and normal again, where they belonged. The next day they had lunch together at a restaurant nearby, and he walked her to her office, where he met a number of her co-workers. The place was spartan and busy. Maps all over the place, bland walls from another period, typewriters and teletype machines, old wooden and metal desks and cabinets bought used on the local market. But the spirit of the place was high. Everybody wanted to be there for one reason or another. It seemed odd to Will that he and every G.I. he knew would fight one another for a seat on the next plane out of this place, but the press people would have to be threatened to get them aboard the same flight. Well, they were reporting the war, not fighting it.

They took longer to separate this time than when he'd arrived the previous day, and he promised to find a way to get back, though he preferred that she leave and go back home to her family and routine. No way, not until he left.

That night Mary was alone and had just bathed. Marge was still out somewhere, an interview with somebody at military headquarters not that far away. She dried and wrapped a thin gown around her and combed at her wet hair, which was drying quickly.

There was a knock at the door. It was Alex Knight, her boss and bureau chief. He was dressed in his usual style, only the colors changing, this time gray slacks, black polo shirt, topsiders. He looked the part of the yacht club type. Mary knew the kind. She'd been around them all her life. And he was drunk, an unopened bottle in his hand, like a key to enter.

"Aren't you going to invite me in?" Alex said. He grinned, his face flush red.

"No, I'm not, Alex. Please leave. I'll call a taxi, if you want. I'm tired. I don't want company."

"I don't need a taxi. I live as close to the office as you do. What in hell would I do with a taxi?"

"Ride it home."

"I don't want a taxi. I want you. You know that. Why do you keep playing these games, torturing me like this? Playing so damn hard to get?"

"I'm not playing. I'm impossible to get. And you're not getting in here. Now leave. Please."

He grabbed at the screen door handle, and she jerked it back from him.

"Let's just talk about it," he said. "We have more in common that you want to admit. I'm not a bad person. You know that. You know I'm easy to work for, work with. Come on, open up. Let's have a drink." He yanked the door handle again, harder this time.

Mary pushed out even harder and knocked Alex off balance. He fell backward against the rail. She stepped out and slapped at him and pushed him hard. He bounced off the rail again and tilted and went head first rolling down the steps. They were wood, not metal, so it could have been worse. Not that she cared at the moment.

He moaned and groaned, and yelped like a wounded puppy at the bottom. "Oh, Jesus. Oh, God," he said. If she hadn't known better, she'd have thought him to be religious.

The rain began after a break and Alex was soaking fast, the blood trickling from his minor wounds.

Mary was stunned by what she did, but relieved even more so. So long, job. "I'll call you a cab," she said. "I hope you're not hurt bad, but you're leaving."

"Oh, jeeze. You bitch. My shoulder. Oh, jeeze." He just couldn't shut up about his shoulder.

Mary told Pam in her next letter that she was glad Alex wasn't seriously injured, but that it felt so good and liberating when she knocked him on his sorry ass.

Marge came around the corner into the alley with her equipment bag and saw Alex there, and Mary at the top of the steps, on the landing. "What the hell," she said. "Alex?" She put down her gear and helped him up. Water dripped from her and her gear.

Mary told her what happened.

"Ah, shit," Alex kept saying, grabbing at his shoulder. Some people are just shoulder guys.

"Let's go home," Marge said. "Stand up." She helped him walk out of the alley to the street. "Lock up tight. I'll be back shortly," she told Mary.

Alex skipped work the next day with a hangover and dislocated shoulder, and several cuts and bruises on his face and arms, for which he sought medical treatment.

And the day after that, after Marge informed Della Myles of the incident, Alex was on a flight out of Saigon and the war zone to some god-forsaken place of little or no news on the other side of the world.

42

Marge Noland was temporary bureau chief until Della Myles could fly in a replacement for Alex Knight, which wouldn't take long because every news hound in the world would die for the job. Then she could get back out of the office, the way she liked it. Her tiny suite had a private bathroom, a ditty left over from the French occupation, and a view of the street, not much different than the outer office, but smaller and with the bathroom. And a lot more time to gaze out the window.

Three days after Will went back to the field, and a day after Alex left, Marge opened her door and motioned for Mary to come in and close it behind her. She handed Mary the phone. "It's Will," she said.

"What?" Mary said. "You're kidding." She took it, and Marge left her alone.

"Surprise," Will said. It wasn't the clearest connection, but it did the trick.

They exchanged I-love-yous. Then Mary said, "How'd you do this?"

"Marvel of Twentieth Century technology. Our battalion radioman has a prick-ten, it's called, a PRC-Ten. It's how we communicate in the field. It's a strong radio. He called a guy at an Australian military base who patched him through to the phone company in Saigon.

And the operator there put him through to your office. But I can't stay on the line long. It's against regulations."

"When can you come back to town?"

"I don't know. Maybe not at all. But I might be able to sneak in a call like this time-to-time. We had a private talking to his mother back home in Michigan this morning."

"Can't you think of a reason for coming here?" Mary said.

"Hell, yes, you know what that is. But the Army doesn't care about my reasons, Hugo."

"Maybe a dental exam or something."

"Never fly. We have field hospitals with dentists, doctors, medics, nurses, the works."

"Stay away from the nurses, William."

"Loud and clear on that. I have eyes only for you. There are no other women in the world."

"Then we're in trouble and I'm going to be very busy."

"You know, you're getting to be real slick and quick-witted. I think you and Pam need to team up when we get back. Doc and I will be your agents and we'll get rich, go on the Carson show."

"You're nuts."

"Kind of."

"You rebel, you."

"Got news for you," Will said. "Guess who's in country now as a journalist. Don't mention any names. The signal can be picked up."

"Oh, you're kidding. You mean a certain frat guy and lineman we both know?"

"You got it. The one and only."

"That was quick. He was supposed to be in Sydney."

"He said he would, so he did. And he's here in Long Binh now. He'll drop in if he can get up over that way. It's only sixteen miles, and civilian journalists can move around with more freedom than we can. They don't have bosses standing over them. Pam and Doc already know it, of course. He told me. I can't say anything here. Keep it to yourself.

"Look," Will said, "I've got to get off. I'll call again, maybe in a few days. We'll be back in the bush a while. Too busy and quiet and unsafe to talk then. Got to go now. I love you, Hugo."

"Stay safe. That's an order, Lieutenant." She sat there at Marge's desk a bit longer in an emotional state between laughing and crying. Nuts. She'd be so glad when they were both back home.

Mary got letters from her family frequently. Her father, Lanny, had arranged through his friend for her to have a place still open in medical school when she returned and finished her last semester of undergrad, long as she didn't stay away more than a year. God forbid. But all that seemed like a million miles away now. The reality and certainty of a normal life again had become a pipe dream. The world and life in it had so many distractions to deal with. Her mother's dream for her, Rene's dream, was waffling.

Mary went to her desk and did her job and simultaneously wrote letters home, and to Shelley and Pam, among others. She asked details about Kenny Miklos being in country now, how it happened.

Shelley wrote back what Miklos had written to Dicky Humphrey, his former roommate now rooming with Alvin Findley. Story was, Miklos got to Montreal and connected with his old high school buddy, who connected him with an acquaintance who had a sideline business dealing in forged papers, I.D.s and the like, for a fee. Presto. Miklos was now Milo Stewart, Canadian-born journalist with a birth certificate, driver license, passport, school history, the works. He got a job with a wire service, where he was in the office long enough to be evaluated and trusted, then sent to their office in Sidney, Australia, for some local stuff, and from there to Vietnam, both North and South, to get anything he could regarding the war. Hopefully, without being shot as a spy by either side. Miklos was now in his element, living his dream. And he'd hook up with Will and Mary when and if he could. Just don't blow his cover. He was still a draft dodger

Mary worked a couple hours late that night, along with Marge.

"Let's go down to Nguyen's, get something to eat," Marge said. "Then all I want to do is come back and clean up and go to sleep."

Nguyen's was a popular little restaurant a couple blocks away that did a good job simulating western cuisine. They sat close to the street to catch an almost breeze that escaped from somewhere to cool things down a bit.

"Girls in the office say I missed it when I wasn't there to meet Will," Marge said.

"They would." Mary grinned. "You know, I couldn't stand him when I first met him. Obnoxious, conceited jock. Like every girl in the world owed it to him, like a birth right or something. I wanted to smack is head off."

"Because that's the way it'd always been for him."

"Yes, according to Shelley, my roommate, who knew him."

"Then it changed."

"Yes, but not right away. He just kept coming back. Becoming more human. More, I don't know, more normal, I guess you'd say. So cute." She smiled.

"Does it every time," Marge said.

"Nobody special for you? Must be somebody."

"There is. But he's married. A lieutenant colonel in the Air Force. He's not happy in his marriage, and neither am I. But he isn't mine, either, and probably never will be. So I'm seeing another married man, from Army Intelligence, down the street from us. A master sergeant. That's life. I chose mine. It's lonely and painful at times, but I'd do it all over again. I love this work. I'd die if I couldn't do it. The thought of doing a normal eight-to-five job, or being home-bound with a house full of kids, would drive me straight up a wall."

They talked and ate and drank the wine. The lights glittered along the street as it got dark. The avenue became less populated. Many here did not trust the night. The Viet Cong were everywhere, and you could never tell who they were or when they might strike. The previous week, on the other side of town, they'd set off a bomb that killed and maimed several civilians who were dining, just like they were now.

Marge said, "Will's unit is moving out for the high country soon. Keep it to yourself. I'm not supposed to know that."

"And how do you?"

"My friend in Army Intelligence. I'm a reporter first, you know."

"Is that necessarily bad, his moving out?"

"It's not good. It means they've located an enemy force in large enough numbers to go way out there and confront them. That means combat. And that means somebody gets hurt. Maybe many. Assuming the enemy is still there. They're slick as eels. Not saying it to worry you."

"A great bedtime story to help me sleep."

"You're a big girl, and he's your man. I'd feel awfully bad if I didn't say anything. His heart is yours. You have a right to know where it is, the way I see it. You just didn't hear it from me. Leaking that kind of information can get somebody in a shitload of trouble. People go to federal prison for less."

"It'd be worse if I was surprised by something bad. So I appreciate it."

"You would've known anyway, when they moved out. Even the Army can't hide that many people stumbling all over the place."

"So where is Alex going?" Mary said.

"To see Della first, and get laced down, like he deserves. Then sent to some dull place a while so he gets the point. He's too good at this to be destroyed or fired. He'd just land on his feet with some other agency. He's very well known. If he hadn't been drunk when he went down those steps, he'd be in bad shape or dead now. But because he was drunk, he was only slightly hurt. It's hard to kill a drunk like that. Too limber, like a noodle."

They talked on about life and work and things, in general.

"So you want children with this guy?" Marge said. She grinned.

"Yeah. Someday, after all the schooling. I want two. Will wants a house full, his own football team."

Mary thought about it and the need to confess. "I have to tell you something," she said.

"Sure."

"Will and I are already married. Please don't tell anybody."

"I won't. But I kind of figured it."

"How?"

"Just a feeling. Your body language, mannerisms. You just don't want him. You already have him. It shows."

"Perceptive. Della doesn't know that. I lied in the interview with her. Or withheld it. Same thing, lied by omission."

"Wouldn't have made a difference, I don't think. Lots of married people in this business. I sleep with my share of them. Who's the beneficiary on your company insurance policy?"

"Will."

"Then she knows. Don't worry about it."

"I just hope that's something neither of us benefits from."

"I'm with you on that. Drink up."

43

Much like Vietnam, the heat and humidity in Tidewater, Virginia, is no picnic in summer either. It didn't get to a hundred and fifteen-or-twenty degrees, but it was sweltering in the salty air, and the moisture stuck to you like glue. At the two-a-day football practices it was important to keep moving to make it harder for the gnats and mosquitos to get through the sweat to the flesh.

We had our usual pre-season scrimmage game with Apprentice School on our home field and didn't do so well. It was the absence of Will and Kenny Miklos. We could tell the difference, the whole team could, especially Turnbull, our quarterback. Their replacements were good, but not as experienced. It was a strange feeling for me. It was the first time since second grade that I'd played a sport without Will being right there, like a twin brother. Our first game was two weeks away and we were going to have a hard time against Furman down in South Carolina, where everybody played hard-knuckle ball. Our new coach had been an assistant at Navy, and this was his first test as a head coach. We wanted to win as much for him as ourselves.

But with all that was going on in the world and the country, the war, the peace movement, anti-government sentiment, women's liberation, the civil rights explosion, it all detracted from and distorted the happy-village life we'd come to enjoy and expect. The world was bass ackward and upside down. News was becoming more than entertainment. A larger view of the world was evolving for our generation of yearlings, and the obit section of the paper was even more popular than the funnies. It was the first time in our history as a nation that we were engaged in a conflict with a country most of us couldn't find on a map.

Aunt Evie was just down the boulevard in the hospital as a patient for the first time in her life since birth, with the same view of the river we had at home. It was the booze catching up with her, the cirrhosis developing. She'd spent all those years hiding in a bottle from the pain of losing the love of her life in the big war. Until now she'd handled it so well, a functional alcoholic. She'd be there a week or two before coming home. It was amazing how someone could be so sensitive and devastated by something she could not recover from.

It was an odd feeling entering the house Saturday afternoon after morning football practice back at school. The quietness was noticeable, like its own noise. No smell of fresh food from the kitchen. No clinking of glass and ice and booze. I'd gotten the message a couple hours earlier, a call from Will's mother, Martha Lynn, who'd driven Aunt Evie to the hospital and gotten her checked in. I picked up Pam and we went there.

Pam always liked Aunt Evie and spent more time with her than I did, it seemed. She was fascinated by the stories from the old days, when Aunt Evie was a teenager, then a newly-married wife of a naval aviator, madly in love and so full of life. The friends, the parties, the never-ending thrill of her husband's company. Never a dull moment. And it made her feel so good when Pam would steer her to the subject of all this and she could talk about and relive it, before becoming incoherent and falling asleep. I think they were both die-hard romantics. And I think I envied them at the time because they could enjoy those kinds of relationships without fear or restraint, something that escaped me.

We were by Aunt Evie's bedside. She looked pretty good after a major dose of vitamins and a nurse's care.

"I'd give anything for a stiff drink right now." She usually didn't say that, just did it, so it had to be bad.

Pam tried to hide a giggle, but not too well.

I said, "No, no, it's why you're here."

"So says you and Bill Thurston," she said of her doctor. "He can drink us all under the table."

"How do you know that?"

"Because I dated him a few times years ago, after he and his first wife divorced. He's a lush."

"So you didn't hit it off?" Pam said.

"He drank too much."

Pam and I laughed. Aunt Evie thought it a perfectly reasonable statement, and raised an eyebrow.

"It wouldn't have worked anyway," I said. "Somebody had to do the driving."

"Martha Lynn is worried sick about Will," Aunt Evie said. "He doesn't say much in his letters, so she knows he's keeping something from her. You wouldn't know more about that. Would you? He tell you much?"

"No, I don't get that many letters from him. He has enough letters to write to Mary and his parents. He didn't go overseas to write letters."

"Don't get fresh, L.D. If he writes about anything bad, keep it to yourself. She's got enough to worry about already."

"And that Miklos boy is over there," she said further. "Y'all's football team and fraternity all dropping out and meeting over in Vietnam or something?"

"No, it just seems like it, I guess."

"No Vietnam for you, L.D. You're going to law school next year. You hear that, Pam? You rope him and tie him down if you have to."

Pam liked the sound of that. "Yes, ma'am, I sure will, Miss Evie. I hear you."

"Do Mary's parents know she's married yet?"

"No, and we're keeping it that way."

"Doesn't seem right to keep it from them. Martha Lynn feels bad about it, herself. How's she going to feel when she meets them and looks them in the eye later and they know she knew all along but hid it from them?"

"Not our business," I said. "Besides, they probably already suspect it. Why wouldn't they?"

"Were me," she said, "I'd shout it from the rooftop. Lucky and I were so in love we couldn't have hid it if we'd wanted to. It was all over us. Our life was just so non-stop. So happy. So alive. Our friends were the same way." Her voice trailed off and her eyes teared up. I'd never heard her discuss this before. And I'd never seen her cry. The booze, her "friend," always had been a mood stabilizer. Maybe her illness was telling her things. Maybe venting some of her pain, relishing some of her memories, was a good thing, maybe therapeutic.

What struck me was her husband's name, which I'd heard many times before, of course. Lucky. Ironic for a man who never made it past twenty-two years old, like so many of their generation. Differences in the way we think, I guessed.

"Mail's on the table," Aunt Evie said. "A check from your mother, I think. Some bills. I'll take care of those when I get home. Laundry's done. If you mess up the kitchen, clean it up, please."

"I will. What can we get for you?"

"Nothing. Just a ride home when Bill discharges me."

"Maybe he can discharge both of you at the same time." Being cute.

She and Pam laughed. I'm so clever.

"I'll have to tell him that. Just don't mention it to him yourself."

We chatted a while longer, then left.

Pam and I went directly to my house and upstairs to my bedroom. I threw open the curtains wide to let the afternoon sun spray in and warm us. We stripped down and went at one another like there was no tomorrow, the whole time looking out at the river and the blue sky, the seagulls, the fishing and skiing boats, the sailboats, and the ships in port at Norfolk.

That night several team and frat members stopped by the house for an impromptu party, mostly a BS session, very low key. Dickey Humphrey and Carol Foley, Alvin Findley and his date, a major looker named Harriet Pomeroy from back home in Richmond— Go Findley. She had a sultry voice. You wondered what she saw in a slightly-built, nerdy guy like Alvin, until remembering that his family owned half of Richmond and Henrico County, and that he was bright and even funny when he wanted to be. A girl like Harriet could have anything she wanted from life. She had vision, anyway.

Ooh, Harriet.

Pam gave me the look, but knew I'd never make a move on a friend's girl. "Enjoy the moment, then come back down to earth," she said.

Findley said to me, "I've got fifty bucks on you scoring in the Furman game, Doc. You and Turnbull both. And I'll be there to see it."

"The pressure mounts," I said. "Do I get a cut?"

"You're a gladiator. You just get free beer."

"I work cheap."

Dickey said, "Speranza and Willets got draft notices." They were two frat brothers. "Willets might get by, but Speranza is a goner, I think. Grades stink. Reminds me of Will. Had everything going for him and pissed it away."

I couldn't argue with that, much as I wanted to.

"Anybody ever hear from Mary?" Carol said.

"I do," Pam said. "She loves her job. Got to see Will once for a day and night. And he called her, too, from the field."

"War, with privileges," Findley said. "I don't get this whole crap going on over there."

"Half the country agrees with you," Dickey said.

"And the other half is nuts or not paying attention, or both."

Pam said, "Mary's job is exciting. She's getting out of the office over there and meeting a lot of important people. Taking photos, helping with interviews. Never a dull moment. When she's not doing it, she's writing and sending the reports over the wire. And Will calls occasionally over the field phone. Don't know how that works."

Harriet liked that about Mary's job. She and Carol and Pam went to the kitchen for something to drink, then sat at the dining room table and talked privately.

Dickey said, "Who all's going down to the Furman game, besides us here?"

"We might have to take a head count, this week," Findley said. "If there are enough of us, we can rent a bus and go Friday after class. Party like hell, down and back."

"Those purple Paladins down there are going to eat us alive," Dickey said. "Their whole first team is back this year, and we're playing with half rookies."

"That's the spirit," I said. "It ain't over till it's over."

"*Then* it's over," he said back, and we all laughed.

We drank beer and wine until almost midnight. Just a couple for me. The season, you know. Then Dickey and Carol, and Alvin and Harriet decided to stay over. They used the two spare bedrooms upstairs, while Pam and I stayed in mine. Aunt Evie's was vacant, of course, off limits. Didn't want to intrude or leave any evidence there.

The noise from Alvin and Harriet was distracting and fascinating at the same time for over an hour. They were not quiet lovers, but obviously thoroughly happy ones. It sounded like Barnum and Bailey in there. Go, Alvin. Go, Harriet.

The next morning we had our equivalent of breakfast at the dining room table. Coffee, toast, whatever we could find in the kitchen on our own that was quick and easy.

I got the Sunday paper from the porch, where I heard it hit earlier at about daybreak. I put it on the table. Pam picked it up and went right to the obituaries. People were doing a lot of that those days.

Pam said, "You see this?"

"Not until you give me the paper," I said. "What is it?"

"Blake Conroy, from Warwick, is dead. Vietnam. He was in the Marines. You remember him."

"Of course. Played ball and ran track against him. Used to see him around. Let me see that."

Warwick was one of two high schools in mid-town Newport News, the other being Homer L. Ferguson, just a couple blocks up, near Christopher Newport College of the College of William & Mary. A long name for a small college. That part of town looked like School City.

I read quickly through the obits.

"Good god. What's the world coming to." It was not a real question.

Findley said, "This is what I mean about the crap that's going on over there. All these guys getting killed and shot up. And for what?"

"I used to see his sister at Buckroe," Pam said. That was the local beach in Hampton we hung out at a lot in summers. "God, I can't imagine what her family must be going through. Like Miss Evie said, L.D., you're going to law school first, before the Marine Corps, not after."

"Thank you for the career guidance."

Dickey and Carol, and Alvin and Harriet left before noon to get back to Williamsburg. Harriet had classes in Richmond the next morning. And I'm sure she wanted to go at it again before she left.

Let's hear it for Findley.

44

Letters from Mary to Pam, and from Will to me, the latter less frequently since guys don't write guys that much, discussed their respective experiences on their jobs. Mary's was positive, the excitement of her work, which she enjoyed in spite of living conditions in Saigon. The almost constant rains of the monsoons. Not exactly Charleston or Williamsburg, but not in the field either. Will's work was dangerous. And wet, of course, with the same monsoons. Slush and mud. And his descriptions, the few he gave, were stoic at best. His way of dealing with the possibility of going out into the bush the next time and not coming back, probably. His company and battalion were almost always losing men when engaging the Cong or NVA, the North Vietnamese Army. I sensed he might want to get into more detail but didn't dare. Maybe because discussing things in depth might expose a side of himself he didn't want to look at or hang out with. And not all the danger was from the enemy. Some young lieutenants and captains, most no older than the troops they commanded, often younger, were "fragged" on occasions, he wrote. Lower-ranking soldiers throwing grenades into the living quarters and showers of their leaders, while they slept or bathed in camp, day or night. You had to watch every-damn-body, friend and foe alike. So many of the men were draftees who didn't want to be there in the first place, and hated the people who led them into combat. They'd rather risk life in prison for murder than death in the bush.

Mary sent gifts home to her family in Charleston and to Will's folks, too. Silk clothing items, paintings and jade carvings, games, the latter to Hank, Will's younger brother. What would he do with a painting or jade carving. She explained to Pam that her mother wasn't particularly happy with her satisfaction in her job, that she likely feared it might lead to permanence and away from medicine. Not a chance, Mary said. But through all the correspondence we sensed they both longed for home and normalcy, and to be together as one again. What else.

Will was told he could expect an R & R break around the holiday season of Christmas and New Year. That was months away. He and Mary would go to Hawaii for ten days, including travel time. The military had its own hotel and resort on Waikiki Beach, in Honolulu. It was the major goal of their lives at the time. Will also had me pass along his good luck wishes for the football team, which I did in the locker room at practice. And Mary was exchanging letters with Shelley Michaels in Montreal. She still could hardly believe Shelley and Kenny Miklos were lovers, living together, when he was home anyway. Though she liked both as friends, she couldn't picture it in her brain, and would have to see it form later in her mind, when they met again at a homecoming or something. Life is full of little surprises.

Will's younger brother, Hank, was coming around the house more frequently now. He'd always stopped by a couple times a week, even when Will and I were up at school. Aunt Evie kept refreshments out for him because, she said, growing young boys were eating machines. He was coming by more often now on days after school and weekends, probably missing Will, his hero. And Aunt Evie and I were his closest connection, next to his immediate family. I guessed he kind of adopted me as his surrogate big brother, like channeling through me to Will. Sure, we'll have a séance, Hank, commune with Will's spirit till he gets home.

Hank was developing well, too, as a football player under his father's tutelage. His dad had been an Apprentice School player, as mentioned. Hank was quarterbacking his rec league team and showed promise as a future high schooler. Always the football thing with our bunch. Send us to war, if you want, but if you take away our football, we'll die on the spot. And he was thrilled at taking over the morning paper route in our neighborhood, now that he was big and strong enough to carry the load on the front of his bike. Collecting on Saturday mornings would be the most fun, of course. He was at the age when his whole life was changing. Growing taller, voice changing. Interest in girls. A chronic need for money to support his evolving social and recreational budget. And for buying his own clothes, not something his mother, Martha Lynn, picked out for him. Sure, independence, Hank. Go for it.

Miklos wrote too. He was moving all over South Vietnam, living his dream as a war correspondent, but having to deal with the reality of conditions of weather and human destruction and carnage, something he couldn't have foreseen, except vicariously. He and Will and Mary were way out in front of Pam and me in the life experience thing. They didn't get into a lot of details, as I mentioned, likely because they were the kind shared without judgment among those who also shared the experiences. Besides, Miklos was the only storyteller among them, and you could see his by-line in papers on occasions under his fake name, Milo Stewart. That must have killed him. The strangest irony was that, only a year earlier, we were all much alike, just a bunch of college kids living the life and wondering where the next laugh or minor thrill was coming from.

We lost our season opener in a tight game against Furman. Pam and I and some of the team players, and frat brothers and their dates, had lunch up at the corner Sunday, after getting back into town earlier that morning from South Carolina and catching some sleep in the dorms. We helped crowd up the place, already jammed with tourists and football fans who'd stayed in town overnight. We licked our wounds and ate our pizza, simultaneously. Defeat was easier on a full stomach.

Later, Pam and I went home. Aunt Evie wasn't due out of the hospital for another two or three days. Her condition was a little more serious than thought previously. We stopped there first. She seemed desperate.

"Just get me out of here," she said.

"Two days," I told her. "Three at most, you'll be busted out. I'll have the getaway car ready."

"Martha Lynn is taking me home. You'll be at school. I'm tired of looking at these walls and eating hospital food."

And not having a drink.

"Look at the view," I said.

"I can do that at home. It's the same view."

"We can sneak you in some real food, if you want, and I'll eat your hospital food. Even trade."

"He'll eat anything, Miss Evie," Pam said. "Take him up on it."

"I just want out."

"What does Jimmy Stewart say?" I was referring to her doctor and former boyfriend, who resembled the famous actor a bit, as mentioned.

"Who?"

"That's who he looks like."

"Oh. Yeah. Monday or Tuesday. I'll die before then."

"No dying for you. The Olympics will be here before you know it. You're going immediately into training."

She laughed at that best she could. "Your momma and daddy are missing some goofy moments with you."

"Doesn't faze them."

"I'm sorry I haven't been there to take care of the house, L.D."

"The house is fine. It doesn't have your touch, but it'll get by. And, by the way, have you heard from my glorious parents? Your wonderful brother and sister-in-law?"

"They don't know I'm in here."

"They'd be happy about that."

"Quit, L.D."

"Part of my antagonizing you back to health."

"How do you put up with him, Pam?"

"She needs psychiatric help," I said. "How else?"

"I think it's melancholy," Pam said. "We lost the game yesterday." She'd been at the game and rode the rented bus down and back with some of the other fans.

"Melancholy is a word she picked up in psychology class," I said. "I never understood it, myself. It has a very nebulous definition."

"Bring me the mail next time you're home," Aunt Evie said. "Tomorrow, maybe?"

"Yes. Should've done it when I came. I'll drop it by tonight."

"No need."

"Yes, there is a need. I want you happy and healthy and back home. It's just a house without you, Aunt Evie. Not a home." Sounded like a song I'd heard.

Pam and I left and went down the boulevard to my house, where we went upstairs to my room, once again. Now almost dark, the lights from the ships speckled the harbor in Norfolk. The beam from a large moon splashed over the river and through my bedroom window. Pam and I stripped and tore at one another in our usual, glorious fashion. God, would I ever get enough of this beautiful girl. I often wondered where our hunger came from. But I did not dare challenge it.

45

There was mail on the dining room table that Martha Lynn had collected from the mailbox and put there for us, apparently without glancing at it. One letter was from Will, a brief thing, because he'd just gotten in from the field and cleaned up and had numerous other letters to write, before resting and going out again. His unit had been out for seventeen days and seen no action. Intelligence couldn't guarantee you contact with an enemy who could disappear in the blink of an eye. This was their land. They knew every square foot of it. You were the hapless interloper. He and his men also hadn't had a shower or change of clothes, either, in those seventeen days. But he said he'd come across marines who'd been out for forty-nine days without a shower or change of clothes. Looked like their clothes, literally, had rotted off them and resembled ribbons or streamers or something, like they were nearly naked. They must have smelled like a locker room after practice, he said. They stank so bad, one of them said, that they quit stinking. Like the odor killed itself, or nobody noticed any more, if that made sense.

Pam spent late Sunday with her family in Stuart Gardens, just down the street and over the bridge from the boat basin. She had classes the next day, Monday morning. I stayed home and caught up on some school work. I didn't have a class until the afternoon.

Then the team meeting before practice, where we would go over the specific reasons for losing the game Saturday. Everything except the fact they were better than us, so we lost. And what we were going to do about the next game. Maybe we'd win it and Hank could have a winning game ball.

I woke up late Monday, never a morning person, though my schedule required it of me most days. Life is a toughy. I took a large mug of hot tea out on the front porch and sat in the rocking chair with the paper, enjoying the solitude. Truth is, I think I was always more of an introvert. Or at least one who required a lot of private time to feel sane. Something I got used to over the years, I guessed. I read the sports page first, the coverage for the next game, critiques, and the forecasts for next week for colleges around the country. And a lot of coaches' blah-blah. A jock's dream.

The weather was balmy, at that place between mild and cool. A slight wisp of breeze off the water. Perfectly comfortable for recuperating from the Furman game. The residual soreness would recede that night at practice, when we'd do a lot of running and sweating, but no hitting. Most college teams didn't do any tackling or hard contact hitting but maybe once a week, usually Tuesday or Wednesday, to avoid injuries. Then, Saturdays, they were all hungry for contact. Because almost getting killed was like reminding you that you were alive. Players get hit real hard just once or twice in a high school game, but in college you get your bones and guts rattled on every play. The best players in the country are there, the few thousand among the million or more, who made the cut. So it's fierce.

The call from Hank came when I was in the middle of all this. His voice was desperate and agitated. Hurt. Barely decipherable. He spoke haltingly.

"L.D.," Hank said. He was sobbing hard. "L.D., Will is dead. They killed him, L.D. They shot him."

"*What?*"

"The soldiers came and told my momma a while ago. She called

Daddy at work. He's coming home. L.D., what are we going to do?" He was a wreck.

And I was shocked, still trying to fit his message into my head. "Hold it, buddy," I said. "Say that again. Are you sure?" What a dumb thing to say to him. But I couldn't think of anything else at the time. It hit like lightening. I was otherwise paralyzed. At least Hank was semi-coherent.

"Go to your momma," I told him. "Stay with her. I'm on my way."

I ran to their house, just a few short blocks away. I forgot to drive, probably got there quicker. Martha Lynn was sitting at the dining table sobbing uncontrollably. Hank was hugging her and crying like a baby. All his current growing up seemed to have regressed, like he was going straight back to infancy, so totally helpless. I had no idea what to do and was dealing with my own emotions. But I had to act strong, even if I wasn't. I was like a family member, having spent so much time with them over the years. I was not going to be a stranger now, while also not sticking my nose into their most private business. I didn't ask for the painful details of the news.

Will's father arrived and hugged his wife and son. His eyes were welled up. You don't often see a grown man cry like that in a lifetime, especially a tough guy like him. You want to help but you can't, and feel kind of stupid and out of place. So the best thing to do is exit and leave them to grieve as a family. I hugged Martha Lynn and Hank and Mister Wythe, or Coach, as we kids in the neighborhood called him. I told them I was there for them and would be at home waiting to help in any way I could, just call. I wasn't doing anything but waiting to help.

Will dead. How surreal. I had time to grasp the concept and reality of it when I got home and sat in the living room, fidgety, not knowing what to do or how to do it. I had no experience in dealing with the death of someone close. I was an expert with absence, but not death. He was like a brother. I just wanted to break down and cry, but did not dare. You see people you love hurt and you can't help, but feel you must remain alert and protect them somehow. Noble thought, but not that practical at the time. I remembered Coach O'Neal's little speech the previous year, before we loaded up and drove to Tim Davis's funeral in Fairfax. Something he'd said about how no one suffers or hurts like a mother losing a child. That was Martha Lynn at the moment. There wasn't a damn thing I could do. And it's not your place to interrupt. They have to do it alone. Worst condition possible.

I couldn't reach Pam at school, but I called the coach and told him I'd be absent from practice a day or two, and why. He was understanding and offered his condolences to Will's family, if I'd be so kind to convey them. "I'll inform the team," he said. "I'll see you tomorrow or the next day. Sorry, Cavanaugh."

I wanted to drive up to school and tell Pam, but was afraid to leave, on the outside chance I might be needed by Will's folks. Whatever I could do without getting in the way.

But I did go down to the hospital and inform Aunt Evie. She wept, as expected. She and Will's family, particularly Marth Lynn, were close too.

"I've got to get out of here and help, be with her," she said.

"Not until Jimmy Stewart says so," I told her. Gallows humor, I guessed.

Back home I sat on the front porch, no tea this time, looking out over the river and not seeing it or any of the things in and around it. This time the river did not comfort me.

It must have been an hour later when the phone rang again, inside. I jumped and went to it, afraid to miss it and fail somehow. It was Kenny Miklos, calling from Long Binh, near Saigon. His raspy voice was even harsher but clear enough, coming from the other side of the world.

"You know by now, I guess," Kenny said.

"About Will. Yes. The Army informed his mother a few hours ago. I'm sorry as hell about all this."

"You and I, both, brother."

"Do you know what happened?"

"Yes. He was hit in the torso, several shots. A firefight with NVA. They lifted him and another guy to the battalion aid station, but it was too far back and he bled out on the way. Died before he got there. Nothing they could do."

"Were you there?" I said.

"No. One of our guys was with their headquarters company. He passed along the information to me, the names of the wounded, and dead, just routine. So I saw the name immediately. I hadn't seen him in a couple weeks when we had a few beers together at the O Club, on base. Oh, man. I tell you." Kenny almost lost it. "His platoon sergeant helped put him on the chopper. Before the choppers came in, he said, he kept saying *Hugo. Hugo.* The last words he ever spoke. Some guys call out for their mothers, you know. I've seen that up close. Others to God. Others mumble. Some don't say anything. "

Will's mother would never hear that from me. If put on the spot, I would say he called for her, Martha Lynn.

"But that's not the only reason I called, Doc, bad as it is."

"What else, Kenny? You need something? What can I do?"

"I don't need anything. But you might need to sit down somewhere. Mary's gone too."

"*What?* You're shittin' me."

He let in sink in a moment. "Wish I were. She was with a reporter, her boss, I understand. Woman named Noland, from NSD in Saigon, where she worked. Came out here to cover the operation as the troops were gradually returning to base. Mary got the word that Will was hit, and they hitched a ride on a chopper to the aid station, out in the field. It crashed. No survivors. Not sure if it was shot down, or a malfunction of the craft. They died a couple hours apart. She never knew he was already gone. Couldn't have."

"Sonofabitch. What in hell." I could not speak clearly, but I could curse.

"I'm so sorry, man," Kenny said. "This shit is a lot more to handle than I figured on. You still there?"

"I think I am. But I'm not sure."

"I'm sorry, Doc. I'm so damned sorry. I know how close you two guys were. They were my friends too. Not as close as you, but they were terrific." His own voice was almost breaking. "I'm going to miss the hell out of them. Shelley is not taking it so well. I called her just before I called you. She and Mary were in touch frequently. I'm just the grim reaper, I guess. Never knew I'd be this close to a story over here, so personal. What can I do for you from here?"

"Just take care of yourself, is what you can do. Keep your head down, as they say. And come by here when you get back. Keep me informed of anything you learn, if you can. Anything his family would want to know. I'd appreciate that, and so would they."

"Loud and clear on that. They'll send his belongings home anyway. Standard procedure. I'm sure the reps told his mother that."

"Not sure what they told them."

"Did Mary's family know she and Will were already married, you know of?"

"I don't think so. They would have said something."

"Well, they'll know it now, I suspect."

"If they don't, I'll make damn sure they do know. She's a Wythe. And I'll be at her memorial service, when they have it, to guarantee it."

"Stay out of this part of the world, Doc, when you go on active duty, if it's still going on then. You hear me? It's a big, nasty mess. It's not World War Two, or even Korea. It's a monster. It's not worth it, is the prevailing opinion of everybody, top-to-bottom, whether or not they admit it publicly. You hear what I'm saying?"

"I hear you on that. I already see the proof of it, and it hurts like hell."

"It is a hell, and I know it firsthand. So I'm telling you as a friend and a brother. Let me know how things go back home. Give my regards to the team. Make sure none of these shit birds flunk out of school. You see how that can go. Pound it into their heads. And say hello from Miklos to that ragged bunch of fence-ape frats up on the corner."

"I will. And you stay safe."

"Got it. Semper Fi, Marine. And Sigma Phi, brother." I thought I heard a lump in his throat when he said bye and hung up. I know there was one in mine.

When we were off the phone, I lost it. I'd held up well about Will, toughed it out like a man, thus far, even after seeing his family ache at the news of his death. Mr. Tough Guy. But the loss of Mary, that special, beautiful creature of a young woman, so innocent and loyal and giving and kind, was just too much to hold back the dam breaking inside me. It was like losing a sister. I wanted to let it roll until my eyes were dry and gritty as emery cloth. I was home alone, anyway. I couldn't remember wanting to cry like that since I was a small boy. My eyes welled up, but I didn't break. And I don't know what that said about me, if I was being strong or being hardheaded, or less human.

46

Aunt Evie got out of the hospital a day before scheduled, thanks to the understanding of her doctor and former boy-friend, Bill Thurston, aka Jimmy Stewart. She looked better than I'd ever seen her, though her eyes were a little glassy from medication. Her skin color was vibrant and healthy looking, her step and balance quicker and surer. I wanted her to be like that forever, though I kind of knew better. She changed clothes, then called and drove around to be with Martha Lynn and Coach and Hank. It would be four days before she would take another drink, but till then she really shined.

Will's remains were on the way home from Vietnam to Dover, Delaware, at the Air Force base there, the east coast gateway for the military deceased, a busy place these days. There would be a funeral with military honors at Fort Monroe, in Hampton, at the base's Chapel of the Centurion.

I needed to know about Mary. So I called her uncle, Charles Reedlaw, at his office, at the newspaper in Charleston. I explained to his secretary that I was a close friend to his niece, Mary. I introduced myself as Layton Cavanaugh and offered my sympathies first, which he accepted, gracefully.

"You're the one she called L.D., or Doc," he said. "You played football with Will."

"Yes, sir. We were best friends all our lives, like brothers, really."
I was impressed and flattered that she had spoken of me to him,
and that he'd remembered. Well, he was a newspaper man, so details were his business. "She said she told you she and Will were
married here, when he went in the army."

"Yes. She confided in me about it."

"Do her parents know they were married?"

"If they don't, they will. They should've known earlier." It had
a snap to it. He said it like we both might have been at fault that
they didn't, like some collective guilt.

I shot back at him, gently as possible. Just a little ditty to keep
balance in the conversation. "The reason I'm calling you and not
her parents is because I don't want to bother them at a time like
this, of course. Especially since they don't know me any better than
you do. And since you helped her get the job with NSD, you're the
next closest family member, according to her. You were her favorite
relative, she said." Carry that load yourself.

Charles was silent a moment. I figured Mary's parents might not
have known he'd gotten her the interview with Della Myles. The
thing that led to the job, that led to her death. But how could he
not suspect it? The guy was in the news business. How else would
she make that kind of contact? His sister, Rene, had to know that,
or at least suspect it. The future lawyer in me here, I guessed, all
this figuring.

"Will didn't want her over there," I said. "I just want you folks
to know that. He was flat-out against it, pleaded with her not to
go."

"Yes. She said that. None of us did."

Us again. This guy was strapped with guilt. He needed to know
I didn't have a big mouth.

"How she got the job is none of my business, Mr. Reedlaw. The
important thing is you helped her be near Will. The one thing she
wanted more than anything. And she would have gone there, one
way or another. And you know that. She was able to be close to him

over there, to see him and talk to him the way she couldn't do here. You just helped make her happy, is all. No wonder she said you were her favorite uncle."

"It's really not an issue."

Yes, it is. "What I called for is to ask about the memorial service. I and some other friends of hers will be there for it."

He seemed a bit choked up on the other end, but somewhat relieved too. He gave me the details.

"Thank you for calling me, Layton. I appreciate it. You're always welcome here. Any of Mary's friends are. I'll tell her parents you called. I look forward to meeting you at the service."

Here was a guy whose sister, Rene "Bootsie" Poythress, was going to hold it against him for the rest of his life when she discovered or confirmed, sooner or later, he'd gotten her daughter Mary that job in Saigon

47

Mary's service was two days before Will's, and almost five hundred miles apart. But Martha Lynn and Coach had made the drive in pain out of respect for their newly-wed daughter-in-law, whom they already loved, because she was a part of their son. Pam and I had gotten letters from each of them regarding their wishes, should anything bad happen to either or both of them. God forbid. How they wanted things. Those would be expressed to the families. Hopefully, there would be no objections or nasty rejections to them. Another God forbid.

Shelley flew in from Montreal and we picked her up at the airport in North Charleston. We were together at the church with other friends of Mary's and Will's from school. Teammates, frat brothers, other classmates, as many women as men.

Mary's Huguenot church downtown was packed. The weather was still hot. The summers are long here and the winters short. Not like back home, where the seasons changed overnight and the temperatures in three minutes. It was a quaint, beautiful place, as most churches are. Places of peace and rest and community. And the community, Mary's social circle, was there, standing room only. And that organ music that kills me every time I hear it. It helped people weep. And it was doing its job. Overwhelming flowers and sunlight gave the place the look and feel of a lush, tropical rainforest.

Most were seated when Lanny walked in and down the aisle holding up Rene, who was pale and weak and struggling like a child learning to walk. Much like Tim Davis's mother had been. Here was a woman who'd lost both her children before the oldest would reach twenty-two, and before she could turn fifty. The sadness made the air heavier and harder to breath.

Charles was behind them escorting Mary's grandmother, Marie. He'd met Martha Lynn and Coach and Hank minutes earlier in the lobby. He reached out in front of him and touched Rene's arm and whispered to her. She and Lanny stopped. Rene leaned over and hugged Martha Lynn's shoulder and kissed her on the forehead. Then she and Lanny sat across from them.

Marie did the same, but offered a kind word to Martha Lynn. "Your son was a wonderful young man," she said. "He won my Mary baby's heart. So he had to be special."

Martha Lynn lost it.

Marie joined Lanny and Rene in their pew. Charles and his family sat with them.

Shelley was a wreck.

Giles and Nell Collier sat nearby. Nell's eyes welled with giant tears. Giles was like a zombie. He'd lost the love of his own life, an unrequited one. He looked as stunned as he did sad.

The pastor, a slender, older man, began and ended the service with the same words, numerous in attendance offering eulogies in between. "She said she would go anywhere in the world he would go. That he would go nowhere without her in this life. And she'd meant it. She followed the one she loved to the very end of her brief, beautiful time here with us."

48

Will's and Mary's thinking ahead about last wishes seemed awfully prophetic for people so young. But they had been in a place of precarious fate when they stated them to Pam and me in letters home. They wished to be cremated upon their demise, whether now or later in life, that their ashes be placed in urns for their respective families, that half the ashes from each family urn be placed in a third urn. And these ashes be taken to the campus in Williamsburg, to the top of the little bridge over the pond there, and sprinkled over the water, their eternal resting home. So they could be together there, symbolically. The urn would be placed next to the oar marker, and stay with it over time. Hopefully, it would not be removed or vandalized. Their families respected and supported this decision. They got their wishes.

In fact, Lanny rented a conference room at the inn, there in town, for a reception in their honor, prior to the ceremony, and to honor their friends who attended. He was holding up well, in spite of losing his only daughter and remaining child. Rene went along with it, but seemed aloof, not so accepting of her daughter's fate. The expression said it all. It was somebody else who caused her daughter's death. She never once exchanged greetings with or acknowledged Will's father, Will's likeness, except in the slightest way. But she kept the words to herself. Marie appeared to be the strongest among them, able to keep her feelings private, and was gracious with everyone.

After Will's equally moving memorial service at our church in Newport News, the retinue of family, friends and others, including Aunt Evie, and Shelley Michaels, who stayed with us on the drive back from Charleston, met in Williamsburg for the reception and to grant Will's and Mary's special wish, their final resting place. It was a Saturday. There was no game in town, as the team had an open date. The parking was easy, though tourists were about. Charles and his family were with them. And so was Giles and Nell Collier. "The church was just her service," Giles said to me when we arrived there. "This is where she will be forever. So I had to be here." Nobody could accuse him of being a quitter.

We crowded on and around the bridge that arched over the pond, and on the banks, either side of it, just as we had at their wedding only months before. The sun splashed through the leaves flickering light over us. Pam was given the urn to carry to the site, but lost her emotions and handed it to me. I handed it to Shelley as kind of an honor, because she had known Mary longer than I and roomed with her that previous year. I sometimes teased Pam about her sensitivity, saying she'd cry at Halloween. But she was such a sweet soul of a person, just being herself. And that was good enough for me.

The same minister who'd married them presided over this memorial.

As we settled in and became silent in this environment that was and always had been quiet and peaceful, it must have occurred to some others as it did to me that this was it. This was the last goodbye. This was the last time we would be in their presence, except in spirit. Their ashes were the last physical evidence we would see. All else would be memory. The lifetime, in some cases, of laughter and pranks, and ball games, and nights out, and dinners, and pains and injures, and hurt feelings, and parties with friends, and victories and losses, and bonfires on the sand, parties on the boat. Of days and nights on the river, walks on the boulevard, days at the beach, the skies brilliant and blue, the waters of the Chesapeake and Atlantic sparkling emerald green and speckled with boats and ships and sails and seagulls and swimmers and romance, and the weight of it all resting on the shoulders like a single vison flashing before the eyes in an instant.

Mary had confided in Shelley and Pam, in her last letters home, that she'd recently had a premonition of a darkness looming, some-thing she'd never experienced. But in Saigon, where she'd spent the last weeks of her short life, premonitions became realities rou-tinely.

The minister gave his brief sermon. Some gave brief eulogies.

Then, as Pam, now recovered, and I together tilted the urn over the side of the bridge and slowly poured the ashes into the pond, the minister spoke the words Mary had conveyed to Pam and Shel-ley in letters only weeks before, when she further explained her feelings for Will and why she insisted on being near him in Vi-etnam, no matter the risks.

The minister said, "They were two young lovers who stood holding hands by the side of the road and stuck out their thumbs for a ride with the times. And the times picked them up. As Mary said to Will on this very spot not that long ago, when they married, 'Together in love. Together in life. Together in death. Forever in eternity. Come and be with me in this place forever.' She said them, and she meant them."

EPILOGUE

Things changed a lot in our lives over the years. Pam and I have been married now for two decades. The smartest thing I ever did was marrying her. At least my mother got that right. It's been a joy that never ends, and gets better every year. We have two wonderful children, Collette, who is fifteen and a spitting image of her mother in every respect. There is a very lucky young man out there somewhere who doesn't know it yet. Wythey, as we call him, a take on his middle name, Wythe, is twelve and looks more like my grandfather and father than me, though his temperament is mine. They fight all the time, but love and look out for one another where it counts. When not calling each other dorks.

We live in the same big house overlooking the river. Most of the older families have moved away as the neighborhood is rapidly and constantly changing. When the older folks die off, the younger settle in other places. It's not like my parents' generation, when people stayed in the same place forever, it seemed. But southerners were migrating these days too. It is a transient world now, but one with ever-expanding opportunities for the young and hopeful.

My father died in his late fifties of a massive heart attack while on another job in Singapore. I was in my second year of private practice at the time, after a three-year tour in the Marine Corps. He never got back home, except to be buried on time. He was always punctual if absent. My mother moved back to live with us. Well, it's her house, and we live here and maintain it symbiotically. Sounds like a clinical term, I know, but I'm not always good with words. She's been great with the kids over the years. Doesn't talk as much as she used to, but has always been there for them. She gets up every morning and showers and dresses in nice clothes, as if about to travel someplace, eats breakfast, then sits on the front porch if the weather is good, or in her chair by the window, and looks out past the river and into the ocean at another time and place.

Aunt Evie died three years after that first bout with cirrhosis. I spent those same three years after Will and Mary died feeling guilty about my selfishness and trying to make up for it to her and Pam. I wanted to be more like my friends who'd died young but had a commitment and loyalty second to none that I envied. I still eye the pretty women, even flirt a bit, but my greatest achievement is remaining loyal and faithful to Pam. I'm a true hound by nature, I guess. But whenever I feel the urge to wander, I visualize my wife and children standing there watching me. Then I don't do it. So it works.

Will's father, Coach Wythe, died only five years ago. Martha Lynn now lives with Hank and his family in Raleigh, North Carolina, where he and his wife teach school and coach sports. He was quite the quarterback in college. Not pro material, but close.

Dickey Humphrey and Carol Foley married and live in Virginia Beach, and we see one another on occasions, being so close. Dickey is a counselor working with the visually impaired, and Carol sells real estate and drinks. Some things never change.

Alvin Findley married Harriett Pomeroy—Go, Findley—and they live in Richmond, where he practices law with his brother, and serves in the Virginia State Senate. Harriett is the principal of a private school and volunteers for anything benefitting handicapped children. They have two of their own, both healthy. I still can't get over her stunning looks. Ooh, Harriett.

Shelley Michaels and Kenny Miklos married after coming back home from Canada, after the war. They live in D.C. Kenny manages the news agency he worked for in Vietnam, even appears time-to-time as a commentator on the Sunday morning T.V. news shows. He and his father and grandfather reconciled before they died. They were even proud of his stand on the war, though they disagreed on policy to the end. Shelley is on staff at the Smithsonian Institute and teaches college classes at local and nearby schools. Once or twice a year she travels to dig sites for the work she really loves. They have no children. Not enough time.

We all get together whenever we can, usually at Homecoming weekends in Williamsburg. The V.M.I. game. Sometimes we meet in summer for a week on the Outer Banks in North Carolina, where Pam and I have a beach house, or at Alvin's and Harriett's place on Hilton Head Island, South Carolina.

And we always, together or separately, when back at school, go into the little patch of woods on campus, where the bridge arches over the pond, and pay respects to the memory of our friends who died too young, to feel close to them. We see the oar marker and make sure it's well tended to, though the urn is long gone. This is where their spirit looms forever, the place they claimed as their own. Pam and I claimed it too and were married there ourselves.

She and I often sit together on the front porch overlooking the James River. The ships in the port of Norfolk across the way still look the same, though they move in and out daily, like the tides, from places all over the world. The boats and sails and working boats, the seagulls, never seem to change. They're all the same as when I was a boy playing and crabbing and clamming in the sand at low tide across the boulevard from my house. The blue sky and emerald green water. The horizon beyond the mouth of the river leading into the Chesapeake Bay and the Atlantic Ocean carrying a million dreams and memories to sea.

An old timer, a client of mine, said to me once, "You don't pick the family you're born into. It's a crapshoot. But you do get to choose your friends. And you're damned lucky if you have even one in this life, because the requirements are narrow and very few meet them."

All my friends meet them. And my greatest, private hope is that someday, when this is all over, we can play on an open field of a thousand yards of lush, green grass and mild breezes, where we throw the football and run like horses, where we can all rally again in that halcyon of all places. Like Mary said to Will in her vows to him, "Come and be with me in this place forever."

THE END